GW01057458

FIVE FARTHINGS

A London Story

by

MONICA REDLICH

Margin Notes Books

Published by Margin Notes Books, 2011

First published by J.M. Dent, London in 1939. Every effort
has been made to trace the copyright holders and to obtain
their permission for the use of copyright material. The
publisher apologises for any errors or omissions and would be
grateful if notified of any corrections that should be
incorporated in future reprints or editions of this book.

Margin Notes Books have been unable to trace the heirs to the
estate of Monica Redlich. Royalties have been set aside and the
publishers would be pleased to hear from the heir.

Design and layout © Margin Notes Books 2011
Introduction and Notes © Margin Notes Books 2011

All rights reserved. No part of this publication may be
reproduced, stored in or introduced into a retrieval system, or
transmitted, by any means (electronic, mechanical,
photocopying, recording or otherwise) without the prior
written permission of the copyright owner and publisher.

A CIP record for this book is available from the British Library

ISBN 978-0-9564626-1-9

www.marginnotesbooks.com
info@marginnotesbooks.com

Published by Margin Notes Books
5 White Oak Square
London Road
Swanley
Kent BR8 7AG

Printed in Great Britain by the MPG Books Group,
Bodmin and King's Lynn

MONICA REDLICH

Monica Redlich (1909-1965) is perhaps most known today for *The Nice Girl's Guide to Good Behaviour* (1935, republished 2004). She was the daughter of a clergyman and brought up in Lincolnshire and London, but mainly lived abroad after her marriage to Sigurd Christensen, a Danish diplomat, in 1937. Life in Denmark, the U.S.A. and Spain gave her material for a number of travel books including *Everyday England* and *Danish Delight*. However, she had previously published a number of novels for adults and children.

Five Farthings (1939) was her second and last book for children after *Jam Tomorrow* (1937). *Five Farthings* received very favourable notices in the contemporary broadsheet press and later from the critic Marcus Crouch who neatly summarised the novel as 'a story of an exceptionally nice family'.[1] Unlike the more well-known *Jam Tomorrow*, it was never reprinted and is now a very scarce title. Both are family stories dealing with genteel poverty and a family's attempts to improve their prospects. While *Jam Tomorrow* is the story of a widowed rector and his chaotic family in a small village, *Five Farthings* introduces the reader to an ordinary family, two parents and three children, forced to move from Sussex to the City of London while the father is treated in hospital. Mrs Farthing returns to work in a smart department store and the three children find that London life has its own unexpected freedoms and opportunities.

---

[1] Marcus Crouch. *Treasure Seekers and Borrowers. Children's Books in Britain 1900-1960*. London: The Library Association, 1970 (updated edition). p. 78.

A NOTE ON THE TEXT

This is a complete and unabridged version of Monica Redlich's novel *Five Farthings*. First published by J.M. Dent in 1939 it was never reprinted. Errors in the original texts, such as repeated words over a line, have not been amended.

While the author has used terms such as 'nigger' or 'queer', which may have changed in their meaning or effect, they have not been updated or omitted in this new edition.

'You owe me five farthings'
Say the bells of St Martin's

FIVE FARTHINGS

A London Story

by

MONICA REDLICH

FOR MERCY CLARKE

CONTENTS

BOOK THREE
CHAP

A NOTE ON THE FARTHINGS' LONDON

The Farthings' London is a little different from that to be found in the directories or on any map. Overton House, where their flat is, will not be discovered by any one walking round St Paul's Churchyard. Magnificat Alley and Watchman Lane do not exist, even under another name: nor does St Sebastian's Church, though it contains many features which I feel certain Sir Christopher Wren would certainly have put in if he had designed it.

My publishing friends in London will find no portraits of themselves in this tale, for Messrs Laurence Broadstreet is an entirely imaginary firm, and the people in it are imaginary also. The actual Book Fair which I have described has not yet taken place, though it may do so at any moment! There is, of course, a Book Fair in London every autumn, the *Sunday Times* National Book Fair, which I strongly recommend to readers of this book.

One cannot find Messrs Greencoat's shop anywhere in London, or Whitefriars School, or St Monan's, or the hotel in Kensington, or Badger's Mews. Otherwise, however, everything which the Farthings discovered is still there for other people to discover also.

M.R.

1939

BOOK ONE

CHAPTER I

THE FARTHINGS ARRIVE

IN a small hotel in South Kensington, five new-comers to London were getting ready for lunch. The Farthings had been in London before, but only as visitors, and they were trying hard to get used to the very strange fact that, from to-day on, they lived there.

They did not much care for their new surroundings at present. The air in London was stuffy, the streets were dull and smelled of petrol, and the hotel where they had just arrived was duller still and smelled of yesterday's cabbage. Vivien Farthing, washing her hands at the little wooden washstand in the bedroom she was sharing with Dinah, gave a sigh which her young sister would certainly have remarked upon if she had not been busy with her violin, plucking gently at its beloved strings to see how it had survived the journey.

Like the rest of the Farthing family, Vivien faced the day with very mixed feelings. She was seventeen. She understood better than either Dinah or John what a big upheaval this move to London had meant, and how long it might be before they could have a settled and peaceful home again. But if Mr Farthing could be cured, as the doctors said he could ... well, then it was a thousand times worth it. Vivien looked round the dingy, cramped bedroom, twisted the soap in her hands, and, forgetting that she had washed already, began carefully to wash again.

'Oh, come on, Vivien. Aren't you ready yet?'

Dinah bounced on the bed to show her impatience, and got up again even more quickly when she found that below its layer of springs her bed had some exceedingly hard foundation. A clock outside struck one, and immediately afterwards a gong boomed out from downstairs—a majestical and dignified boom, which hardly matched the smell of warm mutton fat that had now joined the smell of cabbage.

Vivien looked at her nose in the spotted mirror, and took out her powder-box. She briefly inspected her sister.

'Have you washed?'

'No.'

'Aren't you dirty from the train?'

'Not in the least'.

Dinah shook herself haughtily, then put her head on one side, looked up, and smiled. Dinah's smile was a revelation. Her curly red hair, fair skin, and hazel eyes in themselves made her remarkable; when she smiled her whole face lit up with life and the force of her personality. It was John's considered opinion that Dinah would be beautiful when she grew up—'I mean, if her teeth don't grow crooked and her nose get long,' he would cautiously add.

Vivien too thought Dinah had a good share of the family gifts—striking looks, an outstanding talent for the violin, and a personality so strong that Vivien often felt blurred and indecisive beside her. Yet Vivien herself was at least as good-looking as Dinah. She had the same fair skin, and had very thick chestnut hair with gold lights in it. Her eyes were dark blue, with long lashes which made them seem even darker. Her nose was short and straight, her mouth charming. She was slim like her mother, was by no means tall, and moved gracefully. At seventeen she was not nearly so sure of herself as Dinah at twelve; but, unlike Dinah, she had one great ambition always in front of her, though unlike Dinah she did not tell all the world about it.

Vivien was going to write. She had in fact written a lot already, though no paper except her school magazine had had the pleasure of publishing any of her work. But from to-day on, her career was really beginning. She had written a story which she knew without question was the best she had done yet: a story which was as near as she could possibly make it to those she was always reading in the *Woman's Journal, Good Housekeeping, Good Homecraft,* and other such magazines. It was in her handbag at this moment, copied out very neatly, and enclosed, with a stamped envelope addressed to herself in disguised handwriting, in a package which would be posted to the editor of *Good Homecraft* the moment she could escape from the family and look up the address in a telephone directory.

'Shall we go down in the lift?' she inquired, having powdered her nose to the accompaniment of Dinah's loud, patient sighings.

'No, let's walk,' said Dinah cheerfully. 'I want to see some more of this perfectly beastly place.'

The atmosphere of the hotel got if anything thicker as one went deeper into it, and by the time they had passed two landings identical with their own, and come to the ground floor, Vivien felt she could hardly breathe. Strange, tropical plants and ferns clawed at them with huge leaves. The hall was dark as well as stuffy. They could hear the muffled clatterings of a meal from some room on their right, and they could hear Herbert, the hall porter, whistling softly through his teeth close at hand, though it took them some moments for them to make out where he stood. A stout, bent man with white hair came shuffling through the hall, and peered at them intently as he passed.

'Let's find the others,' said Dinah in a rather subdued

voice.

They went to the drawing-room, where they had all agreed to meet. John was there before them, disconsolately turning over a three-months-old copy of the *Lady*, and Mr and Mrs Farthing arrived only a moment afterwards.

'Are you hungry? Sorry to keep you waiting—Daddy dropped the soap into his suitcase.'

'Yes, and it was wet,' added Mr Farthing, his eyes twinkling as if, whoever might be an invalid, it was certainly not he. 'Well, we 'd better go in to lunch, if you 're all ready. The manageress gave us a strong hint that we 're expected to be punctual for meals here, and we haven't any too much time if Mummy and I are to get off to the specialist.'

Vivien had been curious to see what the other inhabitants of this strange hotel could be like, and when she was settled between her father and John at the table which had been reserved for them, she took a good look round at all the other people in the room. There were not many of them, and they were all, to say the least of it, as much interested in the Farthing family as Vivien was in them. Two grey-haired ladies, thin, straight-backed, and looking as if it was only by mistake that they had left their lorgnettes upstairs, sat at the next table. When Vivien looked up they looked down, and when she looked down they looked up, as if they were playing some complicated game of hide-and-seek. The stout, white-haired man she had seen in the hall was sucking in soup with a burbling noise for which Dinah would have been severely reprimanded, and dropping occasional drops of it down the napkin tucked under his chin. A sad-looking husband and wife with very yellow faces sat at the table in the window, and beyond them was a party of three stout ladies who alone of everybody there seemed bold enough to talk in their natural voices and carry on a conversation. They were talking about somebody called Milly, and their opinion of Milly's husband was decidedly low. The only other guest was a little woman no taller than Dinah, with grey hair sticking out in thin, frizzy corkscrew curls and a face rather like a bird, who gave the impression of hopping up and down every time she took a mouthful.

Vivien gave a little, involuntary shiver. Was this really what London was like? Was it here that she was to find dramatic, real-life subjects to write about, and begin her career as an author? She took a tight hold of the handbag in which her story was hidden, and gave her attention to the typewritten menu which her father, with a smile and a careful absence of comment, was holding out for her to study.

The Farthings had lived since 1919 in Sussex, on the coast not far from Worthing. More fortunate than many demobilized officers, Mr Farthing had been able to take up again after the War the work which he liked and was qualified for, and had become agent on the estate of a distant cousin. It was in Cousin Raymond's house that he met the eighteen-year-old Margot Bradley, who had scandalized half her family and delighted the other half by running away from home to go to London and work in a big dress shop. They fell in love on the front at Worthing—it was a story that the children demanded from them over and over again; were married on a wet Friday morning in the village church; and had continued the story in proper fairy-tale manner by living happily ever after.

In their little house among woods looking over the sea, Vivien, John, and Dinah had been born. The beach, the sea, the woods, and the downs, had been their hunting-grounds since they could remember anything, and though Vivien and John had both been away at boarding school, no other place had ever seemed half as exciting as Berrings. Towns were all right for an occasional expedition. London was exciting, certainly, but in a vast and even frightening manner, and they generally came away almost with relief from visits to their relations there; but home was the place where one could bathe, and bask in the sun, and take Sammy Spaniel for long walks over the downs, and find the first snowdrops long before other people had even thought of them.

But lately, things had changed. The walks over the downs had slowly been turning into walks down a row of red-brick villas. The bathes now took place from a beach lined with two rows of bathing-huts. Sammy Spaniel had been run over and killed by a motor bicycle from the bungalow colony just at the bottom of the lane. The place where every spring of her life Dinah had picked snowdrops was now the back yard of a house with the name of 'Wy-worrie.' It was heartbreaking to see it all; and Mr Farthing's cousin, heartbroken just as they were, and crippled by estate duties and increasing income tax, had at last been forced to sell his house and grounds to the ever-hungry builders.

The Farthings' home, like his, simply ceased to exist. New 'sun-houses' were to be built, with flat roofs, glass-covered balconies, and a dozen other improvements which, as Vivien angrily said, 'we have all managed beautifully without for years.' Mr Farthing's work ceased also, and they were faced with the serious problem of what to do next.

'Why not find another place like this?' said Dinah, as if it were the simplest thing in the world.

'Not much hope, I'm afraid,' her father answered.

There are ten chaps like me for every place that still needs us. No—as a matter of fact, Mummy and I have been thinking of London.'

'*London?*

'London! Well, of all places in the world——'

The suggestion was greeted, as he knew it would be, with horror; but he explained that his cousin could get him into a big London firm for property management, and that a safe job like that, no matter where, was not to be turned down lightly. The family were obliged to admit that this was true, and they said no more at the time, though they said a good deal to each other on their last sad rounds of all their favourite walks.

Vivien, John, and most of all Dinah, had always felt well able to look after their own private affairs: but where the family as a whole was concerned Mr and Mrs Farthing as a matter of course explained to them whatever was going on. They knew the family income, and they helped to decide how it was spent. Dinah's violin lessons, for example, were agreed by all of them—Dinah not excluded—to be of the first importance; but when Vivien had wanted to go winter-sporting, the answer had been that she could go if she liked, but it would mean so much less for their holiday in the summer. Holidays, dentists and doctors, parties, school—everything in the Farthing family was a matter, not for orders, but for discussion. Cousin Raymond's generation thought it strange, but they seemed to get along very well all the same, and not even Aunt Harrison herself could have denied that they were happy.

But before they left their home something else happened: something which made London inevitable. During the War, in Salonika, Mr Farthing had developed some obscure fever which he had never since properly got rid of. Aggravated, perhaps, by the hard work of arranging the sale of land and property, this suddenly became worse, and on some days he was obliged to stay in bed and was hardly able to move. The specialists in London were convinced that by some special electrical treatment this could be cured. If he took the London post which was open to him, he could go for treatment in the evenings after work, and they hoped that in a few months he would be quite well again.

All other plans were left undecided until it could be seen how this worked. They hoped most keenly that they could soon make a home of their own in London. Mr Farthing's pension, and Mrs Farthing's very small private income, would make it possible for them to manage somehow through the first difficult months, but they would not have even half as much money as they had been used to, and they would have to be extremely careful. Dinah and John were of course both to go to school—where they did not yet know, though Dinah had an idea that a school in Kensington, St Monan's, would suit her very well. Good violin lessons were the only aspect of school that really interested her, and a friend of hers who was at St Monan's said that it had a good violin master and a flourishing orchestra. John was now thirteen, and until lately there had been no doubt that he would go on to Shrewsbury, where his father and all the Farthings had been before him. But now, suddenly, there was not enough money. He was not up to scholarship standard, and unless the family affairs took a sudden turn for the better, all they could do would be to send him to one of the big London day schools.

As for Vivien herself, no one in the family knew yet that she had her own future all planned out. They knew, of course, that she was interested in writing and in reading, but they had so little idea of the real state of affairs that Mr and Mrs Farthing talked of her taking a course in either journalism or domestic science, whichever she preferred, as if literature was to be considered on the same level as scrubbing floors and learning to make milk puddings. Vivien thanked them, and said only that she thought she would like the journalism course best. There would be time to tell them later; and she looked forward most heartily to the day when she could first show them her name in print, and prove to them that her career had settled itself.

CHAPTER II

THREE TO PICCADILLY

WHEN lunch was over the Farthings escaped as soon as possible, and without waiting for coffee and conversation in the drawing-room went up to Mr and Mrs Farthing's bedroom. It was a great relief to be able to let off steam a little, and Dinah and her father entered with delight into a spirited comparison of their views on the hotel and its inhabitants. Mr Farthing was half Irish, and on days such as this, when many people would have been silent and depressed, there was such gusto in all he said and did, such a flow of fine-sounding words, and such animation in his dark eyes and lined, lively face, that Mrs Farthing was always either laughing or looking uneasily round to see who might be within earshot.

'When you two have quite finished,' she said, as Dinah concluded a life-like imitation of the bird-like little lady eating mutton, 'we ought to think about this afternoon. Andrew, you and I must be getting off soon to Sir William. And then we have to go and see your aunt afterwards, if we can manage it. But what about you?' she went on, turning to Vivien and the others. 'Do you know what you 're going to do?'

'Oh, just wander about, I suppose.' Vivien spoke without enthusiasm. She wanted to post her story, but beyond that London at the moment held no interest at all for her, and she would just as soon have retired into a book and tried to shut it all out.

'This hotel 's not much fun,' said her father, as if he saw what she was thinking. 'Why not have tea out somewhere?'

'Yes, that 's a good idea,' added Mrs Farthing. 'I 'll tell you what. Andrew, have you got three half-crowns? Look—here 's half-a-crown for each of you, and it 's got to be spent before dinner-time! Not a single penny of it may come home again, and you mustn't bring anything else either—I mean books or chocolates or anything. That 'll make you think!'

'Oh, what fun,' said John, his quiet face lighting up. 'Where shall we go?'

Dinah, at any rate, did not find this hard to answer.

'We 'll go and have tea in the biggest and grandest place we can possibly find,' she said. 'A place with a band and waiters'.

'All right,' said John. 'But how are we going to get there?'

'Oh... oh, we just go out, and walk a bit, and then take a tram or a bus or something, and get off when we see the right sort of place. That 's right, isn't it, Daddy?'

'In a way, yes,' said her father, amused. 'But it 's best to start in the right direction. Vivien, you know the way from here to Piccadilly Circus, don't you? It 's the same from Aunt Harrison's. I think that 's the most likely direction for Dinah to find the kind of place she wants.'

This plan seemed to suit everybody, and Vivien left Dinah and John discussing its possibilities while she escaped, glad of a chance to consult the telephone book and have a last look at her story before she addressed the envelope to *Good Homecraft* and stuck it up. It was a good story—it really was: about a young married couple who quarrelled and then had a motor accident and discovered that they loved each other all the time. She had called it *The Long Lane*—a neat hint, she felt, at the fact that it is a long lane that has no turning, and that everything was going to come right in the end. The address found in the dark telephone booth in the hall, she sat on her bed and read over again the letter she had written to the editor. It seemed all right: a brief explanation of the story, a mention of who she was (though not of her age), and a polite hope that the editor would like it and would let her know as soon as possible whether they could publish it or not. Picking up the envelope affectionately, Vivien put the contents back inside, stuck it up, and began to get ready for the afternoon.

'What 's that you 're posting, Vivien?'

'A letter.'

'It 's a very fat letter.'

'Some letters are fat,' said Vivien, wishing that young sisters of twelve cold be brought up to be seen and not heard, and not to ask questions. But Dinah luckily had been reminded that she meant to write to their old maid down in Sussex.

'I 'll get Bridget a picture post card,' she said, 'She 'd like that best, and there won't be so much to write. I wonder how she 's getting on without us.'

'I don't like to think of the house,' said John suddenly. 'Quite empty, and all our furniture gone.... There were weeds on the path already this morning, even before we came away.'

'Was it really only this morning we were down there? It seems years ago already.'

'Oh, I wish we were back,' said Dinah, all pretence of not minding broken down.

'So do we all,' said John shortly, his voice so ferocious that Dinah, after one sidelong glance at him, said no more.

The Farthings walked along the road for some little time in silence. It was a warm April afternoon. One could smell spring in the air—but mixed with the smell of petrol, of smoke, and of dust. The little breeze brought no tang of the sea, no fresh scent of turf from the downs; only the reminder of thousands of rows of houses, running parallel to this one, and at right angles, and all over the place, under the vast, stuffy, smoky inverted saucer that in London they called the sky.

Still in silence, not thinking of London at all, they walked on along the wide, empty street until they came to another one crossing it at right angles. Vivien gave an exclamation of surprise.

'Why, this is Queen's Gate, where Aunt Harrison lives. I 'd no idea we were so near. Now I know just where we are. If we go on this way we come to Knightsbridge, where she always goes shopping, and up on the left somewhere are Hyde Park and Kensington Gardens.'

'We won't go to Knightsbridge,' said John hurriedly, as if the mention of Aunt Harrison and shopping combined was too much of a good thing altogether. 'Let 's go up to Hyde Park or the Gardens, and see what it 's like in there. We needn't go past Aunt Harrison's,' he added, urging them across the road. 'We can just as well go up the next street.'

The next street, like Queen's Gate, was very long and very wide, and Dinah to her amusement found that it was called Exhibition Road.

'What a silly name,' she observed. 'I wonder how it got it. You know,' she added gravely, 'these great enormous empty roads give me megoraphobia.'

The silence which greeted this remark was not as respectful as she could have liked. She looked a little doubtfully from John to Vivien.

'Try again,' suggested John amiably.

'Well, megalomania, then.'

This time there was no doubt at all about the grin on Vivien's face. For a moment it seemed as if Dinah would be angry; but she swallowed hard, and at last said: 'Well, you know what I mean.'

'Agoraphobia, isn't it? A horror of open spaces.' John looked up the long street, at the far end of which they could now make out a suggestion of green trees, with tiny red buses moving past them at intervals. 'That 's the Park up there, I suppose. That ought to be cooler, at any rate. It 's beastly hot here.'

It was certainly cooler in the Park when at last they arrived there—cooler and much more lively. The tall trees were refreshingly green, and on the grass in their shadows people were moving about, children playing games, nannies in groups pushing prams along or sitting talking on benches, a party of schoolchildren playing netball. The smell of petrol vanished, and the wind among the branches made a pleasant rustling noise.

They plunged in under the shadow of the trees, looked around to get their bearings, and after a few moments' hesitation went on a little, turned, and set off at a brisk walk down the path beside Rotton Row. The long tan stretch was empty of horses. It was still too early in the afternoon for many people to be out except nannies and children, and they seemed mostly to have congregated elsewhere. The whole place was quiet and peaceful. In the dip on their left the Serpentine shone pale and clear in the sunshine.

'If London were like this,' said John, 'it wouldn't be too bad.'

'Perhaps it is like this.' Almost with surprise Vivien heard herself saying the words. 'I mean, we really don't know much about it yet, and I dare say there are plenty of decent places if one can only find them.'

'Let 's hope so,' said Dinah severely. 'Where are we going now?'

'Straight along for a bit. Then we can either walk all the way to Hyde Park Corner, or else go down that little passage by the Barracks and take a bus from there.'

'Oh, the Barracks,' said Dinah at once. 'Can we see the soldiers?'

'I don't know. Only one, I think.'

After another five minutes' walking they reached the Barracks, and by peering in under an archway Dinah was able to see a sentry in a very fine red uniform. A few moments more and they were in Knightsbridge.

It was a strange contrast so soon after the peace and solitude of the Park. There were buses pouring past from four different directions, with little groups of people waiting for them at their various stops. There was an underground station. There were shop windows as far as the eye could see—clothes shops, mostly, which Vivien marked down with a silent resolve to come here alone as soon as possible and do some intensive shop-gazing. There were taxis, delivery vans, private cars, large policemen, hurrying pedestrians—an enormous activity, always changing, always the same, never stopping for an instant.

'Oo-er,' said Dinah very quietly to herself.

John was trying to see what bus they ought to take. It was so difficult to tell. They all stopped at different places, and everybody seemed to know by instinct where to wait and which bus to make for. Vivien, John, and Dinah, standing in a little group, began to feel very much like country cousins, and slightly ashamed of it.

'Let 's ask somebody.' said John at last. He made for the first passer-by before his courage could sink again—an old gentleman with a white moustache and a bowler hat.

'Please, sir——'

'What 's that? What 's that?' The old gentleman looked startled.

'Please, sir, would you be so kind as to tell me what bus we take to get to Piccadilly?'

'Oh—h'm. Yes, certainly.' The old gentleman suddenly became human. He gave them a friendly smile and raised his hat.

'No. 9,' he said. 'You get it just here—you can see the notice.'

He pointed to a notice which they had not seen before, close beside them, at the edge of the pavement. It did indeed mention No. 9, and a few other numbers as well.

'Not at all, not at all,' he said politely when they thanked him. 'In fact, here 's one coming now.'

They hurried to the notice, and waited anxiously while the No. 9 bus came roaring up beside them. At first it seemed to be stopping farther back, and they ran back also: then a car somewhere else moved away, and the bus shot forward to its proper stopping place by the notice. Vivien, John, and Dinah ran after it, and Dinah jumped on the step.

'Passengers off first, please,' said the conductor, putting out his arm, and she had to jump off again.

At last all the passengers had got off—and a number of new-comers, who had certainly not been there a moment ago, had mysteriously shot past Dinah and got before her on into the bus. With a final effort they all three clambered on to the step, and got themselves at last into the safety of the conductor's platform. For the first time in their lives they had managed by their own unaided efforts the difficult feat of boarding a London bus.

They settled down on the top, which was almost

empty, and John noted with admiring eyes the newest type of inside staircase. When the conductor came up he asked with admirable assurance for 'three to Piccadilly.'

But taking tickets, it proved, was almost as hard as finding a bus and getting on to it.

'Whereabouts?' inquired the conductor. 'Ritz? Circus?'

'Oh,' said John. 'I don't——'

'Circus, please,' said Dinah firmly, turning round in her seat.

'Circus. Right. Tuppence, that is.'

John produced a sixpence, and looked up to see the conductor studying him closely.

''Ere,' he said. 'You ain't fourteen. Nor 's yer little sister.'

'No,' said John uneasily. 'No, but——'

'Well, *that's* all right'. The conductor gave him a beaming smile. 'Penny for you. Penny for 'er. You 're halves, see? And don't you ferget it,' he added, punching two white tickets and a blue one. 'Might save 'undreds of pounds.'

Vivien leaned forward.

'Can you please tell us when to get off?' she said. Here at any rate was somebody friendly—she felt they had better get all the help they could.

'Well, where do you want?' The conductor was entering into the spirit of it all. 'What is it you 're making for?'

'The Circus,' said Dinah coldly. She was not pleased at being no more than John's little sister.

'Yeah, but what *for*?' the conductor insisted. He gave her such a twinkling smile that Dinah relented, and suddenly, to his obvious surprise, gave him one of her best in return.

'Well, as a matter of fact,' she informed him, 'it 's for

31

tea.'

'For tea. Well, now.' The conductor pushed back his cap and scratched his head. The six other people on the upper deck turned round with undisguised interest.

'Yes. We 're going somewhere big, and grand, with music.'

'Oh. Oh, you are.' The conductor scratched his head again. 'Do you happen to know what it 's called?'

'Really, Dinah, I——' Vivien began to remonstrate.

But Dinah was enjoying herself.

'Which do *you* think is the best?' she inquired, as one connoisseur exchanging notes with another.

'Well, the missus and me——' The conductor meditated, as if to make sure that he was stating matters fairly. 'The missus and me always say that there 's nothing as good as the Pop.'

'The Pop.' Dinah nodded wisely. 'That 's exactly what we say, too.'

Had the conductor not been obliged at that moment to go back to his duties, there is no telling how the conversation might have developed. Luckily, though, he was too busy for the rest of their ride to do any more than murmur, on his next round of the upper deck, 'I 'll tell you when to get off—don't you worry.' Dinah was left triumphant at her own strategy, and Vivien and John had time to get over their embarrassment with no stares from their fellow-passengers.

Sitting side by side in the seat behind Dinah, they gazed down into the street; and it was then, as they watched the strange new world that was moving past them, that they had their first inkling of what London might one day have to offer. They left Knightsbridge behind them, catching a sudden glimpse of Rotton Row through the Park railings on their left, and came out on to a huge, tilted open space that Vivien recognized as Hyde Park Corner.

Full though it was of traffic, it still looked empty, so high and clear and wide was the sky all above it. There were trees, and statues on high pedestals, and in the distance more trees, with a big archway in front of them on which a gigantic lady with wings was doing her best to manage four horses who seemed determined to plunge down over the edge. But the prevailing impression that they got was one of sky—sky and a strange, beautiful light over all the trees and statues and pavements and grey stone buildings. Here for the first time they saw that London could have a weather of its own; a weather quite unlike that of the country, but making all the difference in the world to the city which lay beneath it.

John caught his breath, and almost said something. But there was no need: Vivien understood. Before they were ready to talk again they were in Piccadilly, spinning along at a fine speed with another park on their right. And soon, on their left at first and then on both sides at once, came shops; lovely, enthralling shops of every conceivable kind, at which they gazed speechless until all of a sudden the conductor called out just behind them: 'Piccadilly Circus and the Pop—'ere you are, miss, and mind 'ow you cross.'

They scuttled down the stairs, and on to the pavement, with polite good-byes to the conductor as they passed. Dinah looked round her hurriedly, in the hope of identifying the Pop before the others could tell her what they thought of her.

'It's over the road, at any rate,' she said defensively.

'It's there,' said John, pointing to a building almost directly opposite. 'There—don't you see? Lyons Popular Café. The Pop. Let's go over.'

The Pop came up to all Dinah's most extravagant expectations. It was big. It was grand, and rich-looking, and warm, and full of people, with waiters running about in all directions and boys pushing trolleys loaded with astonishing cakes. It had an orchestra, which when they came in was playing selections from *The Gondoliers* with tremendous vigour. An elegant gentleman in black led them to a table near the wall; an elegant waiter hurried up and took their order; and before they had really relaxed and got settled down there was a steaming tea-pot in front of them and a plateful of delicious-looking sandwiches.

They soon revived, and that tea-time became for many years a landmark in Dinah's life. It was their first adventure in London. It was the grandest place she had ever been in, and they had achieved it all by themselves without any assistance from well-meaning aunts or parents. In fact, the only person who had assisted was she herself, by her brilliance in the bus. Dinah, having eaten all that she possibly could, leaned her elbows on the table, admired the playing of the first violin (whom she found extremely handsome), and was ecstatically, inexpressibly happy.

CHAPTER III

SHADOW OVER KENSINGTON

THE Farthings arrived back in South Kensington that evening at half-past five, their half-crowns well and truly got rid of. They felt almost like Londoners already. They had been to Piccadilly. They had caught a No. 74 bus home from there almost as if they did it every night of their lives. Infinitely more cheerful than they had been when they went out, they went into the dark hotel hall and straight upstairs to see if there was any news yet from the specialist.

Mrs Farthing answered their knock, and they went into their parents' room. Mr Farthing was sitting in the arm-chair, Mrs Farthing in front of the dressing-table.

'Hallo,' said Mr Farthing. 'How did you get on? Did you have a good time?' His voice was still lively, but he looked pale and tired.

'Oh, yes, thank you, Daddy. Lovely. What about you, though?'

'Oh, me—not too good, I 'm afraid. Not *bad*, but just rather tiresome.' He exchanged a quick look with his wife, which all three of the children noticed. 'Don't bother to take your things off—I 'm afraid Aunt Harrison 's asked you to go round and pay your respects to her.'

'She would,' said John disgustedly. 'But what about you, Daddy? What did the specialist say?'

'Nothing very much,' replied his father. 'That 's really the nuisance. You see...' He thought over his words carefully. 'He examined me very thoroughly, and he 's more or less sure that it 's in my spine, in which case he has some injections which he 's practically sure will cure

35

it. But it may be due to that fever germ I picked up in Salonika. He can't be sure without more investigation. And so he says—and so he 's asked me to go into hospital for a short time, so that he can really make all the proper tests.'

There was a short silence. Mr Farthing did not look at them, but sat waiting, giving them time.

'Into hospital!' Dinah's voice was alarmed. When he heard her, he turned and smiled.

'Yes,' he said. 'But you mustn't be frightened. It 's nothing, really. I 'll be just as well there as I am now, only they want to have me handy to see the result of their tests. That 's only reasonable, one can see. And it won't be long.'

'How long?'

'Oh, a week or two, I should think. Not much more.'

Vivien tried to take hold of her fears.

'Do you know what hospital?' she asked.

'Yes. The London Hospital. It 's in Whitechapel, in the east of London.'

'That 's a very long way away,' said John.

'Yes, it is. I 'd have liked to be in a nursing home, near here—there are dozens of them in the neighbourhood. But he says that 's the best place in London for making these particular tests—they rather specialize in my kind of germ. And of course it 's infinitely cheaper, and that matters rather a lot. So it 's a great advantage that he can get me in there.'

'Oh! Well, when are you going?'

'Very soon, I 'm afraid. In fact, to-morrow.'

'*To-morrow!*'

'Sir William rang up,' said Mrs Farthing, 'and there happened to be a bed. We couldn't miss the chance.'

'Oh. Can we come and see you?' asked Dinah, gazing

intently at her father as if she must at all costs remember what he looked like.

'Yes, of course you can. Very often, I hope.'

'But where are we going to be? Are we going to stay in this—this place?'

Mr Farthing shook his head.

'That 's what we don't know,' he said. 'Mummy and I have been talking it over. It isn't a very nice place, but it 's cheap, and if I can't go to my job just yet we 've got to consider that. And you see, we want to make sure how we stand before we make a real home anywhere. I mean, we don't yet know where it would be best to live, or anything.'

'Not in South Kensington,' said John, looking up with his head on one side.

'But it *must* be somewhere here,' Dinah rounded on him quickly. 'What about my school?'

'Huh!' said John. 'Ever heard of buses?'

'Easy now, easy. We can argue about it all later on, when we know a bit more what there is to argue about. For the next week or so, at any rate, I 'm afraid Mummy and you will have to stay on here.'

A visit to Aunt Harrison was not the most exhilarating cure for bad news, and the three Farthings were very subdued as they went round to obey her summons. All the fun had suddenly gone out of being in London. They forgot the Pop, and the trees of Hyde Park Corner, and the friendly conductor. They thought of hospitals, and dingy hotels, and London, once again seemed a huge, smoky, dirty, hostile place. Vivien suddenly remembered the scent of the trees on a cool evening down at Berrings, and wished again with all her heart that they were back there.

37

Aunt Harrison's house in Queen's Gate looked outwardly almost the same as the hotel where they were staying: white, stuccoed, with many rectangular windows and a pillared porch. But inside it was a world entirely of its own—a world of some fifty years ago, unchanged through all the changes that had taken place in the world outside. Aunt Harrison was rich. Her husband was dead, her son grown up and married, but she lived on as she had always lived, alone in a house that would have held twenty people, waited on by her elderly maids and an elderly butler called Wheeler. The house was dark and sumptuous, and to the Farthings' taste extremely dull, full of large mahogany furniture which they understood to be 'good.' Aunt Harrison herself, with her piled-up white hair, her dignified movements, her fine but out-of-fashion clothes, and her stiff, ceremonious manners, belonged so completely to such a house that wherever she went she carried its atmosphere with her. To see her at Berrings had always made the children feel acutely uncomfortable—they almost preferred to visit her in Queen's Gate, where at any rate she looked at home.

To-day, having seen their parents just before and heard of Mr. Farthing's illness, Aunt Harrison had a congenial subject to talk about.

'It *is* so unfortunate that your dear father's health is so bad,' she said when they had been greeted and directed to suitable chairs near her own. 'He doesn't appear to have the Farthing constitution.'

They could find no answer to this, so they all sat silent.

'I suppose the specialist knows what he is about,' Aunt Harrison went on. 'There are so many cranks nowadays. But a hospital—a public ward, I understand, in an East End hospital…. These are indeed strange times.'

She really means to be sympathetic, I believe, thought Vivien, listening in a kind of dull misery as Aunt Harrison went on. She watched Dinah's fingers playing a tune on her knee, and John's toe rubbing against the leg of his chair, and knew exactly how they were feeling. A clock struck, and the three politely blank faces became even blanker as they worked out how soon they might go.

But a visit to Aunt Harrison had one advantage, at any rate—it roused their spirit considerably. They were so angry by the time they went away that the minute they were out in the free air again they all three burst out at once.

' "A public ward, I understand...!" '

' "So unfortunate for your dear mother!" As if we didn't know that!'

'And what a pity it is that they brought us all up with them to London! That really made me wild,' said John, stamping his feet down angrily on the pavement.

'Me, too,' said Vivien.

'I 'd like to have seen them trying to leave us behind,' observed Dinah grimly. 'Here we are, and here we stay, and if it 's only to annoy Aunt Harrison, I 'm going to *adore* being in London.'

Their wrath entertained Mr and Mrs Farthing so much that somehow their own spirits began to rise again as they let off steam.

'Well, you 've done your duty for a bit now, at any rate,' said their father. 'Poor old Aunt Harrison. She used to be just the same to me when I was a boy. By the way, don't you think it might be a good idea to go to the cinema after dinner to-night? I 'd like to see the new Charles Laughton, and this isn't the liveliest place in the world to spend our evening!'

His suggestion was warmly welcomed by them all, particularly by Dinah, who perceived that no mention at all was being made of her bed-time. Dinner at the hotel was rather an ordeal, but at any rate it did not last long. The old ladies and the white-headed old gentleman said 'Good evening' to them, but everybody's ambition seemed to be to eat the full allowance provided for them in the shortest possible time, and they were all too busy competing for the waiter's attention to spare much interest for anybody else.

They got out of the hotel as quickly as possible when dinner was over, not wanting to have any coffee. A taxi took them to Piccadilly Circus, and in less than twenty minutes they were sitting in the warm, comfortable darkness of a huge cinema, laughing hard at the hoarse misfortunes of Donald Duck.

Donald Duck was so funny, and the new Charles Laughton film so magnificent, that by the time the performance was over their troubles seemed to have mysteriously withdrawn far away into the distance. Happy and sleepy, they collected themselves together. They joined the crowd that was slowly moving towards the doors—and then, suddenly, they came out into the rich, million-lighted darkness of a London night. There were people everywhere; there were lights everywhere, flashing, winking, making many-coloured patterns and pictures on the fronts of high, strange buildings. Everything was alive, and London was suddenly somehow friendly again.

What a strange place it was, thought Vivien. Did it just seem to change according to how one was feeling, or was the character of its many different parts so strong that they could change one's whole outlook? It was enchanting almost in the old fairy-tale sense of the word—a huge, living, scarcely credible city, that could weave as strong a spell as any magician.

Whatever it might be, the whole family seemed to feel it. They said little, but each of them knew the others were content again; and it was a quiet, peaceful, unafraid family that clambered into a taxi and drove back through the bright London streets to South Kensington.

CHAPTER IV

EXPLORERS' DISCOVERY

'GOOD-BYE, Vivien. Good-bye John. Tell Mummy I 'll write this evening.'

Mr Farthing turned to go with the nurse who was waiting. A porter took charge of his suit-case, and before Vivien could realize that he was really going, her father had disappeared round a corner of the hospital's big, dim entrance hall. She swallowed, and told herself once more that it was ridiculous to be afraid—nothing but good could happen to him here, and he would soon be back with them again. But telling oneself did not make one stop, all the same.

For a moment, she and John stood without speaking, gazing at the corridor down which their father had gone. Then John turned abruptly round.

'Well,' he said. 'We 'd better go.'

They went out of the hospital, and down the entrance slope into the wide street. Trams, buses, and cars roared past them. Children were playing on the pavements, women gossiping in the sunshine. Gay, cheap little shops offered Paris hats, best beef, fruit, or permanent waves. It was London all right, but quite a different London from any they had seen as yet. It was Whitechapel Road.

'There 's the tube station, just over there.'

They had been advised to go back by tube, and given full directions. Vivien looked at the tube station, and then at John.

'Don't let 's go back,' she said suddenly. 'Why should we? Mummy and Dinah are out.'

John gave an enormous sigh of relief.

'No,' he said. 'Let 's not. Not to that beastly hotel. I want to walk, or something.'

Feeling more miserable than either of them cared to admit, they set off to the left, in the direction from which the taxi had brought them only a few minutes ago.

'Let 's go on and on walking,' said John. 'I saw a No. 9 bus at that place Daddy showed us—what was it called?—Bank, or something. We can always get home from there.'

They walked on again, not speaking; wondering about their father, wondering what the doctors would find, wondering what was going to happen to him, and to all the family, in the future that looked so obscure. And then, all of a sudden, Vivien thought of something else.

'I wish I knew what Mummy 's gone for,' she said. John nodded. It had puzzled them both that their mother should have an appointment, to-day of all days, so important that it prevented her from coming to the hospital with Mr Farthing. Unless, of course, Vivien reflected, she had preferred to say good-bye to him quietly, alone, and not in that distressing hospital atmosphere: that, too, was possible. But it was difficult not to suppose there was something more as well.

'It 's nothing to do with Dinah, I think, although she took her.'

'No, I think you 're right. Dinah had to have a new coat, and perhaps this was just a good chance or something.'

'Well, anyway, we 'll know soon, I suppose.'

'I suppose so.'

They walked on, and on, and on, and on. The buildings got higher, until they towered like grey cliffs on either side of the road. The bright little shops had ceased. There were tea-shops now, and stationers, and typewriter shops—the sort of shops that would be needed by people working in offices. They were out of the East End, and were coming into the City. Soon they reached the big traffic junction where they had seen their old friend the No. 9, but by mutual consent they did not look for the bus stop.

'It goes down this street here, so we might just as well go on,' said John. 'We can get one as soon as we want to. It's rather interesting, walking about like this,' he added.

His voice sounded almost cheerful again, and Vivien realized when she heard him that she was also beginning to recover. It *was* fun, to be walking through the City. The streets and the shops and the offices were again quite a different London from the others they had seen. The people were different, too; young men from offices, very tidy, some talking and laughing as if they were at leisure, others hurrying along with dispatch cases under their arms, and here and there young women from offices also, just coming out for their lunch—very smart young women mostly, walking in couples and talking as if they had a whole morning's silence to make up for.

'Let's have some lunch up here somewhere, and see what it's like,' said Vivien.

'Oh, that's a good idea. Which reminds me,' added John in an interested voice, 'I'm beastly hungry.'

They began to look out for a suitable tea-shop, but did not immediately see one. They had not the least idea where they were, but a No. 9, swinging round a corner just as they came to it, assured them that they were still on a safe route and were not completely lost. Suddenly, looking up to their right, they found they were just coming up beside an immense grey building which had a narrow little green garden running round it.

'What on earth can this be?' said John.

Through the high railings and an open gate they could see flowers, grass, trees, and benches on which a number of people were sitting in the sunshine. Many of them were eating out of little paper packages; some were talking, some knitting, but by far the most were busy reading.

'It looks like a park, but it's a very tiny one.'

'Yes, but the building. Can it be a church, or something?'

'Oh—I know!' Hurrying forward, Vivien rounded a corner of the vast building—there was no garden now any more—and looked up. 'Yes, I thought it was,' she said triumphantly. 'It's St Paul's.'

John looked about him. They had emerged into bright sunshine, and were now on a large asphalt space in front of the cathedral. The road and the offices skirted round its edge, and tipped down a hill in front of them. There was a statue in the middle of the open space. There were pigeons flying about in clouds and people calling to them to come and be fed. There were people everywhere, all of a sudden, walking and talking and laughing in the sunshine; and on their right, up a long, wide flight of steps, was the grey, pillared, beautiful front of St Paul's Cathedral.

John gasped.

'Oh, what fun!' he said. 'Come on and look.'

They hurried out into the middle of the open space, near the statue, from which they could enjoy the whole scene. A big motor coach drew up at the pavement close beside them, and a crowd of people tumbled out and instantly turned their heads towards the cathedral. '*Saint* Paul's,' shouted someone, with a heavy accent on the 'Saint.' 'Twenty minutes.'

The crowd hurried past, and thronged up the flight of

steps. 'Coo, ain't it big,' said a voice as they passed. 'Ed, where 's your Kodak?' In half a minute they had all disappeared inside the shadowy doorway, and the asphalt was left to those whom Vivien and John already felt to be its natural inhabitants.

There was so much to see that they hardly knew where to look next; but the first thing to do, they had not the slightest doubt, was to go into St Paul's itself. They turned with one consent, and followed Ed and his companions up to the doorway. The shadow of the great portico fell cool upon them after the warm sunshine, and somehow, even outside the cathedral, they could feel the promise of something grand and exciting just within its doors.

Vivien was half-afraid that the bus-load of tourists would fill up the cathedral with their exclamations and clatter, but she need not have worried. They were far away down the other end when she and John came in, and so huge, so magnificent was the nave of St Paul's that the people in the building shrank into tiny, unimportant beings beside its towering grey columns and the high, graceful arches of its roof. From where they stood, the arches of the nave soared away in front of them, and far down its length rose into an even higher, grander space, which Vivien realized must be the inside of the great dome; and beyond that again, tiny in the distance, but perfectly distinct, was the choir and the high altar.

Neither Vivien nor John wanted to speak. Here was something different from any place they had ever seen before; vaster, more calm and yet more inspiring, with a character all of its own. For several minutes they stood where they were inside the door, gazing ahead of them. Then, quietly and almost timidly, they went down the nave to see the rest of the cathedral.

It was all in keeping—spacious, dignified, and lovely. They saw the dome, they saw the exquisitely carved seats of the choir, and the grandeur of the altar. They saw more than they could possibly take in on a first visit, and yet knew very well that they had not seen a quarter of all there was. And before they went out they went back to the place where they had first come in: for it was that view, down the nave to the dome and the altar, that they thought they could never forget.

'We 've got to come back here,' whispered John as, with a last look back, they opened the door. It was the only thing either of them said, but there was no need to say more. They understood each other.

'And I don't know about you,' John added in his ordinary voice, blinking as they came to the strong sunlight of the big open space below the steps, 'but I 'm hungrier and hungrier. Shall we go over to the shops and look for somewhere to eat?'

'All right. It 'll have to be a Lyons, though, or something like that,' added Vivien cautiously. 'I haven't much money.'

They crossed a road, and came to the further pavement, and began as John had suggested, to walk along past the shops. The whole scene was dominated by the great cathedral, but it was a very human scene all the same, full of vans and buses and people and pigeons and shops, and as they wandered along and peered into shop windows they felt almost like the old habitués who were doing the same thing on every side of them.

'Oh—just a minute. Here 's a nice shop.'

John stopped, and began to flatten his nose against one of the shop windows. It was a little stationer's and printer's, and Vivien studied its contents with interest also, though without John's passionate absorption in the

47

new printing gadget which was the centre of attraction. People went past them, talking, and they heard nothing of what was going on: but suddenly they heard something so unexpected that it caught the attention of them both.

'Where are the sausages, Pete?'

'Under the gramophone, I believe—and the butter's on the roof, of course.'

Vivien looked up, and John also. Two young men had just come out of a doorway beside the stationer's, and were saying good-bye to each other. One had on flannel trousers and a pullover, and was hatless: the other was dressed in a dark grey suit and a black felt hat, and was as neat as the first was untidy. It was easy to see that they were brothers, all the same; both had gingery brown hair, and their voices were so much alike that one could hardly tell which of them was speaking.

'I 'll be back as early as possible,' said the tidy one.

'Right you are. Good hunting, Pete.'

Pete walked way, and his brother, after a thoughtful look round, turned to go back into the building from which they had come. As he did so, he almost collided with a little old woman who was just coming out.

'Oh, I 'm so sorry, Mrs Jones.'

'Dear me, Mr Wilkins, that 's quite all right.' The old woman nodded amiably at him, and the young man, running his fingers through his untidy hair, gave a half-smile and disappeared.

'Do you suppose that they live here?' said Vivien in a low voice, much interested.

'I thought no one lived in the City. I thought it was only offices and things.'

'Oh, *no*, sir, if you 'll excuse me—'

They spun round in astonishment. There was only one person who could possibly have spoken. The little

48

old woman was just beside them, busy buttoning up her gloves and hanging a large umbrella and a shopping basket in their proper places on her arm.

'You must excuse me, sir, and you, miss, but I couldn't help speaking to you.'

She was a charming old woman, thin and upright, with pink cheeks and grey hair on top of which was pinned a massive black hat. John said 'How do you do,' very gravely, and she smiled.

'Plenty of people do live in the City,' she said. 'I do myself. Lived here twenty years, we have, me and my husband.'

'What—in here?' John nodded at the doorway.

'Yes. He 's a caretaker, you see. That 's his building. Them young gentlemen live here too, up on the fifth at the back.'

'Oh! Is it nice, living in there?' The Farthings were always ready for a little conversation, and Vivien was fascinated by the old woman's quiet, friendly manner.

'Lovely,' said Mrs Jones with emphasis. 'We 've got front rooms, you see, and we can have a look at everything what 's going on. My family was ever so sorry for me at first, coming to live here—they hadn't the least idea. Country people don't have, you know.'

Vivien smiled.

'We 're country people,' she said. 'We 've just come to London, yesterday. We certainly didn't know how nice it was up here.'

'Just come to London? Well!' The old woman sounded much impressed. 'Well, now! Are you going to live here?'

'I think so. Only my father 's ill, and we don't quite know till he gets a little better.'

'Oh dear, oh dear.' Mrs Jones contrived very cleverly to be sympathetic and yet to make it quite clear that she was not the sort of person who would keep on asking questions. 'Well,' she went on after a pause, 'I must be getting on to the shops, or my husband will have something to say to me.' She arranged the big umbrella on her arm, and turned to go. 'If ever you 're up in these parts again,' she added, 'I 'd be pleased—real pleased—if you 'd step in and have a drink of tea.'

And almost before they could say good-bye, she was gone—vanished down a little passage so narrow that until that moment they had not noticed it.

'What a pet,' said Vivien.

'Yes, wasn't she? Let 's have a look inside,' added John with great interest, peering inside the dark door way of Mr Jones's 'building.'

'I don't see why not—it 's public, I suppose, in a sort of way.'

It was cold inside the doorway, after the warm sun outside, and so dark that for a moment they could not see anything at all. But gradually shapes began to emerge, and they saw that they were in a small square hall with a staircase and the closed doors of a lift. On the wall on their right was a name-board, and John turned to this at once.

'Overton House,' he read out. 'First floor, Messrs Brown and Hippalite. Second floor, Messrs Williams, the Coral Copying Bureau, Mr Montgomery. Third floor, the City Distributing Company, Pekin Carpets Ltd, Mr P. Jones (caretaker). Fourth floor, nobody. Fifth floor, N. B. G. Nilpil. What a funny name! And there are no Mr Wilkinses anywhere.'

'Perhaps they 're N. B. G. Nilpil. Oh, look, here 's a notice!'

Vivien peered closer to read the neat, handwritten note which was pinned on to the base of the board.

"De *f*irable suite to be let," she read slowly. "Four light offices and cloakrooms. Beautiful outlook. Or would suit private per*f*ons." She began to laugh. 'I bet Mrs Jones wrote that,' she said. 'That 's how Aunt Harrison always writes her *f*'s, too.'

'Yes.' John's voice sounded abstracted 'Here—let me see a minute.' He stared at the little notice, not saying anything. Suddenly he caught Vivien by the elbow.

'Vivien—Vivien!'

'Yes. What?'

'Vivien, look at that. Four rooms—beautiful outlook, and would suit private persons. Why shouldn't we—why shouldn't we come and live here?'

Startled, Vivien turned and stared at him. Slowly his enthusiasm began to communicate itself to her. They looked at each other, and back again at the handwritten notice.

'I can't imagine how it could be worked,' she said at last, 'but it *would* be fun if we could.'

CHAPTER V

QUEER PEOPLE

THEY might have stood there for another half hour, discussing the possibilities, but they suddenly remembered how exceedingly hungry they were.

'Come on—lunch,' said Vivien firmly. John needed no persuading, and they set off at the brisk pace which, as Vivien had already noticed, distinguished those City inhabitants who had not yet had a meal from those who had finished. They found a Lyons only a very short distance farther on, and hurried hungrily in. It seemed at first to be completely full, but people were coming and going so fast that soon a table just beside them fell empty. They settled down, and on the advice of a friendly waitress had what she described as 'steak pudding twice with veges,' and ices and coffee afterwards.

'It 's good fun watching all the people,' said John, when his hunger was sufficiently satisfied for him to take notice of their various neighbours. 'That 's one of the big advantages of London, at any rate—there are always queer people to look at.'

'Yes, that 's certainly true. Queer people and queer places. It does make up for Berrings a little. It 's a bit like the adventures we used to have when we were small— finding places to picnic, and new ways up on the downs, and that kind of thing.'

'It 's London adventure instead of country adventure,' said John, seeing at once what she meant. 'It 's rather nice, I think. But the people *are* queer, aren't they? Not only in here, but everywhere. Nobody seems to be ordinary at all.'

Vivien looked round at the tables near them. There

were thin sad men, fat thoughtful men, small lively girls, studious boys with gangster stories, chattering girls, meditative girls, old men with lunch-time newspapers— dozens of people, but not a single one of whom they could instantly have used the word 'ordinary.'

'The old woman we met, for instance,' John went on, warming to his subject. 'She wasn't ordinary. Nor the two queer chaps who kept the sausages under the gramophone. And none of the people at the hotel are ordinary— they 're as queer as queer can be! I 'll tell you what, Vivien—I 'm going to start a collection.'

'What of?'

John propped his elbows on the marble-topped table.

'Of queer people we meet—un-ordinary people. In fact it can be a competition, if you like. Yes, that 's even better. We each get a mark for any one we meet who the other agrees isn't ordinary. We 'd have Dinah in it too, of course. What do you think of that?'

Vivien was not quite sure. It was a good idea, in its way—but collecting queer people was her own special province, as an author looking for material. She did not much care to share so important a matter with two irreverent children.

However, John was busy elaborating his idea.

'We ought to start fair, so I won't bag that old woman,' he said magnanimously. 'We 'll begin to-morrow. Let 's say that the first person to claim a Queer, after two at least of us have been talking to him (to the Queer, I mean), gets a point if the other one agrees. Wouldn't that do?'

'Very well,' said Vivien, sacrificing her rights as an author for the good of the family. 'It sounds quite fun.' After all, what did it matter? The others could collect Queers as they might collect cigarette cards, but they could not do anything else about them. But the day might come when they would read about these very people, whom they had collected and forgotten about, in stories by Vivien Farthing, or perhaps even in a book. And Vivien, cautious enough to say nothing about her schemes until she had something concrete to show for them, wandered off into dreams of the future while John, concentrating on the present, ordered himself another ice.

Mrs Farthing and Dinah, it seemed, had also been having an interesting time.

'We 've been at Greencoat's, in Regent Street,' said Mrs Farthing in answer to John's questions. 'My very old friend Margaret Hadfield is a buyer there. She came down to Berrings once, if you remember.'

'I remembered her perfectly,' said Dinah. 'She 's rather fat now. She and Mummy talked for hours.'

'Yes, I 'm afraid we did. But Dinah was well amused, going all round the place with one of the young assistants. You see——' Mrs Farthing hesitated a moment before she went on. 'Margaret and I had something special to talk about. I can't tell you now—I wish I could. I promise faithfully I 'll tell you the first moment I can, and that will be when we hear a little more about Daddy.'

'Oh. When will that be?'

'We can't be certain. He rather hoped he might be able to tell us something when he writes to-night.'

'Oh. I see. I suppose,' said John slowly, 'it 's no good talking about anything, really, until we know about Daddy. I mean about where we 're going to live, and that kind of thing.'

'Well, not much good,' said Mrs Farthing. 'Nothing can be finally fixed, you see, until we know.'

John shot a meaning look at Vivien, who nodded in

agreement. It was no good talking about those rooms in the City for the moment. They could, however, talk about all their other discoveries, and they gave Mrs Farthing and Dinah a spirited account of them all, ending up with John's newly invented competition.

Dinah was not as scornful of it as she might have been. 'That 's not so bad,' she said. 'Could I have Aunt Harrison and the fuzzy-headed old lady downstairs?'

'Why should you have them any more than me?'

A hot argument at once developed as to who should have whom of all the people they knew, and at last, Mrs Farthing intervening, they agreed that the competition was only to start the next day, and that nobody to whom any of them had ever talked should be included.

'And if you ever meet any one whom you all think ordinary, let me know!' she said. 'What *is* an ordinary person, by your rules?'

This took a bit of thinking out, but John at last said that it was somebody of whom one could say that he (or she) was very nice, and absolutely nothing more.

'That sounds dull enough, certainly,' said Mrs Farthing. 'Talking of which, we really ought to go and sit downstairs soon for a bit. This room isn't much fun to sit in, and we ought to be polite a little now and again.'

'Why?' said Dinah promptly.

Mrs Farthing laughed.

'If ever one was in danger of becoming conventional, children like you and John are a very good safeguard,' she said. 'Well, I suppose, partly to give you some practice— you don't get any too much! And it 's expected if one comes to stay in a place like this, and as we 've nothing urgent to do we might just as well give the old ladies something to talk about. Are those enough reasons to get on with?'

'H'm. *I* 'll give the old ladies something to talk about,

if you like,' answered Dinah without hesitation.

'Dinah, you will not.' So firm was her mother's answer that Dinah, with a startled glance, subsided, and her behaviour downstairs was so unnaturally sweet and polite that Mrs Farthing and Vivien, catching each other's eyes, had great difficulty in not laughing aloud. The old ladies were in the drawing-room in full force, and when the Farthing family arrived they set to work without a moment's delay to find out as much about them as they possibly could.

'It 's like being interviewed for a job,' murmured Vivien to John while Mrs Farthing was dealing with the volley of questions. 'All they 've forgotten to ask is whether we are sober, willing, and honest!'

However, by the time they had found out where the Farthings came from, who Mrs Farthing had been before she married, whom Mr Farthing had worked for, what he was suffering from, what the family proposed to do in London, what schools John and Dinah would be likely to go to and what were their favourite subjects, the old ladies seemed more or less satisfied. Conversation turned to more general topics, and at one time Dinah and Vivien were engaged upon a keen discussion of Princess Elizabeth (of whose doings they knew nothing at all) in one part of the room, while Mrs Farthing discussed new novels in another and John joined in a brisk argument about the latest behaviour of the Government. It was funny, but it was also extremely boring, and when seven o'clock came and the gong began its majestic boomings in the hall the Farthing family leaped to its feet with a punctuality that would have earned the approval of the manageress herself, and joined very willingly in the dignified yet somewhat hasty procession that at once made its way to the dining-room.

CHAPTER VI

A FLAT IN THE CITY

WHEN Vivien came down to breakfast the next morning, Herbert, emerging with a broom from behind one of the palm trees in the hall, told her in a loud whisper that her mother was in the drawing-room.

'But my sister 's gone in to breakfast,' said Vivien, puzzled, 'and John too, hasn't he?'

'Yes, miss, but your mother asked me to be sure and tell you where she was.' Herbert nodded as if to say that if ever any one wanted messages delivered, he was the man who could be trusted to deliver them properly.

'Oh. Thank you.' Vivien hurried to the drawing-room, where she found her mother reading a letter close to one of the windows.

'Good morning, Mummy. Herbert said you wanted me.'

'Good morning.' Mrs Farthing looked up and smiled, but her face was white. Vivien guessed easily enough that the letter was from her father. She caught her breath.

'Have you heard——'

'From Daddy? Yes.' Mrs Farthing turned over the letter once again, as if she had read it many times already. It was written in pencil: and the glimpse of those scribbled pencil words, instead of her father's usual tidy letters, brought a sudden, painfully vivid picture of him lying writing in bed in the hospital.

'Yes, he 's written a long letter.' Mrs Farthing looked up into Vivien's eyes. 'Vivien, darling, we shall have to think hard to-day.'

'Why—what 's happened?'

'Nothing 's happened, luckily. But Daddy says that—

that they are very doubtful whether they can cure him at all quickly. They want to keep him longer in the hospital, for one thing—anything from three weeks to three months, he thinks—and they can't promise that he 'll be fit to work at once when he comes out.'

There was a short silence. Vivien's heart began to beat very fast.

'Then—what are we going to do?'

'That 's just what we 've got to think,' said Mrs Farthing. 'As you can see, if Daddy is going to be laid up for a few months—it won't be more, he feels sure—then we 've got to find some way of living during that time. We haven't enough money for everything unless somebody earns some.'

'Couldn't I——' began Vivien quickly. But her mother had more to say.

'I told you I went to see Margaret Hadfield yesterday,' she went on. 'I met her in the old days, you know, when I ran away from home and worked in a shop. That was a terrible thing to do when I was a girl—not at all like it is now. Margaret has a very grand job nowadays, buying all the model dresses for Greencoat's; and by a queer stroke of luck, she 's temporarily lost one of her assistants, and she offered me the job.'

'*You*, Mummy?'

Mrs Farthing laughed at the tone of Vivien's voice. 'Oh, I 'm really quite qualified for it. I used to deal with just the same sort of work, though of course on a much less important scale.'

'Yes, I don't mean that. But——'

'You mean it 's all wrong for me to go out to work,' said Mrs Farthing quickly. 'I know, darling. It *is* wrong, in a way. But we can't see anything else to be done, the way things are for the moment.'

'Does Daddy know, then?'

'Oh, yes, he knew why I was going to see Margaret. He hoped it wouldn't come to this, of course—he hoped he'd be out of the hospital soon and able to work. But he wasn't *very* hopeful, I think.

Mrs Farthing sighed. Vivien tried frantically to catch some of the dozen different questions that were whirling about in her mind.

'Then—then—where are we going to live?' she said at last.

'Yes, that's the biggest question, or one of them. Not here, certainly,' said Mrs Farthing with a little smile. 'I suppose in rooms or a maisonnette somewhere in one of the cheaper parts of Kensington. We shall have to begin looking out. It must be on one of the underground lines, so that we can get to Daddy and I can get to work; and I must say, I wish it wasn't quite so far away from the hospital.'

'From the hospital?' Vivien looked up quickly. There was a sudden flicker of hope in her eyes. 'Oh, Mummy!'

'What is it, darling? Have you got an idea?'

'Oh, yes, I do believe I have.' Vivien's voice was eager. 'But John ought to be here too, really, because the idea was his first. May we wait till after breakfast and talk about it then?'

Mrs Farthing laughed. She looked much less white now.

'All right—that's fine,' she said. 'And let's go in to breakfast straight away. Madam won't be at all pleased with us if we're very much later.'

Vivien said nothing to John at breakfast—it was not possible to explain it all in so public a place, and they were kept busy answering observations on the lovely spring weather from the nearest old ladies, and telling them that yes, thank you, they slept very well in London and did not notice the noise. As soon as all four of them had finished—and Dinah was last, having taken a fancy to eat all through the breakfast menu for a change—they went upstairs.

Mrs Farthing's room was being done, so they went along to the one Vivien and Dinah slept in, and were pleased to find that the beds had already been made and everything put tidy. Mrs Farthing sat down in the wicker armchair and Vivien on her bed, while John and Dinah, looking rather puzzled, stood in the middle of the room.

Mrs Farthing began at once to explain matters, and Vivien was glad she had been told beforehand, for Dinah and John managed to make a considerable uproar before they finally understood everything to their own satisfaction. Their questions, it could not be denied, were perfectly reasonable ones: but it would never have occurred to Vivien to ask, as John did, what kind of X-ray had been used for Mr Farthing and whether he might see the plates, or, as Dinah did, whether her mother would be required to act as a mannequin and if they had measured her figure for it. At last, however, they began to quieten down.

Vivien caught her mother's eye.

'Now may I——?' she inquired. Her mother nodded, and Vivien quickly began to speak.

'John and I were in the City yesterday,' she began. 'While you were at Greencoat's, you know—after we left Daddy. It 's lovely there, in front of St Paul's, and we walked about, and then we met an old woman whose husband is caretaker in one of the office buildings. It turned out—we saw a notice of hers—that there was a suite to let in her building which could be used as a flat, and John suggested that it might be a good place for us to go and live.'

She looked at her mother. Mrs Farthing looked surprised, but decidedly interested, and Vivien quickly went on.

'We didn't see how it could be worked, yesterday,' she said, 'but now everything is so different that it really looks—it really looks like an idea. You see, it 's near Daddy for one thing——'

'Yes,' put in John, who had listened with admirable patience to her explanation of his scheme, 'and it would be good for Mummy too, as it 's on the Central London railway, almost, and she could go to Oxford Circus from St Paul's Station.'

'And it wouldn't be any dearer than Kensington, would it?' added Vivien.

'It might even be cheaper,' said Mrs Farthing. 'I 've always heard that City rents are fairly low.'

'And John and Dinah could get to school just as well from there, couldn't they?'

'Well, that *is* a question,' said Mrs Farthing thoughtfully. 'If Dinah wants to go to St Monan's, up here, that 's a very long way away. But we can see.'

Her tone was not at all that of someone raising objections, but that of someone who likes a scheme and is trying in every way to see if it cannot be managed.

Vivien and John exchanged a quick, delighted glance, and Vivien hurried to produce the principal point of her argument.

'And then, you see, Mummy, what I thought was that if you are out all day, and the others are at school, it could be my department to run the house and do the cooking.

Mrs Farthing looked at her keenly.

'But, darling, what about that journalism course? I

61

hoped that now you really would get a chance to do something you wanted to.'

Vivien avoided her mother's eyes.

'Oh, that,' she said, as if she had almost forgotten it. 'Oh, it doesn't matter at all, truly. I 'd much rather stay at home. We 'd have to have a maid otherwise, and that would be a waste of money, and you see I can go and see Daddy every day, and we did talk of domestic science too, and that 's practically speaking what it will be, and in fact it 's much the best arrangement. Don't you think so, really?'

Mrs Farthing sat for a moment without speaking.

'If it can be worked, I do,' she said slowly. 'It 's not what I should have liked, any more than my going to Greencoat's is, but it will only be for a short time, we hope. Thank you, Vivien.'

She looked across at Vivien with a quick little smile. Vivien was delighted—delighted, and almost ashamed. It had sounded so noble, somehow, the way she had said it: and the truth of the matter was that, though she did very keenly want to help, she had also in her mind the fact that, with the family out all day, she would have more freedom than she had ever hoped for to get on with her writing. A whole flat to herself, no one else there, stories, publication, money, wealth for the family, all difficulties at an end—as always her imagination needed only one scrap of encouragement to go galloping away with her. It was with some difficulty that she recalled it and came back to attend to what her mother was saying.

'But of course,' Mrs Farthing went on, 'the first thing is to have a look at the flat—or office suite, or whatever it is. Daddy would be scandalized to hear us making plans like this without knowing what it is we 're planning about.

'You 're going to see him this afternoon, aren't you?'

'Yes. So we ought to get along there some time this morning. In fact,' said Mrs Farthing, looking at her watch, 'we ought to start the very moment we are ready, for it 's a long way to go, and we 've talked so much that it 's late already.'

They took a 74 bus outside the hotel, and at Hyde Park Corner changed on to their old friend No.9. Nobody talked much: there was so much to think about, both pleasant and otherwise, that they all wanted time to sort it all out in their minds. Even Dinah was subdued. She looked rather scornful about 'this City idea,' as she called it, but matters were too serious for her to say what in ordinary times she would certainly have said about a scheme arranged when she herself had not been present.

The journey took a long time, much of which was spent waiting in traffic blocks; but at last the bus began to climb Ludgate Hill, the beautiful, towering dome of St Paul's came closer, and it was time to get off. They climbed down the swaying staircase, and when the bus drew up beside the cathedral hopped off left foot first as if they had been Londoners for years.

'Now where is it?' inquired Mrs Farthing, looking round.

'Just over there. That red one, with the Stationer's window in it.'

'Oh, there. What a lovely position. There must be a beautiful view.'

'That 's just what Mrs Jones said.'

They hurried across the pavement as if every moment were valuable, and went into Overton House. There was a light in the lift this time, and the door was open; and inside, sitting on a stool and reading a newspaper, was an elderly man who they knew at once must be Mrs Jones's husband.

'Excuse me—good morning,' said John politely. The elderly man looked up. He was thin, and rather small, and he had a long, thin, drooping grey moustache which made him look like a sad but friendly walrus. He put down his paper and stood up.

'Aren't you Mr Jones?'

'Yes, I am,' said the man, surprised. 'Good morning, sir. Good morning, madam.'

'We understand,' said Mrs Farthing, 'that there are some rooms to let here. My son and daughter were here yesterday, and happened to meet your wife; and then they saw the notice about rooms to let, and we 've come to ask if we might see them.'

Mr Jones gave a sudden very charming smile. 'Why, the missus told me about you,' he said, looking at Vivien. 'She said as how you had a conversation, just outside here.' He turned back to Mrs Farthing. 'Yes, of course, madam. I 'm on lift duty, so I can't show you them myself, but if you 'll just step into the lift I 'll give a call for the missus on our way up.'

The family stepped into the lift. It was a very old-fashioned one, of carved mahogany with mirrors let into the back and sides; but as a contrast to this magnificence there was a perfectly ordinary rope running right through it in the front left-hand corner, and Mr Jones simply gave this rope a pull when he wanted to start and (mysteriously) another pull at the third floor when he wanted to stop. Having stopped it, he stepped out into the corridor and called 'Minnie! Minnie!'

'Coming, Phineas.'

It was Mrs Jones's voice, from not very far away, and in a moment she appeared, wiping her hands on the huge white apron which covered practically all of her except her head, her hands, and her toes.

'Good gracious me!' she said, when she saw whom the lift contained. 'Well, I never did! Good morning, madam, I 'm sure—and you, miss, and you, and you, sir.'

'This lady would like to see the fourth floor suite, Minnie. Will you go?'

'Of course, Phineas. Just wait while I shut the door.' Mrs Jones hurried back, and returned a second later putting a key into her apron pocket. She stepped into the lift, Mr Jones pulled the rope again, and in a moment they were up on the floor above and were all getting out. The lift bell rang, and Mr Jones, apologizing for his hasty departure, got back into the lift and swiftly disappeared.

'It 's just in here,' said Mrs Jones, producing a small bunch of keys from yet another pocket. She unlocked and opened a door, and ushered them all in.

'In here, madam—this is the principal room.'

The moment they got in they all rushed to the window. 'It does—it does look that way,' said Vivien delightedly. She pointed down, and there, far below them, was the pavement over which they had just walked from the bus, while on their left, clear down to the very faces of the statues, was the enormous pillared front of St Paul's.

'Well, that 's grand,' said Mrs Farthing with enthusiasm. 'We should never be dull with that to look at, anyway.' She turned round and looked more closely at the room they were in. 'It 's a beautiful big room, too,' she added. 'Isn't it unusually big for an office, Mrs Jones?'

'Yes, it is, really,' Mrs Jones answered. 'The ones underneath are divided into two or even three, all except ours. And then, you see,' she added, crossing to a door on the right, 'it joins on to the other front room, so there 's a good big stretch if ever you was to want to walk up and down and do some thinking.'

'That's one way of looking at it, certainly,' said Mrs Farthing, amused.

'Oh, well, you see, we have the rooms underneath, and they're just the same, so I know. My husband, he's a great one for a walk when he wants to think. Then this is the small front room, in here, and there's one big room and one smaller one at the back, opening out of each other.'

'It sounds as though it might just do for us,' said Mrs Farthing thoughtfully. 'But is there a bathroom, and so on?'

'Bathroom no, lavatory yes, on the bend of the staircase,' answered Mrs Jones rapidly. 'But there *is* running hot and cold water in the little cloakroom, what the last tenant had put in.'

'H'm. . . . No bathroom is a very big drawback, you know. But let's see the rest of the rooms, if we may.' The two rooms at the back were also very nice ones. They had of course no view like those in the front—in fact they looked on to a flat lead roof with other windows all round it. But they were airy, and clean, and had just been newly painted. Vivien realized that she would once again have to share a bedroom with Dinah, but in the present state of affairs that was hardly to be avoided.

'It *is* a nice flat,' said John. 'Do you think it will do for us, Mummy?'

Mrs Farthing, who was talking to Mrs Jones, turned round at his question.

'I'm more inclined to think so now Mrs Jones has told me the rent,' she said. 'It's most astonishingly cheap— I never imagined it was possible to get anything of the kind for such a price. Let's see the kitchen, or whatever it is, now, please, Mrs Jones, and then I'll talk to my husband this afternoon and get in touch with the landlord if he thinks it the thing to do.'

The kitchen, or cloakroom, or whatever one cared to call it, was a tiny room also facing on to the lead roof, with a forlorn-looking gas-ring standing on a metal-topped table in the corner.

'You see, there *is* gas,' said Mrs Jones, not without pride. 'The young ladies used to make tea in here, when these was offices.'

'Yes—but where is the hot and cold water?'

'Oh, that 's next door, where they all used to hang their clothes.' Mrs Jones led the way into another door, just behind the lift, and there to their surprise they saw quite a tolerable-sized little room, with a shining new wash-basin in one corner and a geyser on the wall above it.

'Why, we could fit a bath into here, easily, if we wanted to. This makes it *much* more promising,' said Mrs Farthing. 'I really couldn't imagine how we could manage without a bathroom of some kind, but this looks like the answer.'

They went round the rooms once more, discussing what each could be used for and how their furniture—or at least a very small proportion of it—could be fitted in. The big room, of course, would be their sitting-room, and the other front room Mr and Mrs Farthing's bedroom, while John would most likely have the outer back room and Vivien and Dinah the inner one.

'I almost begin to feel as if we lived here,' said Mrs Farthing at last, looking once more out of the window at the cathedral and the busy streets below.

'I 'm sure I hope you will do, madam,' said Mrs Jones warmly. 'Who ever would have thought, when I met Miss Vivien and Mr John yesterday, that I should have seen them again so soon. We 'd be real pleased to have you living here, and that 's no lie, and if I could be of any help any time with a bit of cleaning or anything of the kind, I 'd be only too pleased.'

'Thank you very much indeed,' said Mrs Farthing. 'Now I really think we must go—but I have a kind of feeling that in a very short time you will see us back again.'

CHAPTER VII

DINAH SEES TO THE FUTURE

MRS FARTHING was right. Less than forty-eight hours later the whole affair was settled, the lease signed, the delivery of their furniture arranged for. In a very few days they would once more be, not homeless wanderers in a private hotel, but a family with a genuine home of their own to live in. Not a genuine ordinary family—that was impossible as long as Mr Farthing was ill in hospital, and Mrs Farthing out all day at work; but at any rate they would have what Vivien called a burrow, and they were all immensely cheered at the thought of it.

Meanwhile, the time passed quickly. They had a great deal to see to, for Mrs Farthing was to start at Greencoat's on the following Monday, and before then not only the details about the flat, but the urgent question of schools for John and Dinah, had got to be finally settled. The days were not long enough. Every afternoon Mrs Farthing was allowed to go and see her husband, and with the long journey to and from Kensington that left her little spare time between lunch and dinner. Mr Farthing was in good spirits, and very comfortable, he said, but had nothing to report of himself except that the tests were proceeding as Sir William had arranged. For the short time she had left Mrs Farthing went to see him alone, for when she was working she would never be free to visit him except on Saturdays and Sundays; but as soon as they were living in the City Vivien or John or Dinah would be able to go and see him regularly.

The inhabitants of the hotel were fascinated and a little shocked to hear of the Farthings' new plans.

'In the *City*?' said one old lady over and over again. 'In the City? But my dear Mrs Farthing, in the *City*?'

'Yes,' said Mrs Farthing pleasantly. 'In the City.'

'But in the *City*! You know you can get the most delightful little maisonnettes in any of the streets round here, and this is such a *refined* neighbourhood.'

Their opinion of the City was easy to interpret; and when they learned, not only that Mrs Farthing was going to work in a shop, but that Mr Farthing was in a public ward in a big public hospital, there was a period when they almost began to feel that they could not know such an unrefined family any longer. However, their fundamental kindness of heart triumphed in the end, and they decided that the Farthings were so brave and unfortunate that the only thing to do was to be sorry for them—a course which all the family found extremely trying except Dinah, who got a large box of chocolates from the white-headed old gentleman to console her for the family misfortunes.

It was Dinah who suffered worst of them all from the present unsettled state of affairs. John was quieter, and to Vivien's surprise was taking a keen interest in the domestic details of their settling into the flat; but Dinah, who in any ordinary Easter holidays would have been half her time playing the fiddle and the other half running wild in the countryside around Berrings, was restless in the confined life of the hotel. She came shopping with them, but was soon tired of it. She came for long walks in Hyde Park and Kensington Gardens, but asphalt paths and flower-beds were a poor substitute for the downs, and without music life lost most of its interest.

'If only I could practise a bit it wouldn't be so bad,' she said one morning. 'But I got out my fiddle and tried, last night while you were downstairs, and Madam sent

Herbert rushing up to tell me I mustn't.'

'It *is* a shame,' said Mrs Farthing, worried. 'I wish we could think of some way out of it. You wouldn't care to go and practise at the school, I suppose, if we fixed things up with Miss Carruthers?'

One look from Dinah was enough to answer her; desperate things might be, but they were not yet sufficiently desperate for Dinah to wish to go near a school in the holidays. It had been more or less settled that she should go next term to St Monan's. A friend of hers had been sent there, and spoke enthusiastically of Mr Hepplewhite the violin master and of the orchestra which he conducted, and Mrs Farthing liked the head mistress and the school buildings and grounds. What Mrs Farthing liked much less, though, was the amount it would cost if Dinah were sent as a boarder. Yet the long journey to school and back every day would be extremely tiring; and Mrs Farthing was still hesitating, hoping against hope that perhaps enough money might turn up.

'Well, there 's another possibility,' Mrs Farthing went on. 'What about asking Aunt Harrison if you could go and practise there?'

'Oh . . .' This was clearly not much more to Dinah's taste than St Monan's; but matters were sufficiently serious for her to think it over carefully.

'There 's a piano in the schoolroom, and it 's at the top of the house, so nobody would hear you.'

'H'm. . . .' Dinah ran her left toe up the back of her right stocking, as she always did when specially deep in thought.

'Let 's go round to Aunt Harrison's, anyway, and see how she feels. We 've got half an hour or so now, and it 's about time we paid her another visit.'

'Bags not go,' said John hurriedly. 'I went last time.'

'All right,' answered his mother. 'That 's fair. Are you coming, Vivien?'

'I might as well, I suppose.' Vivien was not enthusiastic, but it was rainy weather, and neither a walk in the Gardens nor a morning in the hotel drawing-room was a very alluring alternative.

They rang up first to say that they were coming, and found Aunt Harrison enthroned in state to receive them in her high, upright armchair by the empty fireplace. She was very gracious. She was always very gracious, and Vivien, as she listened to her questions and Mrs Farthing's polite answers to them, wondered yet again whether Aunt Harrison was really fond of anybody, or really cared about the health or prospects of the people she asked after so courteously.

She very soon received a surprising answer to these meditations. Aunt Harrison, having worked through the more senior members of the family, said suddenly:

'My dear, I have been thinking that perhaps you found some of your plans rather difficult to arrange, now poor Andrew is in hospital. I have a small suggestion to make. Would you rather we talked about it alone? It is no secret, if you are willing that Vivien and Dinah should hear it at once.'

'Oh—please do exactly as you think,' said Mrs Farthing, slightly startled. 'The children know everything that we are planning.'

'Well.' Aunt Harrison took a firm grip of the gilt arms of the chair. 'You said at one time that you hoped John might go to St Paul's School in Hammersmith, and Dinah to St Monan's. You also said some thing about a course of domestic science for Vivien. Now that you are going to live in a neighbourhood so very far away, it seems to me that the children will have much more travelling than is at all good for them.' She raised her nose slightly in the air, and Vivien saw Mrs Farthing grip her hands together and force herself to remain politely silent.

'I am wondering,' Aunt Harrison went on, 'whether you would care for either Vivien, or Dinah, or John, to live here during their term-time while they go to whatever school you have decided upon. I would be willing—I would be pleased to undertake all the school expenses, if so.'

There was a silence—a silence of astonishment, and hurried thought, and then of all the suppressed things that the Farthings would have liked to say to one another if they had been alone. It was broken by Aunt Harrison herself.

'This is a big house,' she said, in quite different tones, 'and it sometimes seems very empty now James is grown up. It would be nice for me to hear someone young in it again.'

Again there was a pause; then Mrs Farthing cleared her throat.

'It 's most immensely kind of you, Aunt Ethel,' she said. 'I really don't know how to thank you. It 's a very, very kind suggestion, and I believe it will help us to solve one of the biggest of our difficulties. Of course you 'll understand that we want to talk it over, and see who would be the best to come, and so———'

'Mummy—Mummy.'

Dinah was on her feet. She was looking at Aunt Harrison as if she suddenly saw her as quite a different person, and she began almost to dance about in her anxiety to speak and be heard.

'Mummy—please couldn't I come? Please couldn't it be me?'

If Dinah had suddenly grown wings Mrs Farthing

could hardly have been more surprised. She waited, and Aunt Harrison waited, and Dinah went on excitedly:

'John can go to another school—you said so—and Vivien's going to do the cooking at home. But I *must* go to St Monan's, and you said that if I was a boarder it would be too expen—— I mean we couldn't manage it, and there's a piano in the schoolroom here where I could practise, and so you see . . .'

Vivien, watching her great-aunt's face, saw it suddenly break into a smile quite different from the gracious one with which she had welcomed them. Aunt Harrison was pleased. One might almost have said she was happy, if she ever could be anything so undignified.

In ten minutes, thanks to Dinah's outburst, the whole affair was fixed up. She was to go to St Monan's in three weeks' time. She was to come home to the City every week-end, and for the rest of the week to stay with Aunt Harrison. They went off to inspect her bedroom, a pleasant room facing on to the garden; it looked small, because it was full of massive mahogany furniture, but actually, Vivien realized, it was almost as big as their biggest room in the City. Dinah was enchanted, or so she said, and she and Aunt Harrison, when they said good-bye five minutes afterwards, were obviously both in doubt whether it might not be a good thing to kiss each other. They decided against it, and parted with the customary solemn hand-shake; but Dinah was in the highest spirits as she set off between her mother and Vivien to walk down Queen's Gate back to the hotel.

But if she was sure she had been clever, Mrs Farthing was not so easily able to make up her mind about it.

'You're quite certain, Dinah darling?' she inquired as they walked along. 'Remember, it's not just for a short visit, with one of us—it's for everyday life, all through

74

the term.'

'Yes, I 'm quite certain,' answered Dinah lightly. 'I think it 's a lovely idea.'

'What ever made you make up your mind like that all of a sudden?' said Vivien, puzzled. 'I thought you hated Aunt Harrison's.'

'Oh, it was when she said that about the house being empty,' answered Dinah. She put her head on one side, and looked meditatively into the distance. 'She wants someone young, you know, to cheer her up—I do think it 's so romantic.'

And Dinah gazed starry-eyed up into the future, while Mrs Farthing and Vivien, after a startled glance at each other, turned hurriedly away and did their best not to laugh.

There was a letter waiting for Vivien when they got back to the hotel. She saw it immediately, gleaming white against the green baize letter-rack with tapes across into which it had been pushed. Dinah unfortunately saw it too.

'Hallo, there 's a letter. Is it me? No, Miss Vivien Farthing. Bother you, Vivien.' She took it out of the rack and gave it to Vivien. 'But, I say—that 's your own handwriting, surely? It looks a bit queer, but it is yours, isn't it?'

'What if it is?' said Vivien, glowering and anxious, taking it quickly from Dinah's hand. The envelope was thick—much too thick…She knew the feel of its contents.

'Is it a free sample?' persisted Dinah, as Vivien tried to escape upstairs. 'Is it one of those books about how to be radiant and attractive and get married? What is it? Oh, I do think you might tell me.'

But Vivien steadfastly refused, and at last Dinah gave up her attempts, and turned back to the more interesting matter of her suddenly altered future. While she was telling John the whole startling story, Vivien at last got a chance to open the envelope, sitting on her bed just as she had done when she packed it up.

It was her story all right; and any lingering hopes that they had liked it really were soon extinguished by the little piece of paper which came with it out of the envelope. The editor of *Good Homecraft* presented her compliments, but regretted that she was unable to make use of the enclosed material.

That was all. Vivien sat with the little slip in her hand, and tried to tell herself that it was only what she had in her heart expected; that no one ever had a story accepted at the very first try. But it was really not possible to pretend that she was not disappointed. She gave a great sigh, and half opened the story, then shut it again as she caught sight of those well-known words, written and rewritten and rewritten, and then copied out in her most careful handwriting. The story was all right—she refused to believe anything else. Much more likely they had never even looked at it. Vivien realized suddenly how extremely quickly it had come back to her, and for a moment felt very indignant. How could they have considered it properly in so short a time?

Yes, if they had only read it over more carefully they might easily have found that they liked it after all. But then, it was rather a silly sort of magazine; really—just a popular paper. Perhaps, indeed, that was just the trouble. That was not the right kind of magazine for *The Long Lane*. It should go somewhere more intelligent; somewhere where they appreciated stories that were subtle and psychological rather than melodramatic. Yes, that was it. Full of relief and resolution, her hopes soaring again almost in spite of herself, Vivien went to her dressing-table drawer and took out two new envelopes.

CHAPTER VIII

THE FLAT TAKES SHAPE

'AND how is the flat getting on?'

Mr Farthing shifted slightly and carefully in his bed. If one had not watched his face closely, it would have been hard to tell that he was in pain. He settled himself again, looked up, and smiled as he saw Vivien's expression.

'I 'm getting on all right, darling—it 's only moving that 's a little difficult. Have you got all the furniture in yet?'

'Oh, yes—the last of it arrived this morning. It came just when the City lunch-hour was beginning, and we had a crowd of typists and errand-boys commenting on everything as it came out of the van!'

Vivien began to tell him of the various excitements of their moving in; of the consignment of bedclothes and saucepans which had gone by mistake to a startled business man in a second-floor office, of the doll's pram (Dinah had demanded that it should be brought out of store in case she should ever happen to need it) which had started to run away down Ludgate Hill and been run after by a delighted crowd of pursuers, of the couch which could not be got into the lift and the wardrobe which, once in, could not be got out of it. It was a good story, and even the silent man in the bed next to Mr Farthing's turned on his elbow and began to listen.

But all the time she talked, Vivien was acutely aware of the sound and look and antiseptic smell of the ward all around her. This was the first time she had been to see her father—the first time she had ever been in a big public ward—and it was all strange and a little alarming.

Not that there was anything at all alarming to be seen; the men in the beds up and down the long ward lay peacefully enough, many reading, some talking quietly to a visitor or to their neighbours. A little boy with a bandaged head was doing a jigsaw puzzle; an old man next door to him was laboriously writing a letter.

Nurses hurried quietly about, some with trays of tea, some with bandages and instruments in enamel trays. The sun came streaming in at the high windows, making long splashes of light on the polished floor, and all the time a subdued murmur of talk and movement combined with the faint antiseptic smell that hung in the air. It was not at all an unhappy world, but it was certainly a strange one to a new-comer.

It was strangest of all, and much the worst thing, to see Mr Farthing. In such unfamiliar surroundings he looked almost shockingly out of place, when one had been used to seeing him walking about out of doors, sitting at the table, taking part in ordinary everyday life. His face looked so brown against the white pillows that it was scarcely possible to believe that he was ill. And yet— there was that huge testing apparatus by his his bed; there was the look on his face when he moved; there was the chart hanging above his bed on the wall....

Vivien brought her mind back as much as she could to her account of the family doings.

'Mummy went at a quarter-past eight this morning,' she said. 'She says she won't have to leave so early when we 're living at the flat, and when she knows better about her work.'

'Is it only one more night you 're sleeping at the hotel?'

'Yes, we hope so—if we can get the flat into any sort of order by this evening. Mrs Jones is being an absolute dear, and she 's done almost all the cleaning for us.'

'Phineas and Minnie—I do like their names,' said Mr Farthing, amused. 'They 're an unusual sort of couple to find in a mercenary place like London; it sounds as though they would belong much better in a cathedral city or a little country parish.'

'Well, I hope that never occurs to them—they 're simply invaluable to us. Mrs Jones treats us as if she had been our nannie. It is queer, finding ourselves living in a flat like that,' Vivien went on. 'Queer and nice. I do hope you 'll like it, Daddy, when you come.'

'I 'm perfectly sure I shall. What 's happening now you 're away—have the movers finished?'

'Oh, yes, and we 're putting things away in cupboards—at least, the others are. I really must go back soon, and do some more myself.'

'They 'll turn you out of here in another quarter of an hour,' said Mr Farthing. 'It 's been simply great to see you, darling. Can anybody spare time to come to-morrow?'

'Yes, of *course*,' answered Vivien. 'John wants to come, please. He would have liked to come to-day, only I bagged first. But of course one of us will come every day that we possibly can.'

In a few minutes more she said good-bye to her father, and hurried away, down the long floor of the ward between the beds, out into the stone corridor and down the staircase, into the entrance hall, out into the warm sunshine of the Whitechapel Road, and on to a bus. Ten minutes more, and she was in front of St Paul's—arriving home.

It was strange to think that this was arriving home. The evening exodus from the City was just beginning, and a steadily growing crowd was making its way from

79

the offices down to the bus stops and tube stations. They were all going away to their homes, but she was coming home in the opposite direction. She looked up at the windows of the flat, and saw Dinah leaning on the sill, waving a tennis shoe to welcome her.

'We 've practically finished,' said Dinah airily when Vivien arrived. 'We 've been working like niggers ever since you went.'

'Yes, I really think we can come and live here to-morrow,' said John, coming in at that moment with a pile of plates. 'It would be fun to start, anyway. How 's Daddy?'

As soon as Vivien had told them about her visit to the hospital, they went on a tour of inspection. The flat really was in astonishingly good order. They had brought as little of their Berrings furniture as possible, so that even these small rooms did not look overcrowded, and with carpets on the floors and all the chairs and tables standing in the right places, everything was beginning to look recognizably like a home. The beds were not made up, there were no pictures on the walls, and no lamp-shades up, and books and clothes and china were standing about wherever room could be found for them; but it seemed to Vivien that they could easily make the flat habitable by the following evening.

'Let 's tell Mummy that,' she said at last, when they had been all round. 'We three can come here early in the morning with all the luggage, and then she can come back here after her work. She 'll be glad, I know—she and Madam certainly don't like each other.'

'Madam 's an old cow,' said Dinah dispassionately. 'We' d better go back soon, or we 'll be late for her beastly dinner.'

They arrived back at the hotel only just in time to

wash before dinner, for the buses were crowded and they spent a large amount of time waiting in traffic jams. Mrs Farthing was not back by seven, so they began dinner without her; and they had finished, and so had everybody else, before she arrived. At last, at ten minutes to eight, she came hurrying in.

'I *am* late,' she said, pulling off her coat. 'George, can I have my soup, please?'

The waiter went off and she began to ask how they had been getting on. Almost immediately, though, he came back and said apologetically that they could not serve soup now.

'Oh?' Mrs Farthing was surprised. 'Is it finished? Well, then, bring me the next thing.'

'Excuse me, madam, but we don't serve the next course either.'

'You don't serve the next course? Well, what do you serve, then?'

'I 'm very sorry, madam, but orders are that no hot dinners can be served after seven forty-five. But I 'm sure I could manage to get you a little cold mutton.'

'Oh.' There was a moment's silence. Mrs Farthing stared across at the opposite wall. 'No, thank you. Don't bring me anything. I will go and speak to Madam. Don't you three wait,' she added, getting up. 'If you like to go and sit up in my bedroom, I 'll come as soon as I can. But I can't stand that woman any longer, and I shall most likely tell her so.'

With a quick smile of good-bye she was gone. The three got up and went uncomfortably upstairs.

'Cold mutton, after a hard day's work,' said Dinah with feeling. 'Didn't I say she was a cow?'

Mrs Farthing did not come for twenty-five minutes,

81

but when she did she was cheerful.

'I 've had a hot dinner, and I 've been refreshingly rude to Madam,' she said as she came in. 'I feel *much* better now. We 've only got two more days of our week here to run, so we shan't have to endure it very much longer.

'We needn't endure it any longer, if you like,' said Vivien. 'We can go to the flat to-morrow.'

'To-morrow?' Mrs Farthing was delighted. 'Have you really got on so far as that? Well, that 's splendid.'

'The beds aren't made up, and of course it 's in a mess, but apart from that it 's perfectly ready for us to go in,' said Vivien cheerfully.

'Mummy, what did you do?' Dinah was tired of domesticities. 'Did you mannequin?'

'No, indeed I didn't. I sold one cotton dress, at fifteen and sixpence, after the customer had tried on twenty others, and I began to do what 's called learning my stock—knowing about the things I 'm supposed to sell—and I added up a bill wrong, and I discovered which of my colleagues are nice and which aren't, and I walked about thirty miles, I should think, up and down the shop. It wasn't at all bad, though, for a first day,' Mrs Farthing added hurriedly.

'Poor Mummy,' said Dinah. 'You must be horribly tired. But to-morrow we won't be in this cowish place any more, and you can lie down on an elegant sofa in our elegant sitting-room, and you 'll get an elegant dinner, perhaps—if Vivien 's any good at cooking—and anyway it 'll all be much better.'

'It certainly will,' said Mrs Farthing, looking quite revived at the beautiful prospect held out to her.

'We 'll be cockneys now, won't we?' said Dinah all of a sudden. 'All people are who live in the City.'

'No, of course we shan't.' John was scornful. 'You 've got to be born within sound of Bow bells.'

'Oh, it 's born, is it? I thought it was if you lived there. Where are Bow bells, anyway?'

'I don't know. 'I do not know,' says the great bell of Bow"—Listen!' John began to sing very quickly:

"Oranges and lemons," say the bells of St Clement's;
"You owe me five farthings," say the bells of St Martin's;
"When will you pay me?" say the bells of Old Bailey;
"When I grow rich," say the bells of Shoreditch;
"When will that be?" say the bells of Stepney;
"I do not know," says the great bell of Bow.

'Five farthings—five farthings! That 's us, don't you see! It 's an omen! It proves we were meant to live in the City. Daddy will soon come home, and then we really will be five, and——'

'And we don't know when we 'll grow rich, any more than the great bell of Bow does,' put in Vivien. 'That's fun, John. It 's the first good joke I 've ever heard about our surname.'

'It 's not a joke, it 's an omen,' John insisted. 'A very, very good omen.' And though they all laughed, there is not the slightest doubt that they agreed with him.

CHAPTER IX

SETTLING IN

AT eleven o'clock on the following morning a heavily loaded taxi pulled up outside a small red-brick office block in front of St Paul's Cathedral. Three young persons and ten suit-cases emerged from the inside of it, and the driver began to unstrap a trunk from beside his seat, casting a thoughtful glance at the large selection of other luggage which awaited his attention on the top of the roof.

'I hope Mr Jones is at the lift,' said Dinah, clutching her violin case. 'I 'll go and see.'

Mr Jones was at the lift, and Mr Jones, as always, was very willing to help them, and with the help of the taxi-driver (who seemed to think the whole business very comic) the luggage was eventually unloaded and taken up to the flat on the fourth-floor landing. When it was all assembled Mr Jones and the taxi-driver sank out of sight in the lift, and the Farthings were left alone in the sudden quiet of the landing.

They went into the sitting-room, and stood looking round them at the chaos of suit-cases and furniture.

'We 're here,' said Vivien at last 'We live here.'

For a moment no one said anything. It was a queer-looking place to live in, in its present condition: more like a box-room than a flat, and a very small box-room at that, filled up as it was with luggage and objects which did not belong there.

'We 'd better begin to tidy,' said John, 'but what on earth shall we begin with?'

They considered the matter for a few minutes, and at

last decided that each of them should take one particular kind of thing and see to that as far as possible. John was going to do all the furniture, and get the sitting-room in order somehow. Dinah was to put clothes away, find bed linen, table linen, and towels, and make the bedrooms as tidy as possible. Vivien was to collect all the kitchen equipment, china, glass, and so forth, from the various strange places where it had been put, and try and get everything ready enough for meals to be prepared.

They expected their jobs to be long ones, and they were not mistaken. By one o'clock the flat looked, if anything, in a worse muddle than when they had arrived. The suitcases were all open. The Farthing family's garments, which littered every chair and table and most of the floor as well, reminded Vivien of the sixpenny old clothes stall at a jumble sale. Books were standing in high, tipsy-looking stacks against the walls, and the bookcases were full of more clothes and mysterious parcels the contents of which everybody had forgotten. The bedclothes had been discovered, but Dinah reported that they were full of straw. John had managed to put one lampshade up, but it was so wildly crooked that it made one feel giddy to look at it.

The only real signs of progress were in the kitchen, where Vivien had managed to get all their china put away, the saucepans and cooking utensils arranged near the gas-cooker, and a few tins of soup, sardines, fruit, and such-like stand-bys disentangled from the general turmoil. Even so, though, the china was too dirty to use, and there were as yet none of the essential stores such as butter, milk, eggs, flour, and vegetables.

'It certainly is a job,' she said wearily, leaving her work and coming in to see how the others were getting on. 'It 's far worse than moving out, and that was bad enough. How are things going?'

'I 'm sick and tired and exhausted to death,' Dinah emphatically. 'And I want my lunch.'

'So do I,' said John, smearing a black hand across his damp forehead with the natural result. 'And besides, it 'll soon be time for me to go to see Daddy.'

'I want mine too,' said Vivien almost indignantly, as if to say they were not to blame her for all this simply because she was older. 'Shall we open a tin, or what? Oh, no, we can't, because all the plates are dirty and we haven't any glass-cloths.'

'Let 's go out,' said Dinah. 'Let 's go to the very first place we come to and eat the very first thing on the menu. That 's all I 'm capable of.

In their present exhausted state this strange suggestion appealed to them all, and with slightly renewed vigour they had a hasty cold wash, put on coats, and rang the bell for Mr Jones's lift. Mr Jones was very sympathetic as he took them down to the street, and said that never, never, not if he was to live to be a hundred, would he forget the day when Minnie and him moved up to London from the country

The Farthings staggered out of the lift and out into the warm, sunny street, looking interestedly round to see what kind of restaurant they had obliged themselves to eat in. As it turned out, Dinah's scheme did them pretty well, for the first restaurant they came to was a milk bar. They had never been in one before, and were a little alarmed by the sight of so many people standing about and talking with glasses in their hands; but when they went in they found a clear space at the counter, and a menu lay there for them to look at, and a girl was waiting with her hand on the shining taps to produce whatever they ordered, so it was not so very difficult after all.

'Raspberry Milk Shake,' read Dinah. 'That sounds rather nice. Let's have three of those to begin with.'

The Raspberry Milk Shake was admirable, and so were the tongue sandwiches which they ate with it, and twenty minutes later three much more cheerful Farthings made their way back up Ludgate Hill and up to the flat. Mr Jones had gone from the lift, and in his place was the small but lively-looking boy who relieved him while he was having his lunch. The boy seemed a little puzzled at first by the appearance of three bare-headed and very un-Citylike young persons, and chewed some chewing-gum thoughtfully while he studied them.

'Fourth floor, please,' said Vivien.

'Oh, fourth—you're *them*, are you?' said the boy with interest. He shot them up to the fourth floor with double Mr Jones's usual sober speed, and stood in the open lift looking on and chewing until the bell rang and he had to go down again.

It may have been due to the lunch, or it may simply have been that so much foundation work had been done in the morning, but certainly the next hour's tidying produced results. John went off quite soon to see his father, and Vivien and Dinah in a very short time had the sitting-room in order, the beds made up, and all the old clothes, shoes, and mysterious brown-paper parcels put somewhere or other out of sight. They worked quietly, not talking except when they had to, and when St Paul's clock chimed three they both looked up in surprise.

'That *is* better,' said Vivien with relief, surveying the result of their labours. 'Now it really isn't bad for Mummy to come back to.'

'What's she going to have for supper?' Dinah picked up one of Mr Farthing's shoes which had escaped on to the sofa, and took it out into the bedroom.

'I don't know yet. I must go and find some shops. I suppose there *are* food shops somewhere round here,' Vivien added. 'It mostly seems to be stationers and restaurants.'

'And gentlemen's outfitters,' said Dinah, who took a great interest in the patterns of men's ties and suits, and had had some very good times already studying the shops on Ludgate Hill.

'I know—I 'll go down and ask Mrs Jones. I 'm sure she won't mind.'

'Have you been inside her rooms yet? No, you haven't. I 'll come with you, I think—I 'd like to see them.'

'I know just what they 'll be like,' said Vivien. 'Clean and cosy and very full of things, with upright arm-chairs and lace curtains.'

'And a cloth with bobbles round the edge,' completed Dinah happily. 'Come on—let 's go and see.'

From Mrs Jones's rooms came a clatter of tea-cups, and when she opened the door they saw that the long kitchen table behind her was completely covered with tea-trays. She welcomed them warmly, and insisted that they should come in.

'Just for a little sit-down,' she urged. 'You must be tired. A cup of tea would do you both good, I 'm sure it would.'

'Well, thank you very much indeed,' said Vivien. 'It would be very nice, if you 're sure it 's not a bother.'

'No bother whatsoever,' said Mrs Jones instantly. 'I make tea for twenty every afternoon. Charlie, Charlie, where are you?'

The chewing-gum boy appeared at her call, and was dispatched to find out how many teas would be wanted to-day on the first floor. This done, Mrs Jones installed her visitors in chairs, and politely inquired how they were getting on.

'Very well, really, thank you.' Vivien did her best to ignore Dinah's triumphant signals, but it was difficult. The chairs they sat in were old-fashioned upright ones with little lace head-rests. There were lace curtains looped up at the windows, and pictures all over the walls; and Dinah, with every sign of delight, nodded towards the tablecloth on the centre table, which was of dark red cloth with bobbles all round its edge.

Mrs Jones was full of useful information; she knew a nice clean little dairy, a reliable butcher, a handy grocer's shop, a shop for home-made bread, and the best place to buy wooden spoons and scrubbing brushes. When Charlie, reporting that the day's total was twenty-two teas, had been given the various tea-trays and sent to take them round, Mrs Jones took a cup of tea and a little sit-down herself while she entered into further details.

'Weaver's is up through this passage,' she said, nodding towards the back of the house, 'but all the others is in a little street just behind St Paul's. Watchman Lane, it 's called—you can't miss it if you turn to the left outside here, walk down to the end of the Churchyard, and go straight in the little alley opposite. It 's the street with St Sebastian.'

'Is that a church?'

'Yes—the one with the spire,' said Mrs Jones. 'You can see it from your window. Well, down there you 'll find the dairy and Billings's, and Harvey's, and the oil-shop, all close together on the same side as the church. Have another biscuit, do, dear,' she added to Dinah, who had had at least six already

Dinah had another biscuit willingly, and another after that, but by that time even she had eaten almost enough, and soon afterwards, with many thanks for their tea, she and Vivien left and went upstairs to get their coats and go shopping.

They found Watchman Lane very easily—a narrow, curving street where the high buildings seemed almost to meet above their heads. St Sebastian's spire could not be seen from so close underneath it, but they identified the church at once by its grey front with flat pilasters and large, round-topped window. Close beside it, sure enough, was a tiny dairy, its shop-window almost filled by a huge stork made of very shiny green and brown china.

They went in, and arranged with the young woman in charge to deliver milk to the flat every morning, and also bought butter, milk, eggs, and some cream to take back with them. When she heard that Mrs Jones had sent them she at once became friendly and conversational; and the same thing happened at the baker's, at the oil-shop where they bought soap and soda, and at the grocer's up the tiny lane behind their house where they bought ham, corned beef, sugar, flour, and a big tin of potato crisps.

'That really is grand,' said Vivien as she and Dinah staggered home with their load of parcels. 'Mrs Jones solves everything—finds us a flat, cleans it for us, sends us to the right shops—did you see how they all seemed to like her? I don't feel nearly so worried now I know where we can buy all the things we want.'

'Were you worried?' said Dinah. 'I wasn't. You haven't told me yet what we 're going to have for supper.'

'Bother you, I don't *know*,' said Vivien. 'Let 's see—what have we bought?'

It was not perhaps the most practical way of arranging a menu, but when they got home and spread out their purchases on the table they were able to plan quite a tolerable meal out of them. First a big tin of soup, from their Berrings store-cupboard: then ham fried with an egg on top of it, with potato crisps: then tinned fruit salad and cream. It made them almost hungry to talk of it, and though it was still at least two hours too early Dinah insisted on setting the supper-table, so that they could be sure Mrs Farthing would have a cheerful sight to welcome her when she arrived home.

'It does look nice,' said Vivien, coming in to admire Dinah's work. 'One could hardly believe this was the same room now it 's all tidy. I wish we 'd bought some flowers, though.'

'I 'll go out and get some,' said Dinah instantly. 'I 'd like to explore a bit.'

'Oh, will you? Good. And we ought to have some fruit, too—apples, or oranges, or something.'

Dinah's exploration was a longish one, and Vivien was just beginning to wonder if anything had happened to her when she heard voices on the landing, and Dinah and John arrived together. Surprisingly enough, it was John who was doing most of the talking.

'Vivien,' he said the moment he came in, 'Daddy knows where I 'm to go to school.'

He sounded enormously cheerful, and began at once to enter into details.

'It 's called Whitefriars School,' he said. 'It 's a very old school, and you have to be certified or something by two people who live in the City of London. Two of the doctors at the hospital are going to do it. It 's down by the Thames. They 've got a fives court, but they play games miles and miles away down in the country. The history master is awfully good, Daddy says.'

'Oh, John, I *am* glad.' For five minutes more John continued to talk about the tremendous advantages of Whitefriars School, and even Dinah listened without wanting to change the subject. The school had only one drawback, it appeared: that it required an entrance examination, and that the examination was going to take place precisely eight days from now. John supposed he would get through it somehow, but he also supposed it might not be a bad thing if he were to do a little work. He accordingly turned every stack of books upside down and at last produced a book of theorems, which he settled down to study; but when Vivien came in from the kitchen twenty minutes later he was standing at the window and gazing up at the sky, lost in beautiful dreams.

Just as St Paul's was chiming seven Mrs Farthing arrived back. They heard her footsteps on the stone landing, and a moment afterwards she opened the sitting-room door and came in.

'What 's this!' she said, looking round her in bewilderment. 'What a wonderful sight!'

'Do you like it, Mummy? Do you think it looks nice?' Dinah, delighted, was jigging about on one foot in the background.

'It 's magnificent,' said Mrs Farthing warmly. 'I simply can't recognize the place. You must all have been working like niggers. Aren't you tired?'

'Oh, no, it 's been great fun,' said Vivien, entirely forgetting the exasperations of the morning. 'And we 've got all sorts of things to tell you about. But how have you been getting on, Mummy?'

'Oh, much better than yesterday, thank you,' said Mrs Farthing. 'It 's a great deal easier already.'

'Now, please, Mummy, will you absolutely promise—'

'I won't promise anything,' said Mrs Farthing, who knew pretty well what was coming.

'But you *must* promise, because, you see, if you won't you can't have any supper. Will you absolutely promise faithfully, strike you pink, that you won't try to help us but will sit on the sofa and be a lady?'

Mrs Farthing looked round at the severe faces of her family. 'All right,' she said. 'I can see I 'll have to. Strike me pink, then.'

It was the most solemn oath in the family, and when they heard it they knew that it was to be trusted. Mrs Farthing, having washed and changed, sat on the sofa with her *Evening Standard*, while Vivien and Dinah struggled with such unforeseen problems as how to warm plates for the soup and the eggs, and whether to cook the eggs and ham before they had the soup or to keep everybody waiting in the middle of the meal and have them freshly fried.

'And I don't ever remember frying making such a smell down at Berrings,' said Vivien when, having decided to cook the ham and eggs right away, they had them all sizzling in the frying-pan. 'Oh, do get out of the way, John.'

'I 'm only saying that if you turn the flame lower it will cook just as well,' said John in an injured voice, flattening himself again the wall while Vivien stirred the soup. 'All right, if you don't want me I 'll go.'

'I 'm sorry,' said Vivien, realizing that her temper was getting a little worn. 'But the kitchen is so tiny, and it 's so hot, and there are such a lot of things to do— Dinah, will you get the plates ready now? We can put the ham and eggs in the oven till we 've finished the soup.'

By some sort of miracle the meal was ready without disaster, only half an hour later than they had said it would be. Vivien, hot and exhausted, reflected unhappily that she would most likely have to cook meals like that, in that tiny kitchen, for the next few months at the very least, and her heart sank. Cooking and washing up, and cooking and washing up....

But the others were so cheerful that she soon began to recover. The meal was a success: the soup, the ham and eggs, the tinned fruit salad, were all delicious, and everybody began to look perceptibly better by the time they had had something to eat.

'Our very first meal in our very own flat,' said Dinah. 'This is better than the hotel.'

'It certainly is,' said John. 'Though I rather miss all the old ladies.'

'Do you? I don't. Bags Mr Jones, by the way—nobody thought of him yesterday!'

'Bother you! All right. Is he queer, though? Isn't he ordinary?'

'He's sweet and he has a walrus moustache,' said Dinah quickly. 'That's not ordinary, for a lift-man! And I found *such* a nice assistant in the fruit-shop.'

'You seem to have made yourselves at home all right,' observed Mrs Farthing, much amused. 'You know all the shops in the neighbourhood, and most of the inhabitants, and John has a school to go to, and you've conjured up a real proper flat out of four empty offices! We needn't have been worried about whether you'd settle down!'

'It's like Book One of a story,' said Dinah. 'Now we're settled, and now the fun can begin.'

'The fun's begun already,' amended Vivien, now completely recovered. 'Queer people, and new places, and exploring, and getting the flat straight. It's been fun all the time—and it's going to go on being fun.'

BOOK TWO

CHAPTER I

SIR CHRISTOPHER WREN

VIVIEN put away her duster, took up a packet of soap flakes, put it down again, and went into the sitting-room to see the time from St Paul's. The flat was tidy now for the day. There should be time to wash stockings, if she really gave her mind to it.

But on the other hand there would also be time to tidy that shelf in the kitchen—or to write to Aunt Rosamund for her birthday. Or to take a look at yesterday's newspaper, which she had not yet seen. Vivien took two steps in one direction, and two steps in another. She looked out of the window at the sunshine, and remembered that she must soon go out to buy a joint. A joint meant potatoes, and potatoes meant peeling. Potatoes it would have to be: the other things, as usual, would have to wait.

Vivien was alone in the flat. Mrs Farthing was at Greencoat's. Dinah was spending the day with Mary Connor, the Kensington friend through whom she had heard of St Monan's—early next week their term started, and they were making all they could of the last of the holidays. John, having come successfully through the written part of his entrance examination for Whitefriars School, had to-day gone off, painfully clean and rather frightened, to be interviewed by the provost.

Through the windows, and up the staircase from the offices below, came the sounds of the City at its daily work, but up here it was peaceful and unusually quiet. Vivien was glad to be alone for a little while, but she would have liked it considerably better if she had also been free to get on with her own affairs.

She went into the kitchen, filled a basin with water, and tipped some potatoes into it. It was only ten days since they had moved into the flat, yet already these things seemed so much a routine that she could hardly believe she had not been doing them for months. Potato-peeling, dusting, making beds, cleaning the bathroom, washing up—that was what running a household seemed to consist of. As for those dreams of having time to write, for the present they had vanished like smoke in the wind. There was never time—or if by any chance there was time, there was no peace, in this tiny flat, with John and Dinah all over the place all day. She was sometimes almost angry when she thought of how her days went by, used up on nothing better than dirtying knives and saucepans which she then had to wash, or dusting furniture that would be dusty again in an hour.

And yet—she was being useful. For the first time in her life she was really doing something which helped the family, and filling a gap that could hardly have been filled otherwise. That was something to console her—that, and living up here in the midst of the City. And Vivien needed consoling.

The story had come back again—just as promptly as the first time, and with a very similar printed note from the editor. But this time someone, meaning perhaps to be kind, had written in ink on the printed form, 'Handwritten MSS. are not considered.' Vivien had been so indignant that she had stuffed the whole package into a drawer, where it still was. Why should they expect everybody to have typewriters, just because they were too lazy to read even the neatest of handwritings? She would send the story to yet another magazine soon, when she had time to think about it, and then, if it came back from there also, perhaps she would have it typed, if she could afford it, at the Coral Copying Bureau on the second floor.

But Vivien was rather tired of short stories. They took such a long time to get published: and moreover, though she had been all this time in London, and had seen so many new and strange people, she had not yet got a single idea for a new short story out of it all. She was slowly coming to the conclusion that, when at last she had time again, it would be much better to write a novel. She remembered that Arnold Bennett, or somebody like that, had said it was much easier to write a whole novel than one short story, and she had an idea for one which seemed to her to be quite excitingly good. It was to be about a girl who lived in London with her family. The father was an invalid, or perhaps the father and mother were both invalids, and the girl served in a shop to make money to keep the home going, and wrote late every night when the family was in bed—not at a novel, but at a play, which was accepted by a famous manager and put on at a West End theatre; and the handsome and cultured actor who was playing the hero fell in love with the girl, and they married and were rich and happy ever after. No one, Vivien felt, could mistake such a story for her own story, or such a quite different girl for herself: and yet it would give her a chance to put in such a lot that she knew about—having no money, and doing housework, and living in London, only of course all made more exciting, more moving, than the ordinary humdrum round.

Vivien thought a lot about her novel. She had not yet written anything of it except a few notes, though when once Dinah was out of the way at school she hoped to do a little in bed every night. But when life got too tiresome, as she peeled potatoes or cooked or polished, she would often wander off into that other world where Pamela (or

99

perhaps she would be called Anne) sacrificed all her time and youth to her family, and miraculously got the reward which she deserved. For without question fiction had great advantages over fact. Pamela (or Anne) would be able to do by instinct, and in no time at all, all the things which Vivien found so tedious and so difficult. Pamela (or Anne), for example, would be able to cook.

Vivien had never been a great hand at cooking, and now, with a hungry family to provide for two or three or four times every day, her mind became a despairing blank every time she tried to think what to give them and how it should be cooked. True, she could ask Mrs Farthing in the evenings. She could even remember quite a lot from the times when, as a treat, she had been allowed to go into the kitchen at Berrings and help Bridget to prepare the dinner. But cooking had been play in those days. Now it was work, and the difference in some odd way took all the fun out of it.

Joints were her stand-by—roast meat with roast or boiled potatoes, and cabbage or carrots or some other vegetable which was not too hard to cook. For sweets she made jelly out of a packet, or bought some ice cream, or gave them stewed or fresh fruit with cream, or simply something out of a tin. It was all quite eatable, except perhaps for her gravies, which she would have been the first to admit were thin and dull, but which went resolutely into lumps when she tried to improve upon them. And the family was very patient about it, and said nothing when the joint turned up day after day, first roast, then cold, until it was finished. But it was deadening work, and Vivien began to think she understood why the cooking in big institutions had such a name for being dull.

However, life was fortunately not all cooking. Apart from that and the housework and her own lack of time, living at the flat was proving every bit as pleasant as they had hoped it would. It was so fantastically unlike anything they had ever done before that that in itself made everything exciting. To come out on to a large stone landing every morning to take in the milk; to see red buses roaring past down in the street below, and St Paul's for their next-door neighbour; to go down in Mr Jones's mahogany lift, in company perhaps with typists carrying a tray-full of letters, when one wanted to go out shopping: it was so infinitely far away from Sussex that it might have been another world. They missed the fresh country air, and they terribly missed all their friends in the village, where they had known everybody in every cottage ever since they were small. But they had one another to talk to, and Mr and Mrs Jones, and they were on friendly terms with all the people in their usual shops. Mrs Farthing found Greencoat's quite tolerable, and often came back with good stories about the queer people with whom she came in contact. Dinah was looking forward to St Monan's, John to the cricket season. They had all London to explore, and a thousand strange things and strange people to comment on. As long as Mr Farthing was ill and in hospital, there was nowhere in the world where they would rather have been than here.

The potatoes finished, Vivien washed her hands and considered whether it was time to go out. John had said he would not be back for lunch; she was completely free until the time came for her to visit her father. She could have lunch in, she could have lunch out in a shop—she could do exactly what she pleased. To stay in would mean the luxury of a little time for reading, and she had just got a new novel from the library down the street. To go out, on the other hand, would mean the pleasure of a stroll in the City, and of sitting in some crowded tea-shop and listening to the talk of the people all around her. It was a fine day, and she suddenly remembered again that there was meat to be bought. That settled it. She would go out.

She put on her outdoor clothes, and went down in the lift with Mr Jones and out to the sunlit pavement of St Paul's Churchyard. It was always fun to come out here—there was so much going on, and the great grey cathedral in the middle gave a special meaning and permanence to all this everyday life, which went on around it as it must have gone on for over two hundred years. Going vaguely in the direction of the butcher, but intending to explore a little on the way, Vivien browsed her way contentedly along the Churchyard towards Cheapside, studying all the shop windows very thoroughly as she went.

The lunch hour was beginning already. The benches under the trees were filling up, and young women in couples, talking at top speed about their clothes and their boys, were beginning to crowd round the shop windows. Vivien almost began to think that she would not mind having her lunch; but she had not yet decided where to go, so she wandered along and across the road, singing a cheerful little song which passed quite unheard in the general hubbub.

She was in Watchman Lane before her song came to an end: and as she looked up at the sky and round at the shops and offices she suddenly, for the first time, became really aware of the spire of St Sebastian's Church. The street itself was in shadow, but the spire was full in the sun, and when Vivien realized what it was she was looking at she stopped dead in the middle of the pavement to stare at it.

It was one of the most beautiful things she had ever seen. Very slender, lit to a warm glow by the sun, the spire rose into the air as if the sky was its natural home; and supporting it, keeping it to the earth, were groups of stone columns, delicate filigree work planned by some master, through which here and there shone the deep blue of the sky.

'Why haven't I seen that before?' said Vivien to herself in scandalized tones. She gazed for a moment more; then, on a sudden impulse, crossed the road, ran up the steps, and plunged into the church.

It was so dark inside that for a moment she could not see anything. But as her eyes became accustomed to the darkness she began to pick out details—a pillar, a richly carved pulpit, windows with semicircular tops; and she realized with a feeling almost of relief that the inside of St Sebastian's Church was as beautiful as its spire.

She could not have said what it was that appealed to her so strongly. She had seen many fine buildings before, and St Paul's, a hundred times more magnificent, she knew and loved, yet without any of this special excitement. St Sebastian's was almost square, and very small, but two rows of pillars running from the door to the chancel, and a domed roof turned the small square space into a shape that was almost magically perfect. It was painted white, and on the window arches and above the altar there were blue and gold stars.

She was still gazing when she heard quiet, limping footsteps somewhere on her left. Out of some recess came a man with a very stiff leg, and a dark moustache so large that it left practically nothing of his face to be seen except a pair of eyes and a pair of dark eyebrows. He studied Vivien closely, then limped away and with something of a gesture turned a switch. Instantly the whole church roof was bright with light: not strong light, but a light which showed up every detail of the dome and the graceful plaster leaves and scrolls which surrounded it.

Not knowing whether to thank the man or not, Vivien stood a little awkwardly, studying the roof; and she was much relieved when a gentle squeak from the entrance door announced that someone else had come in. The new-comer seemed much more at ease than she was, and went straight up to the man with the limp.

'Grand, that is,' he said warmly. He was a large, rather stout man with a cheerful reddish face, and he nodded up at the illuminated roof with great approval.

'I put it on for the young lady,' said the other man in a hoarse whisper, delicately looking not quite in Vivien's direction.

'I 've said it before, and I 'll say it again,' the stout man went on in the nearest approach to a whisper that he could manage, 'this is Wren's best.'

'And there you 're right.' The other man perfectly agreed with him. 'There you 're right, Mr Blueley. You can have St Stephen's. You can have St Bride's. You can have St Paul's itself, if you want to. This is the one for me.'

And he drew himself up, and looked down over his moustaches with the air of one who was in no way to be taken in by inferior articles. Vivien, who had by now crept away to a safer distance, watched fascinated. The two were very much in earnest, and they looked so solemn and so engaging that if only she had dared—if, for instance, she had been Dinah instead of herself—she would have gone up and talked to them.

But she was not Dinah, and her main idea was to escape as soon as possible. The door squeaked again; and in the slight distraction of somebody else's arrival Vivien tiptoed to the entrance and edged out, giving a vague and embarrassed smile in the direction of the two men by way of good-bye.

Once outside, she luckily caught sight of the butcher's shop, and being thus reminded what she had come out for, went in in a great hurry and bought half a leg of lamb for the family dinner. It proved to be an extremely inconvenient parcel to carry, and an almost impossible one to stow away in the crowded café where she went for her lunch, and eventually she realized that she could just as well have bought it an hour later and taken it straight home. She did not spare the matter much thought, however, for she was busy thinking about something quite different.

Wren. Sir Christopher Wren. So it was he, was it, who had created that exquisite church? He, too, who had planned St Paul's—and Vivien was almost overwhelmed to think that, while she had been admiring St Paul's all this time, and had been well aware who was responsible for it, she had not spared a single thought for the man who had created it. She and John had already been back there twice: they had been round and round it, and down to the crypt, and up, at John's special request, to the Whispering Gallery in the dome: and yet they had taken it all for granted, as something which simply existed, the same as the other buildings in the City.

That one man could have imagined and brought to life all that huge, superb, complicated building, set on its hill as the crown of all London . . . she could hardly take it in. But that one man had created St Sebastian's—that was another matter, for the lovely little church bore clearly the imprint of one rich and well-defined personality. Vivien walked along, deep in concentration, avoiding the passers-by by a series of lucky accidents, and quite unaware that her half-leg of lamb was slipping out of its wrappings. One thought only was in possession of her

105

mind—that she must get to know as much as she possibly could about this amazing man among whose masterpieces she had now come to live.

CHAPTER II

UPON PAUL'S STEEPLE

VIVIEN asked her father that afternoon whether he could tell her anything about Wren, and got a quite unexpected answer. Mr Farthing was in high spirits, and, nobody at his end of the ward being seriously ill, the nurses were having a hard time to keep him reasonably quiet and stop him from making the other patients laugh more than was good for them.

'Wren?' he said. 'Good gracious me, yes. Don't you know the poem about him?'

'Poem? No, I don't.'

'It 's a beautiful poem. Let me see—how does it go?' And rolling over on his back and gazing up at the ceiling, Mr Farthing recited in ringing tones:

'Sir Christopher Wren
Said, "I am going to dine with some men.
If anybody calls
Say I am designing St Paul's."

'There 's sense for you, Vivien. There 's romance, as one might say, cunningly tempered with realism. If there is any hero in the world I should choose to resemble, it would be a man like that. Wouldn't it?'

He shot the question at his next-door neighbour, a thin but very cheerful Cockney who laughed and answered 'Not 'alf it would!'

'That poem,' he went on, 'is by a fellow called E. C. Bentley. A fellow who, if I had my way, would be called the Shakespeare of the twentieth century. But I haven't, of course,' he added sadly. 'And as for Wren,' he went on when he had thought this over for a time, 'there's a book about him somewhere at home—or there ought to be. Perhaps it's in store, though.'

'Oh, it *will* be nice when we have all our books and things again, Daddy. It's nice now, I mean,' Vivien added in a hurry, 'but I mean it will be even nicer when you are well and we can properly settle down again. What do the doctors say to-day?'

'They say they haven't made the slightest impression on me hitherto, but they now have a new idea which may produce some effect. It's no good minding their ways, Vivien darling,' Mr Farthing went on in a wholly serious voice. 'They're doing the very best they can, and they're sure to find something soon; and when they do they'll know what to do to any other people who turn up with my peculiar disease—and that's something, anyway. So don't be sad, because if you get sad then I get sad, and then if I get sad you get sadder, and then you see in the twinkling of an eye we'll all be most horribly miserable.'

He smiled at her so cheerfully that she had to make some attempt to smile back, but it was not a very good one.

'Tell me,' he said, his high spirits completely returned. 'Haven't you got a secret sorrow? There's nothing I enjoy so much as a good secret sorrow,' he added, laughing at Vivien's startled expression. 'No love affairs? Nothing?'

'Oh, Daddy, you are hopeless,' said Vivien, beginning to laugh in spite of herself. 'No, I haven't any at all, I'm afraid, except perhaps gravy and cold meat.'

'Is that the best you can do, you heartless little creature?'

'But they're most important, Daddy. They really are sorrows. I can't make gravy, and how on earth can one manage not to have to keep on having cold meat?'

'As to gravy, that 's easy,' said Mr Farthing gravely. 'You simply buy some stuff and mix it up. But as to cold meat. . . . Hi!' he caught the attention of his Cockney neighbour, and leaned over towards him.

'What does your wife do about cold meat?' he inquired confidentially.

'Hash, mate,' replied the man, so calmly that Vivien supposed he was used to her father's ways. A man behind him, with a bandaged head, looked up and said slowly 'If you got cold meat you eats it, er course.'

'There you are, Vivien,' said Mr Farthing in triumphant tones. 'You eat it, and if you don't do that you make hash. Don't you ever dare to say I 'm not a help to you. What 's that, nurse?' he added to one of the nurses who had just come up. 'Doctor on his round? All right. Vivien, darling, you 'll have to go now, I 'm afraid. Love to Mummy, and tell her I 'll write to-night. And if John 's had any luck with his interview, you might be so extravagant as to send me a telegram.'

There was no one at the lift when Vivien got back to Overton House. The boy Charlie was most likely supposed to be on duty—in fact as Vivien stood in the entrance hall, she thought she could hear him whistling somewhere along the corridor. Yes, that was Charlie's whistle all right: very cheerful, and whistling some tune which she dimly thought she recognized. It was no good ringing the lift bell. He was delivering letters or parcels, and he would not come a moment before he saw fit to do so. She had better walk up.

She turned away from the lift and began to climb the stone staircase. Four stories was a long way up, but it was fun once in a way to go past all the different offices and see what was going on.

She climbed diligently up towards the first landing. One could almost guess that it was nearly time for everyone to go home. There were all sorts of extra little noises going on—bangs and runnings about and chatterings which suggested that everything possible was being finished off for the night. A young man came suddenly round one of the corners, almost colliding with her in his haste to deliver the files he was carrying. He too was whistling, though more quietly than Charlie; and Vivien realized, when they had both said 'Sorry' and gone on, that he was whistling the very same tune as she had heard Charlie performing downstairs.

It was a lively tune, and one that she knew well—it sounded rather like a peal of bells being rung. Climbing up towards the second floor, Vivien tried hard to remember what it was called. She came round on to the second landing, where someone was standing hopefully pressing the lift bell: and there she found the answer.

A little fair-haired typist was standing there, nonchalantly waiting for the lift and singing to herself as she waited. 'La *la* la la la *la* la la,' she sang, down the scale and then on. 'La *la* la la la *la* la la, La *la* la la la *la* la la…'

It was the same tune again—they had all been infected by it. Vivien did not need to hear any more. She knew it now. It was John's favourite song of the moment, an old, old song which they had learned in their childhood and remembered when they came to live here. *Upon Paul's Steeple* was its name, and John generally burst out into it when he was feeling particularly cheerful.

Vivien laughed out loud, and began to climb a little faster. Tunes are always catching, and she had a kind of idea now what she was going to hear when she got to the top. She was almost disappointed not to find Mrs Jones in full song also when she reached the third landing; but already, one floor higher up, she could hear what she was expecting. A little out of breath, she climbed the last flight of stairs, and came in sight of the open sitting-room door.

John was sitting on the table. He was clearly waiting for her arrival, but for the moment was interested in something outside the window, and was staring into space. He was singing at the very top of his voice. beating absently with his fist on the table as he did so.

'Upon Paul's steeple hangs a tree
As full of apples as can be,'

he sang, loudly and rather huskily,

'And little boys from London town
They run with staves to pull them down,
And then they run from hedge to hedge
Until they come to Lon-don . . . Bridge.'

He finished off with a fine *rallentando*, turned round, and saw her.

'Hallo, Vivien!' He leaped up, his arms and legs going in all directions at once. 'Vivien, I 'm through. I 've passed. They 'll have me, and I 'm four months below the average age of my form.

'I knew it!' said Vivien delightedly, arriving in the door way. 'I guessed it right down on the second landing!'

CHAPTER III

STEW

GETTING Dinah ready to go to school was almost like fitting out an expedition for the North Pole. There were a score of different things that she had to have: a green tunic for this game, a grey sweater for that, a special cardigan to put on if she was cold at break, stockings and gloves of a certain pale brown for wearing with the school hat and coat. If Aunt Harrison had not helped to pay Mrs Farthing would have been in despair, and she sometimes half regretted that they had not sent Dinah to a day school in the neighbourhood, like John, and kept her peacefully at home.

But . . . there was her music. And as for keeping Dinah peaceful, such a thing had never happened yet, and the more she had to do and the more people of her own age she had to run around with, the greater would the chance of her peacefulness become. The flat was much too small a field for Dinah. Vivien was going to be extremely glad to be free of her company in their tiny bedroom; and while they would have been very sorry if Dinah had been going right away, and not coming back for Saturdays and Sundays, both Mrs Farthing and Vivien worked not unwillingly at sewing on name tapes, turning up hems, and counting and packing the large trousseau which was required to get Dinah safely through a term.

'I 'm surprised they don't want a white satin ball dress, in case you 're asked to Buckingham Palace,' said Vivien on Dinah's last evening, when the chaos of packing had reached its maximum height. 'Or a little pink sunshade, in case it 's too hot while you are promenading in the garden. Why don't girls have a sensible outfit, like John? All he 's bought so far is a cap and three cricket shirts.'

Dinah put out her tongue in reply, but it took her five minutes to think of the obvious response that neither a cap nor three cricket shirts would be much use to her. She became very much subdued as the evening went on, and by the time everything was packed and in order she was so quiet that one would have thought she had never made a good retort to anything in her life. She was still rather quiet the following morning, and resented very much that both Vivien and John came with her in the taxi to Kensington; her conversation during the drive was limited to three enormous sniffs, and if she had been alone she would certainly have cried.

However, when they arrived at Aunt Harrison's and Wheeler the butler received them in his most dignified manner, Dinah began to cheer up. The sight of her trunk and three suit-cases being carried in cheered her still further, and when they went up to the drawing-room she embraced Aunt Harrison violently, and gave every sign of being delighted to have arrived. Aunt Harrison was charmed, Dinah was charmed to see that she had charmed her, and by the time Vivien and John had exchanged proper civilities with their great-aunt and had got up to go, Dinah was once again at the top of her form.

'Give Daddy my love,' she said. 'I 'll be home on Saturday at lunch-time, unless there's anything very important I have to do.'

'Won't you write or telephone before that? We 'd like to know how you are getting on.'

'I 'll ring up, perhaps, if Aunt Harrison will be so kind

as to let me use her telephone,' said Dinah in a highly proper voice, just loud enough for Aunt Harrison to hear. 'But if you don't hear, that simply means I 'm all right. Good-bye.'

John managed to wink at her as he went out, but this she ignored completely.

'Pouf,' he said, as they got out into the street again. 'I wonder how long she 'll manage to keep that up. Sooner her than me, I must say.' He suddenly began to dance sideways along the pavement. 'Vivien, let 's go to the Natural History Museum. That 's where Aunt Harrison ought to be, you know—it was seeing her that made me think of it! The whole house looks stuffed, and she 'd be——'

'John, do be quiet!' Vivien recognized the first symptoms of one of John's attacks of high spirits, and she looked apprehensively around.

'I want to see the elephant,' said John in a sort of a chant, looking sideways at her. 'The beautiful elephant that you always like!'

'No—*not* the elephant. You know I hate it. And I don't like stuffed animals, anyway.'

'Well, then, let 's go to the Science Museum. You must keep me quiet somehow,' said John threateningly, side-stepping round an elderly gentleman. 'I 'll race you to Exhibition Road.'

'John, John, you *won't*. Do be quiet!' Vivien racked her brains frantically for something to say to him. 'You 've got to go and see Daddy this afternoon, you know.'

'Yes, of course I know. And to-morrow I 'll be in school—do you know that! Labouring over my books, homesick, bullied, getting thin and pale, probably half starved——'

114

'You 're not likely to be starved if you 're only at school for one meal every day.

'You seem to forget,' said John with sudden dignity, 'that the other three meals are provided by you.'

'Forget it? I only wish I could. I do nothing else but provide meals which you gobble up in about a tenth of the time it 's taken to get them ready.

'Ah, but you 're not an artist. If you were you 'd adore getting them ready. You 'd labour over them for hours and hours. You 'd hover about with a pinch of black pepper or a suspicion of nutmeg. You 'd measure, and you 'd brood, and you 'd have sudden inspirations——'

'Artists presumably don't have to peel the potatoes every day,' retorted Vivien with spirit. 'If you 're so keen on it, you 'd better do some of the cooking yourself.'

John spun round in a circle, finishing up immediately in front of her so that she could not go on. His face was half mischievous, half serious.

'Now you 're talking,' he said. 'Would you really like me to?'

'Oh—well——' Vivien was a little taken aback.

'Don't want your beautiful kitchen messed up, I suppose,' said John, going straight to the point. 'But what you don't realize, my angel-faced monkey, is that I can cook. You don't believe I can, but I can, all the same. I always did it in camp last year, and Aunt Rosamund let me help her often when I was staying with them. *She* didn't mind. And I made such a beautiful treacle pudding,' he added, his voice quite tender at the thought of it.

'Well . . . What do you want to cook?'

'The dinner for to-night.'

'What do you want to make?'

'Stew,' said John without a moment's hesitation. 'A

115

thick, brown, gorgeous, smelly stew.'

'Stew to-night? But it 's boiling hot weather. Don't you really think——'

'Stew or the stuffed elephant,' said John, beginning to waltz along again. 'Or else something even worse. Take your choice.'

Vivien looked at him and laughed—it was impossible to do anything else.

'All right,' she said. 'Stew, then. Come on and let 's buy the things.'

Less than two hours later Vivien was already wondering how she could ever have supposed that cooking was not amusing. To John the whole matter was like some voyage of exploration, or a delicate piece of scientific research. His high spirits remained, but transformed into a passionate concentration on the matter in hand, which not only lasted, but increased, while they made a shopping list, bought the necessary meat and vegetables and a few other stores, and carried their parcels back through the hot City streets to St Paul's Churchyard and the flat.

And when once they got into the kitchen, the world outside ceased to exist, as far as he was concerned. There was excitement enough in here, and he was thrilled and anxious and delighted all at once. He put on an apron of Mrs Farthing's, which covered him from neck to ankles, and in a very short time he had flour all over it and on his nose, and sprinkled here and there in his hair as well; but from the moment he began he was master of everything he did. They had got out an old cookery book, which gave instructions half a page long or the preparing of stews, but after he had read it through once John hardly looked at it.

116

'How on earth do you do it?' said Vivien, marvelling. You seem to know the whole thing by instinct.'

'Well, it 's such fun, you see,' said John, as if that explained everything. 'This flour needs some pepper and salt in before we use it. And look out—the dripping is hot now.'

Making a stew seemed to be a considerably longer affair than Vivien's customary roast meat, but John said that by two o'clock at the latest everything would be finished. There were carrots to wash and slice. There were onions to fry—and it was John, not Vivien, who knew that the way to peel onions without tears was to hold them and the knife under cold water. There was the steak to hammer, to roll in flour, to fry quickly in the same saucepan as the onions until it was brown. But at last everything was ready, meat and vegetables together in the saucepan. Water was poured over them, the lid put tightly on, and the gas turned low.

'That 'll be ready by six, most likely,' said John, 'but we can just turn the gas out and heat it again when we want it. Now what about pudding?'

They had been much too deeply interested to stop for a proper lunch, and took some sardines from a tin, with thick hunks of bread and butter. It was getting late now, and John had to go to the hospital, so they decided to make something simple.

'What shall it be?' said Vivien. 'Jelly?'

'No, something proper,' said John a trifle scornfully. 'Chocolate mousse.'

'Chocolate mousse?' Vivien stared at him. 'I thought you said something simple?'

'That is simple. It 's as easy as winking. I 've seen Aunt Rosamund do it. Where 's that packet of plain chocolate we were eating last night?'

Almost speechless with amazement, Vivien found the chocolate, and stood meekly by while John made efficient preparations. He melted a quarter of a pound of the slab in a double saucepan, and took out four eggs. The yolks he beat up with a fork himself, but the whites he handed over to Vivien.

'Beat 'em as stiff as you can,' he said. 'Then we mix the chocolate and the yolks, and then we put the whites in. Don't you call that simple?'

She could not deny that it was. In less than ten minutes the pale brown, frothy mixture was setting in four Woolworth soufflé glasses, and five minutes later John had washed and tidied himself, removed the flour from his head, and gone contentedly off to see his father.

Vivien, when he had gone, stood for several minutes at the sink, gazing out at the flat lead roof and the windows opposite. She had not been so much surprised for a very long time. John was the last person on earth whom she would have suspected of such a gift for cooking. It really seemed unfair—she felt a little jealous that he, who had plenty of other occupations, should prove to be a genius at something which she had taken on as her own especial department.

She thought of the stew, and the mousse, and John's rapt, happy face as he worked. He did enjoy it—he really did; and as Vivien thought it all over she realized that she had enjoyed it herself. It had been three times as much trouble as the meals she usually prepared, but it had certainly been more than three times as much fun.

Vivien looked out of the window again, then suddenly nodded, and turned to look for the cookery book. It was lying on the side, buried now under an enamel plate with three forks on it, and a discarded saucepan. She unearthed it hurriedly, turned to the index, and began to read through the list of recipes. 'Meat, Roast,' 'Meat, Boiled,' and even 'Meat, Stewed,' she passed by with disdain. Not till she had come to the most elaborate dishes the book could provide did she turn back the pages, prop it open on the window-sill, and begin to read as she washed up the stack of basins and plates and kitchen utensils which their experiments had left.

The window was open, and the growl of the traffic on Ludgate Hill came clearly in on the still summer air. Vivien, trying to concentrate on *Escalopes de Veau à la Crème*, became aware that there were other and nearer noises to be heard, and one in particular which kept on distracting her. She lifted her head.

It was not the typewriters, though several of them could be heard tapping diligently. She was used enough to them. It was somebody talking—somebody telephoning, presumably, as only one voice could be heard. And the conversation, if conversation it was, sounded so extraordinary that Vivien forgot all about *Escalopes de Veau à la Crème* and all about washing up.

'We must have the mat by to-morrow midday—I tell you they 're holding up the machines.'

That was the first sentence that she heard completely. The voice, now properly launched, started off on a vigorous monologue.

'Have you got a pull?' it demanded impatiently. 'Very well. First thing—the caps and the block are both off centre. Yes, they are. Second thing—the body 's wrong. I said Plantin, not Sans. I hate Sans with those caps, as you ought to know by now. Third thing, there 's a fool misprint. It 's "Superb: Sir Hugh Walpole," not "Super: Sir Hugh Walpole." Ever heard a critic say "Super"?' The speaker gave a snort. 'Don't suppose you 've ever heard a critic say anything,' he added, more in sorrow than in

119

anger. 'Well, get that straight, anyhow. Good-bye.'

Vivien put down the kitchen spoon she had been clutching. She looked hastily along all the windows opposite to see if she could make out the speaker. Never in her life had she heard such fantastic conversation—it sounded like something out of *Alice in Wonderland*. And what had Sir Hugh Walpole to do with it? And what mat in the world could have its caps off centre and its body wrong?

There was nobody in sight at all, except two typists at a window opposite whose typing and face-powdering technique she had often studied before. She thought she saw one of the Wilkinses at their window up on the left, which was at right angles to the Farthings' flat: but she did not care for the Wilkinses, and she did not investigate further.

She picked up her mop again, and reluctantly prepared to get on. As she did so, however, somebody suddenly appeared at one of the windows which a moment before had been empty. It was a large man, in his shirt-sleeves, with a long slip of paper in his hands. He looked hot and not a little angry.

'What 's that?' he said loudly, speaking to someone in the room behind him, but not bothering to turn round. 'Yes, half-double, of course. *Sunday Times* and *Observer*.'

He leaned his forehead on the open sash, and stood puffing deeply. He seemed to need fresh air very badly, and Vivien realized that it must be because the warm summer weather had made him open his window that she now could suddenly hear his conversation. He did not stand long, but after a dozen or so large gulps of air went back into the room again, and disappeared from her sight.

What he could be she could not imagine, but he made the outlook from the kitchen window twice as interesting as it had ever been before, and she hoped very much that he would continue to be troubled by the heat, and leave his window open, and have indignant telephone conversations, so that she could find out a little more about him.

However, it was interesting inside the kitchen as well as outside. The smell from the stew was exquisite; if it tasted anything like so good, it would have been well worth all the trouble of preparing it. The cookery book offered other suggestions which sounded fully as exciting, but there was no denying they were difficult. What on earth was *roux*? How much cream was 'a little,' and what was double cream anyway, and did they mean ten minutes or two hours when they told one to simmer a thing 'until tender'? It was all very complicated, and when at last the washing up was finished she took the book off to the sitting-room, sat down with it, and was lost to the world until she heard John arrive home.

John's first thought was for the stew.

'How is it getting on?' he demanded. 'Have you looked after it?'

'Oh, yes,' said Vivien, the more emphatically as she had forgotten all about it for nearly an hour. However, it was in admirable condition, to her great relief. They both stood admiring it for a long time before they put the lid on again, and John looked at it every ten minutes or so until it was finished, reporting on its progress every time.

Dinner-time came at last, and John himself brought the stew to the table. Mrs Farthing said she had never smelt such a delicious smell in all her life. Its taste was every bit as good as its smell, and Vivien noticed with a little pang of conscience that Mrs Farthing ate twice as much as the tiny piece of meat which was usually enough for her dinner

When all the news of the day had been pooled, and they had eaten the stew and gone on to John's excellent chocolate mousse, Vivien suddenly remembered about the strange man in the office opposite. She told them as much as she could remember of what he had said, and they found it as peculiar as she did.

'What on earth do you think he could be?' she said. 'A printer?'

'He couldn't be in the Secret Service, could he?' suggested John hopefully. 'That might be a code.'

'If the Secret Service telephoned codes with its windows open it wouldn't stay secret very long,' said Mrs Farthing. 'It sounds to me as though he was a journalist or something of the kind.'

'Oh, yes—that 's very likely it. He did talk about newspapers, and critics.' Vivien put the last of the dinner things on her tray to take out to the kitchen. 'It can't have been anything very dramatic really, although it sounded so queer.'

And without the slightest suspicion what a dramatic part the window opposite could play, Vivien folded up the tablecloth, cleared the last things away, and settled down to a good housewifely talk on cooking with John.

CHAPTER IV

MR WALTER BLUELEY

'WE don't seem to get on very fast with collecting Queer People,' said John one morning at breakfast.

'What 's the score now?' Vivien poured out more tea for Mrs Farthing, who at breakfast time was always left free to read her letters and papers before going out to work.

'I'm 7, Dinah 's 9, and you 're 3.'

'Good gracious, that 's bad. But we haven't met any new ones for a long time, now I come to think of it.'

'You don't tell me,' said Mrs Farthing, looking up from a letter she was reading, 'that you can't find any more queer people in London? I 've never known you think any one ordinary yet.'

'Oh, no, it 's not that,' John reassured her earnestly. 'Only we never seem to get about together now Dinah and I are at school, and it doesn't do if only one of us sees them. And then you see there 's cooking and things, when we *are* free. Perhaps you 'll get a chance to catch up a bit in the hols, Vivien.'

'Oh, the holidays? Yes, I might. We shan't be going away, shall we, Mummy? We can't, if Daddy doesn't get better soon.'

'No, we can't have a real holiday this year. We 'll have to save it up. But I 've just got a letter here from Aunt Rosamund, as it happens, and she says that any of us can go there whenever we like. They 've taken a house in the country.'

'Oh, that 's fine,' said John. Aunt Rosamund, Mrs

Farthing's younger sister was a great friend of the whole Farthing family, and they had often visited her when she was in England before. Her husband, Colonel Charles Edmonthorpe, had had a post at Malta for the last two years, and it had been good news both for their own two children and for the Farthings that now for a time they were going to settle in England.

'Where is it?' inquired Vivien. 'Anywhere nice?'

'It 's in the Midlands somewhere—you know Uncle Charles is never happy unless he can hunt. Let me see. . . . High Melvin, the village is called. She says the house is very nice, and there 's plenty of room. I really think that may solve things for us in the summer. I know she means it when she says it wouldn't be any trouble. We could go down in relays for a week or so each. And what about a week-end now, Vivien? She suggests that too. Wouldn't you like to go?'

'Oh . . .' Vivien thought it over, but only for a moment. 'No, thank you, Mummy. Not just now, at any rate. There 's much too much going on here!'

'Do you truly mean that?' Mrs Farthing sounded almost relieved. 'You 're not dull?'

'Dull? Oh, no. The days simply aren't long enough.'

A few weeks ago Vivien would not have believed that she could have said such a thing. But it was perfectly true. It was not that she was doing much writing. She put down an idea or two for her novel now and again; but she had not got much further than calling the hero Richard, giving him fair curly hair and piercing blue eyes, and roughing out the scene in which he told Pamela (or Anne) that to him she was more beautiful than any actress in the world. Vivien's own days were now so brimful of interest that literature, for the moment, had somehow been almost abandoned in the excitements of everyday life.

The cooking was going ahead fast. There had been startled and none too polite comments from the family at first and one or two failures; but John backed her up nobly, and helped whenever he could spare time from his homework, and already the standard of cooking was such that they were quite surprised if they did not get at least one new dish for dinner every day. Dinah, in an expansive moment, had said Vivien made some things better than Aunt Harrison's cook. The housekeeping bills had gone down several shillings a week, now that no food went into the dustbin, and the various cookery books which Vivien had unearthed or bought were marked on page after page with the date on which she had successfully attempted each new recipe.

All that took up time in the most agreeable manner, and every possible afternoon she spent at the hospital with her father, telling him all about their various experiments and discoveries, and hearing his news. They had always been good friends, but now they got to know each other better than ever before, and the more they talked the more they seemed to find to talk about. There was one new discovery of Vivien's which interested Mr Farthing more than anything else, and about which he always had to have the latest news from day to day: the work of Christopher Wren.

Wren's churches and other buildings were without question what Vivien now liked be in the whole of London. Since her first discovery of St Sebastian's she had found that the City was simply crowded with his creations: many of them she had passed by day after day without knowing that they existed. Every lane in the City seemed to have a Wren church tucked away in it somewhere. Her interest once roused, she had hunted for them in every spare half hour, and she already felt almost as knowledgeable as the two men she had heard talking in St Sebastian's. At first she had marked her quarries down by their spires—those astonishing spires, no two of them alike, which give any sight of the City a quality all its own. She knew St Mary-le-Bow and St Martin's Ludgate, St Andrew's Holborn, St Vedast's, St Stephen's Walbrook, St Lawrence Jewry, St Bride's, and many others also. She had run to earth all the ones with visible spires, and was now finding the others: strange little places, some of them, tucked in between a high office building and a row of shops, but all showing in some way or another the special, magical quality that marked all Wren's work.

She could not say what it was that so much fascinated her. She had tried several times to put it into words—to write it down, even—but the words escaped her. Design, order, space, light: all these things came into it, and yet they were not in themselves enough. Standing one day at her favourite place inside the big west door of St Paul's, gazing down the immense, splendid aisle to the dome and the distant chancel, she felt that she got very near to it—but when she tried to catch her thoughts in words, they escaped her again.

Mr Farthing understood better than any one else what pleasure all these explorations gave her, and she was always glad to be able to tell him of something new. One lunch-time before going to the hospital she suddenly made up her mind to walk up Fleet Street to the Temple, thinking that she would just have time to take a look at the Middle Temple gateway before catching a bus out to Whitechapel. She loved the Temple, with its quiet courts, narrow passages, and gardens sloping far away down to the Embankment: but not until a few days ago had she known that the gateway leading into Fleet Street was the work of Wren.

She strolled quietly up Fleet Street among the lunch-hour crowds, past the huge *Daily Express* and *Daily Telegraph* buildings, past all the strange little alley-ways which always made her think of Dr Johnson, past St Dunstan's-in-the-West where the two giants hammered solemnly on their ledge every time the big clock struck the hour. She came opposite the gateway, and began to study it.

It was lovely, certainly: a smooth, quiet façade of old red brick strapped with stone columns, with windows in the upper stories and an arched gateway below leading into the Temple lanes and courtyards. It looked both out of place and delightfully right among the noise and the shops and offices and hurrying people. Absorbed in her thoughts, Vivien stood and gazed at it. Half the fun of Wren's things, she reflected, was that they now stood in a London so wildly unlike the city they were designed for. She wondered what Wren would have said if he could have walked down Fleet Street at this moment. Buses, huge lorries full of newsprint, errand boys on bicycles, press messengers, typists, hundreds upon hundreds of men in nondescript suits walking along looking nowhere but at the pavement and their own thoughts. . . . Would he have liked it all, or would he have hated it?

It was still too early for her to go on to the hospital, so after a moment's hesitation she crossed the road, went back down Fleet Street, and turned up the short passage that led to the wrought-iron gates of St Bride's. St Bride's Church, she thought, had the loveliest steeple in the whole world—always excepting St Sebastian's, of course. It was like some celestial wedding-cake. And the inside, white and gold, with its oval windows, belonged perfectly to the spire and was no less beautiful. Deep in thought,

Vivien pushed open the lobby door and went into the church.

She had stood for some little time, looking and meditating, before she realized that somebody was looking at her. She turned cautiously round, and saw a large, dark-suited figure a little to her left. To her surprise, the man made a movement of recognition.

'Back again?' he said with a friendly smile.

Vivien frowned in embarrassment.

'Well, yes,' she said. 'But—'

'Is this the one you like best?'

'Er—yes. I mean, no, not quite,' said Vivien, realizing with astonishment what the man was talking about. 'I like St Sebastian's better, really.'

'There,' said the man triumphantly. 'What did I always say? And come to think of it, that 's where I saw you first.'

'Where you saw me?' Startled, Vivien looked at the man more closely. 'Oh—now I remember,' she exclaimed. 'You were the man who was talking to the other man. . . .'

Her voice died away—she did not feel at ease talking like this in a church, and friendly though the man seemed, she still felt a little embarrassed. He nodded, partly as if to show that that was indeed the man he was, but partly to suggest that he quite understood how she was feeling.

'Let 's go outside,' he said. 'We can't talk properly in here.'

Obediently enough, Vivien allowed him to shepherd her out of the church and into the sunlit courtyard. There she turned and looked inquiringly up at his broad red smiling face.

'You know,' he said, speaking with obvious relief in his normal vigorous tones, 'I 've seen you several times. Twice here. Once at St Vedast's. And then that first time

128

at St Sebastian's, when old Persepolis put the lights on.'

'Oh—have you really? I don't think I 've ever seen you, except that once.'

'Ah, but I 'm not a pretty young thing,' said the man, cheerfully but quite impersonally. '*But*,' he added, as if now came the whole point of the discussion, 'when one person that likes old buildings keeps running across another person that likes old buildings, what ought those two people to do? Why, they ought to talk, of course. Am I right?'

Vivien took one more look at his large, square, brick-red face and friendly grey eyes.

'All right,' she said, her doubts set at rest. 'Yes, you are.'

'Fine.' The man nodded vigorously several times. 'Blueley, my name is. Walter Blueley. Here 's my card.'

'Thank you,' said Vivien, taking it. 'Mine 's Vivien Farthing.'

'Thanks very much. Well—we can't very well stand here. Have you time to step into Lyons for a cup of coffee?'

'All right,' said Vivien after a moment's pause, feeling that if she broke the conventions she might as well do it thoroughly 'I 've got twenty minutes.'

They fell into step and walked up Ludgate Hill, Vivien not a little surprised at herself and Mr Blueley extremely cheerful. He talked about the view of St Paul's from Ludgate Circus, and about the weather; but it was not until they were settled at a small table in Lyons, and provided with two cups of coffee, that he really seemed to consider the conversation open.

'I 'll watch the time for you,' he said. 'You don't want to be late back and get in a row.'

'Late back? Oh, but I shan't be. I 'm only going to the

London Hospital, to see my father.'

'What?' Mr Blueley was surprised. 'Don't you work in the City then?' I thought this was your lunch hour.'

'Oh, no—we live here. My parents and my brother and sister and I.'

'Well now, that 's very surprising,' said Mr Blueley, taking a long drink of coffee. 'I don't live in the City. Wish I did, but it can't be done with three small kiddies. I work here, though, as you can see by my card.'

'Oh,' said Vivien, who had forgotten all about it. "Mr Walter Blueley," she read. "Representing Messrs Laurence Broadstreet Ltd, Publishers, Magnificat Alley, E.C.4." Publishers?' She looked up at him, her voice husky with respect. 'Are you a publisher?'

'Well, not exactly. But I travel for them. I 'm their London representative, you see.'

'Oh, are you really.' Vivien was very much impressed. 'How awfully exciting. What do you do, exactly?'

'Sell books, if I can. But we must talk about all that another time,' said Mr Blueley, looking at his watch. 'Tell me, what made *you* think of buildings?'

'What—going and looking at Wren churches and things, do you mean? I don't know,' said Vivien, rather baffled by this direct question. 'Because they looked nice, I suppose.'

'Simply because you like them? Nobody told you to go, or anything? I thought so,' said Mr Blueley warmly. 'The Pure Approach.'

Seeing Vivien's puzzled look, he gave an almost embarrassed smile. 'There I go again,' he said. 'It 's an idea I 've got. Want to write a book about it one day, fool that I am—about architecture, and design, and how people feel about them, and so on. As if there weren't books enough already.'

'Oh, but there can't be too many books,' said Vivien quickly. Mr Blueley laughed.

'What a thing to say to a publisher's representative!' he exclaimed. 'I 'll tell you a thing or two about the book trade, if you like! And if you 'd care to come with me to Broadstreet's one day, I 'll show you for yourself. Do you write, by the way?'

'Er, no—I mean yes, a bit,' said Vivien, startled.

'Yes, of course you do. Who doesn't?'

'Well, I don't really,' said Vivien, not particularly pleased by this calm way of treating her most vital secrets. 'I mean, only privately. No one knows about it.'

'All right, I won't ever say a word. Don't worry. But I suppose every young thing in the British Isles writes a bit, and some of the older ones too, like me, who ought to know better. Ever had anything published?'

'Er—no. But——'

'But you keep on hoping? That 's the way. Thirty-nine rejection slips before you get anything accepted.'

'*What* did you say?'

'Oh, I was quoting from an article in this week's *John o' London's*—a lot of authors were telling how they first came to take up writing. Very interesting, it was. But you 've seen it, surely?'

'No.'

'What? You don't see *John o' London's Weekly*? Or *The Times Literary Supplement*, or the *Spectator*? But how do you keep up with what 's going on?'

'I read the Sunday papers, sometimes,' said Vivien meekly. '*The Observer* and *Sunday Times*.'

'Yes, yes, of course you do.' This was by no means enough for Mr Blueley. 'But how do you work? You 'll be telling me next you haven't an *Author's Handbook*.'

'No, I——'

'Well, really, I mean to say. . . . How do you find out what market your stuff is suitable for—which papers you ought to send it to?' Luckily for Vivien, Mr Blueley was so shattered by her disclosures that he did not wait for any answer. 'It seems to me that I can give you one or two tips, Miss Farthing, if you 'll take them from an old hand like me who 's been pottering about on the job for years.' He looked at his watch. 'Time for you to go,' he said. 'I said I 'd tell you. Well, well. . . . You can take it from me, one of the proudest days of your life will be when you get a signed letter of rejection from an editor instead of the printed slip.'

Mr Blueley seemed quite serious, and there was no doubt he knew what he was talking about. Vivien, getting up to go, looked at him with a consternation which she did her best to hide. Was writing really so difficult? Had every one to go through so much before they got anything published?

But however depressed she might feel, it was impossible to resent what he had said. He looked so cheerful about everything, whether it were Wren or young authors or his own ambition to write a book. She would take his advice, every bit of it . . . one day. In the meantime, he was an entertaining person to have stumbled upon, out of all the City's thousands, and Vivien was more than delighted when, as she left to go to the hospital, he repeated his offer to take her to his firm one day and show her what a publisher's was like.

CHAPTER V

PUBLISHER'S OFFICE

THE family took Mr Blueley calmly enough. John and Dinah both urged Vivien to produce him as quickly as possible for them to see, so that they could bag him for the competition. Mr Farthing made up a poem ending 'I remain yours truly, Walter Blueley,' and Mrs Farthing said 'If you 're sure he 's not going to be a bother to you, I think he sounds rather interesting.'

'Yes, he really was interesting. He 's full of stories about this part of London, and he 's not a bit dull. His firm 's just round the corner from here, you know. He says there's been bookselling around St Paul's for hundreds of years. The publishers all used to live over their offices a hundred years ago or something like that, and he said that in Paternoster Row, just at the back here, their wives were told to sit in the window all day and watch what authors went into the rival publishers opposite, so that they could go and catch them as they came out!'

'That was rather sharp practice! I suppose they 're all much too respectable to do that sort of thing nowadays.'

'I suppose they are,' said Vivien a little regretfully. I do hope he remembers to take me to Broadstreet's. And he wants me to go and see Gray's Inn with him one day, when he 's in the City for lunch, and Staple Inn, and one or two other places. He really does love them all, I think.'

Further acquaintance proved that Mr Blueley was every bit as entertaining as he had seemed at first. Before many days passed he had rung Vivien up on Mrs Jones's telephone and taken her off for a little lunch-hour exploration, and in a short time they were fast friends. He was full of enthusiasm for London and everything in it, and she discovered more in two lunch hours with him than she would have in a month by herself. It was not only Wren buildings that they visited. He took her to the old, old church of St Bartholomew's in Smithfield, to Gray's Inn and Staple Inn and Lincoln's Inn Fields, to the Roman Bath tucked away a few yards behind the Strand, and down to the Embankment Gardens to see the beautiful water-gate designed by Inigo Jones three hundred years ago. He was the greatest fun to go about with—never bothering her with information, but always ready with interesting facts or stories if she asked, and always beaming with good humour. He liked to talk about his family, and to hear about hers, and they very soon felt as if they had known each other for years.

In the intervals of exploration he told her a great deal about writing, and she was more and more amazed to find how much there was to know about the tricks of the trade.

'It seems to me,' she said a little bitterly, when they were talking about it all, 'that being *able* to write is the last thing that matters. It 's much more important to have your work typed with the right-sized margins, or send in exactly the right number of words.'

'No. No.' Mr Blueley would not have this at all. 'No, you 're wrong there. The most important thing of all is to be able to write—to have the ideas and the ability—but it 's very nearly as important to be able to present your work properly. It 's like clothes—nice clothes are all very well, but they 're no good if you don't know how and when to wear them. You want to make your manuscript look professional, of course, well typed and so on, and you can see that it 's vital to send your work to the paper that 's most likely to use it, and to give it the tone and the length that that particular paper prefers. That 's where a book like the *Author's Handbook* comes in—you can look up all the papers that take love-stories, for example, and see what kind they like, and try them all in turn.'

'Yes, I quite see that,' said Vivien, who had bought the book on Mr Blueley's advice and spent some astonished half-hours studying its contents. 'Oh, dear, but it 's all very hard for someone who 's just beginning. And I can't help wondering—do they really read the things that are sent in, do you think? I mean, they come back so quickly, sometimes.'

'You can be quite sure they do,' answered Mr Blueley decidedly. 'After all, they 've got to have the stuff to publish. They can't afford to overlook anything that could possibly suit them. But I know how you feel. I used to feel just the same when I was young and thought I should be a writer.'

'Don't you still think you 'll be a writer? I mean, aren't you one?'

'Well—no,' said Mr Blueley, after thought. 'I had a story or so published, but it seemed such slow work… I get on much better selling other people's work than I ever did selling my own. There 's that architecture book, of course, but that 's something rather different. It 's not begun yet, anyway, and nobody knows about it except you. By the way, don't forget that you were coming with me over Broadstreet's one day.'

'Forget!' Vivien's tone was eloquent. 'May I really?'

Mr Blueley took out his engagement book.

'Of course you may. As soon as you like.'

'And see how the books are made, and everything?'

'Everything there *is* to see. But you mustn't expect anything so very exciting—it 's mostly just a lot of unfortunate people like me sitting at their desks and tearing their hair out trying to think up original ideas.'

In spite of this sad picture, Vivien looked forward to her visit with more excitement than she had felt about anything for a very long time. The day came at last. John, who was free early that afternoon from school, went out to the hospital to see Mr Farthing, and Vivien, putting on her nice hat and powdering her nose with particular care, went down in the lift to the waiting Mr Blueley.

'You know we live just in the next street?' he said as they set off.

'Oh, yes—I 've seen your door. It looks very grand.'

'Grand—my goodness! Well, I suppose it 's not bad, really,' said Mr Blueley, as one trying to be fair. 'It 's a fine old building, and there 's a good hall and staircase, but we 've grown so big that we 're all squashed in anyhow. The sales department lives in a corridor. The advertisement manager has a room cut out of the building next door. Mr Irvine hasn't got a room at all, but a little cubby-hole leading out of his uncle's.'

'Who 's he?' said Vivien, beginning to feel rather bewildered.

'He 's Mr Broadstreet's nephew,' said Mr Blueley, as they arrived at the firm's door in Magnificat Alley. 'He 'll go into partnership with him soon, and most likely take over the business when the old boy retires. Here we are. Come on — there 's nothing to be frightened of.'

There was indeed nothing to be frightened of when they got inside the door, except a very elegant and well-dressed young woman who made Vivien feel she would like to sink quietly through the floor. However, the young woman gave a friendly smile when she saw Mr Blueley, and thought no more about them, but got on with her work, sitting up very straight at a big desk in the corner.

'That 's our Miss Ramsay,' said Mr Blueley as they crossed the big hall and went towards the staircase. 'She 's a grand woman—knows what the old boy 's thinking before he thinks of it himself, and can smell a best-seller almost before she 's begun to read the typescript. Round there, under the stairs, is the sales department. That 's where the finished books are dispatched, and the accounts kept.'

'The finished books? But the hall was full of books,' said Vivien as they climbed the stairs. 'Aren't they to be sold?'

'They 're there to look pretty. Any one can come in and go round looking at them, but all the serious selling is done at the trade counter.'

'What 's up here?' inquired Vivien hardly above a whisper.

'Waiting-room, secretaries, Mr Broadstreet, Mr Irvine, agreements, production, art, filing, and advance publicity, said Mr Blueley rapidly.

He pushed open a swing-door half-way up the big staircase, and the holy calm suddenly gave place to the most varied and intriguing collection of noises, proceeding from the doors on either side of a long corridor and mingling in the middle like some mad symphony. Typewriters were the outstanding feature, clicking away at a tremendous speed and pinging their little bells as they came to the end of a line. Somewhere to the right someone was thumping, the thud, thud coming in like the beat of a drum. Telephone bells rang, buzzers buzzed angrily as if someone wanted someone else and was tired of being kept waiting. And over all the mechanical noises rose the sound of people talking—dictating, discussing, telephoning, near and far away, high and low, men's voices and women's, while somebody in a room near by was quietly and systematically groaning.

'That 's young Sackville,' said Mr Blueley, laughing as he heard the groans and letting the swing-door fall into place behind him. 'That means he 's trying to write a blurb.'

'A—a blurb?' Vivien looked apprehensively at Mr Sackville's doorway. 'I 'm awfully sorry to be so ignorant, but what is a blurb?'

Mr Blueley ran a thoughtful hand through his thick brown hair.

'A blurb,' he said. 'Well, a blurb is—a blurb is——'

'What 's all this?' said a new voice close behind them. 'Are you in trouble, Mr Blueley?'

They both swung round. Gazing over Mr Blueley's shoulder was a young man with a book in one hand and the other hand still on the swing-door by which he had come in.

'Oh, Mr Irvine,' said Mr Blueley with a start. 'I didn't hear you come through. Well, yes, as a matter of fact, this young lady has just asked me what a blurb is, and well, you know, it 's not too easy, if you see what I mean.'

The young man laughed. He had what Vivien considered a very alarming face, rather dark and looking as if he knew a great deal about everything, but when he laughed his nose went into creases all up the sides and he did not look nearly so formidable.

'Perhaps I can help,' he said. 'Won't you introduce us?'

'Mr Irvine Broadstreet, Miss Vivien Farthing,' said Mr Blueley promptly. 'Miss Farthing is a neighbour of ours— her family lives just round in St Paul's Churchyard—and she is so anxious to know about publishing that I took the occasion to give her a quick look round.'

'Really?' Mr Broadstreet sounded interested, but Vivien could not believe that it was anything more than politeness. They shook hands. 'Well,' he went on. 'a blurb is the bit about a novel or some other book which makes you convinced that you must read it immediately. You know—"This dramatic life of William the Conqueror is as thrilling as any detective story," or "The everyday disasters of matrimony are sketched in with a light and witty touch." That sort of thing.'

'Oh, are those blurbs? I 've often thought how difficult they must be to write.'

'They are. They 're ghastly. Sackville 's a genius at it, but it nearly makes him sick every time.' Mr Broadstreet gave her another extremely charming smile. 'Have you been all round yet?'

'No, we 've only just begun,' Mr Blueley answered. I thought I 'd like to show her some of the wrappers and bindings and that sort of thing, if you don't mind.'

'No, no, of course not. And if you want to look in my uncle's room on the way out, don't be afraid. He won't be back from his lunch till well after three. One of the most important parts of a publisher's work,' Mr Broadstreet added, turning to Vivien again, 'is having long and sumptuous lunches at the very best restaurants. We take somebody whom we want to make a deal with—a starving author, for instance—and give him so much food and drink that he can't think any more, and then fix everything up. It 's a very good scheme.'

With a cheerful grin, and something that might almost have been a wink, Mr Broadstreet backed out through the swing-doors as suddenly as he had come. Vivien laughed.

'What fun,' she said. 'What a nice man. Where are we going to now?'

'To see how books are put together. Down here please.'

The next half hour was so absorbing that Vivien

forgot about everything else—time, and Mr Broadstreet, and everything except the inner workings of book making which Mr Blueley so carefully showed her. What he could not explain himself he got somebody else to explain, and Vivien met more new people than she could possibly remember afterwards. She saw the stack of manuscripts, from would-be authors all over the world, out of which the firm of Broadstreet would choose those which it wanted to publish. She saw the reports on them being filed by a cheerful little girl with fair hair, and the unwanted ones being parcelled up to be sent back again; and she felt that just so would any manuscript of hers be parcelled up and sent back, and rightly enough too, most likely. In another room were the proofs of those books which had already been printed—some of them on queer long slips of paper, as long as a newspaper but much narrower, which Mr Blueley referred to as galleys. There were proofs of photographs and drawings too, all printed together on one big sheet, and two young women were cutting some of these up and trying to fit them into place in the books to which they belonged.

But what interested her if possible even more was the room in which a young man with his coat off was planning the bindings and dust-wrappers. He was deeply absorbed by his task, ranging a row of empty book-covers on the mantelpiece and standing back to get a better look at them.

'Here—Blueley,' he said at once when they knocked and went in. 'Come and look at these. It's for *The Grass is so Green*—you know, that autobiography. Do you think the cloth ought to be green, with a title like that, or do you think it's simply silly?'

He gathered up all the book-covers again, came across the room, and thrust half into Mr Blueley's hands and half into Vivien's.

'Take a look at them, like a good chap,' he said, speaking to them both impartially. 'There 's a green, you see, with the title in white, and there 's a blue one, and a pale yellow blocked in reseda. The wrapper 's pale green and gold, with a splodge or two of purple—sort of surrealist stuff. Here 's a proof of it.'

They all bent over the book-covers—neat empty cases of cardboard and cloth, with the title stamped on the back. The young man, whom Mr Blueley addressed as Mr Tyson, was completely absorbed in getting their opinion and comparing it with his own. Vivien was fascinated. Never before had she seen all the pieces of a book like this before they were put together: never even thought of them as existing. She ventured at last to say that she thought she preferred the green one.

'Why?' said Mr Tyson promptly.

That was a hard one, but she was less afraid of everything now.

'Well,' she answered, almost without delay, 'if I was looking for a book at the library and saw one called *The Grass is so Green* and it hadn't a green cover, I should think how silly that was, but if it had a green cover I shouldn't think any more about that but should take it down because I liked the title.'

Mr Tyson, in his own cold way, seemed obliged.

'That 's sense,' he said. 'That 's constructive. Thanks so much.'

He then suddenly woke up to the fact that she was a stranger, and gave her such an extremely suspicious look that Mr Blueley caught her eye and laughed. Introductions were hastily made, but Mr Tyson continued to look so suspicious that after the shortest possible time Mr Blueley said they must hurry away, and took her out into the

141

corridor again.

'And we really must hurry,' he said. 'I 've got to go down and talk to the sales manager in another ten minutes. But you 've seen most of the interesting things now, I think.'

'Oh, it 's been lovely,' said Vivien as they went along the noisy corridor. 'I 'd no idea how exciting it was.'

'Tyson 's a comic, isn't he! We 'll just look into the old boy—into Mr Broadstreet's room, and then I must run away and leave you. Through here this time.'

Instead of going through the swing-door they turned to the right just beside it, and went into a room where several girls were sitting typing. Out of this led another door, and Mr Blueley, opening it, motioned Vivien to go through into the large room beyond.

'This is Mr Broadstreet's room,' he said, his voice suddenly several degrees quieter than usual. 'Fine place, isn't it?'

Vivien, gazing around her with interest, thought that it looked more than anything like the waiting-room of a Harley Street specialist. It was huge, with three big windows down one side and a mahogany desk and arm-chair sitting exactly in the centre of a large Turkish carpet in the exact centre of the room. There was a glass case of books at one end of the room, and one letter lying on the desk, but otherwise no sign whatsoever that this was the place from which a whole busy publishing firm was run.

Vivien was just about to say something when a cough from quite close at hand made her start. She looked up, and saw that, cut off from the room by a carved wooden partition with a lot of holes in it, Mr Irvine Broadstreet was sitting at another desk within a few feet of the door by which they had come in.

He turned round, smiled, and got up and came out

from his little pen.

'Admiring our show piece?' he said cheerfully. 'Huge place, isn't it? You see, Miss Farthing—I 'll tell you another secret about publishing. The bigger the managing director's room, and the emptier it is of everything to do with publishing, the more certain all his visitors are that the firm is enormously successful.'

'But where does he work?' said Vivien, laughing. 'Or doesn't he?'

'Oh, certainly he does. But look in here, and you 'll see where all the hard work gets done.'

He waved at his little partition, and Vivien, peering through it, saw that there, at any rate, there was confusion enough and to spare. There were papers on the floor, papers on the chair, papers piled so high on the desk that the top of the telephone was only just visible; and how there had been any room for him to sit down she could not imagine.

'Have you seen everything?' he inquired. 'What do you think of us all?'

Vivien tried to think of some answer that would express a little of what she felt, but while she was still stammering her admiration she heard Mr Blueley beginning the story of Mr Tyson and *The Grass is so Green*. Young Mr Broadstreet listened to it gravely, and when he heard what Vivien had said he turned to her and once again gave her one of his most captivating smiles.

'That was grand,' he said. 'That was exactly the sort of thing we 're always longing to be told—what the ordinary reader is going to think about the books we design. You don't mind being called an ordinary reader, I hope?'

'Oh, no,' said Vivien, hoping that she was not going to blush.

'Most people think they're extra-ordinary readers,'

said Mr Broadstreet. 'But the ordinary reader is practically the most important thing in the world, as far as we are concerned. It 's he who has to buy our books, or ask for them at the library, and if we can't persuade him to we 'll all go bankrupt.'

He beamed at her, as if the prospect of bankruptcy was not yet terribly near to them, and then turned to Mr Blueley.

'Couldn't we use her now and again?' he said suddenly. 'As an Ordinary Reader? Fire some book or some jacket at her and see what she says of it? It might be extremely helpful to have someone living so close.'

'Good gracious me!' said Mr Blueley, startled by the rapidity of all this. 'Why, yes, I 'm sure we could, Mr Broadstreet. That 's a fine idea. If she doesn't mind, of course.'

Vivien gazed helplessly from one to the other. The blush which had been impending came on in full force, spreading relentlessly upwards from her neck over all her face.

'What do you say, Vivien?' Mr Blueley prompted at last. Would you mind?'

'Yes, what do you say, Vi—— I mean Miss Farthing? It wouldn't be much, you know. Just an occasional five minutes.'

He put his head on one side and smiled, and Vivien was lost completely. She had meant to say no—not because she wanted to say no, but out of sheer fright; but now there was nothing possible to say but yes, and thank you very much indeed.

In two minutes it was all over. Mr Broadstreet had written down her address and Mrs Jones's phone number, and shaken hands, and said good-bye. Mr Blueley had taken her to the staircase, and shaken hands also, and

144

plunged off through the swing-door. She walked down the stairs and through the show-room without the slightest idea of what she was doing. She came out into Magnificat Alley. Her mind a confused and delicious jumble of publishing and proofs and book-covers and the charm of young Mr Broadstreet's smile, she turned down the lane to the left and began to walk home.

CHAPTER VI

HOME FROM THE HOSPITAL

'IT was mean of John to score Mr Blueley,' said Dinah, chopping up a hard-boiled egg.

'Yes, it was,' agreed Vivien with feeling. 'We just ran into him, you know, on Ludgate Hill, and John said "Bags" almost before I 'd introduced him.'

'You 'll never catch up, said Dinah. 'You 're too polite. But John 's ahead of me now. It 's not a bit fair, either, now I 'm away all the week. There are some *awful* people I ought to get marks for.'

She spoke with gloomy intensity, and chopped at the egg as if she were chopping up one of her enemies. Vivien looked down at her rather anxiously. Dinah was being very quiet—much too quiet—about how she got on in Kensington. They gathered that she got on all right with Aunt Harrison, for she had made the discovery unthinkable either to Vivien or John—that Aunt Harrison liked one better if one answered back now and again. But there was something wrong, without the least doubt, though what it was nobody knew. Dinah had chosen Kensington herself, and she was not the sort of person to admit that she had not chosen right.

'Such as whom, for instance?' inquired Vivien cautiously.

Dinah glowered at the chopped-up pieces of egg.

'Heppie,' she said between her teeth.

'What—the violin master?' Vivien could hardly believe it. 'Do you really mean that?'

'Do I mean it!' said Dinah with concentrated

146

bitterness.

'But, Dinah, I thought he was so good.'

'So he is, in his way, for some of them. But he 's absolutely all wrong for me. He freezes me up. I can't tell you what it is. He doesn't like me and I don't like him, and whatever I do is wrong, and he says I 've no technique at all, and I have to unlearn everything I used to do before. He makes me do two hours a day of solid technique. Honestly, I 'm nearly frantic. Mr Vining said I was almost ready to pass Inter when we left Berrings, but I know I 'm worse now.'

'That really is dreadful. What are you going to do?'

'Do?' said Dinah. 'Burst, I suppose.'

'Can't we talk to Mummy, or Aunt Harrison, or someone?'

'Don't you dare talk to any one.' Dinah looked up at her angrily. 'I chose him myself, and you know they 'd only say things. No, I 'll pass Inter and I 'll fix it all up somehow, even if I have to do something desperate.'

More than that she refused to say, and Vivien, after a few further attempts to discuss the matter, gave it up in despair. However, Dinah did not seem quite to have reached bursting-point as yet, and after a short time more she began to look much less unhappy.

'These eggs are done,' she said. 'Is the chicken ready? What do you do now?'

The experiment of the day was a special kind of galantine of chicken, and as John was out playing cricket Dinah had asked to come and help. She enjoyed cooking now and again, though she soon got tired of it; and on this particular Saturday she seemed to find it a relief to her angry thoughts.

'Melt the gelatine,' said Vivien. 'You can do that, if you will. I 'm stirring the bechamel sauce.'

'All right. What 's bechamel?'

'This is—flour and butter and milk. It takes ages to make it properly, but it 's worth it. It 's the sauce that Count Béchamel invented, and then he said "With a sauce like this, a man would find it a pleasure to eat his own grandmother."'

Dinah thought this was extremely funny, and roared with laughter.

'Oh, it 's nice to be home again, where people say silly things! "Eat his own grandmother!" He might have tried eating his hat. Here 's the gelatine. Take it quick, while it 's warm.'

The galantine turned out very well, and the afternoon went by peacefully, troubled by nothing except occasional outbursts of song from the wheezy gramophone belonging to the two Mr Wilkinses upstairs.

'I don't think much of those Nilpils,' said Dinah— the name on their notice-board had struck the Farthings as so suitable that they always used it, whether it belonged to them or not. 'They only seem to have that one record, and it must be at least ten years old.'

'It 's *Rose Marie*. They never play it except at weekends. And did you know they 've only got one hat?'

'Well, that 's all I 've got, except my school one.'

'Yes, but I mean one hat between them. They never go out both together, and whichever is going out takes "the" hat and "the" umbrella, and I think "the" tie as well. I 've heard them talking about it.'

'What a funny idea. Perhaps they 're horribly poor. Like us, only worse. Has Mummy gone to the hospital?'

'Yes. She won't be back for a long time yet.'

But Mrs Farthing, to their surprise, arrived home when they had only just finished tea and begun to wash up the tea-things. When they heard her footsteps they thought at first that it must be a stranger.

'Vivien—Dinah—John,' she called. 'Are you at home?'

They hurried out on to the landing, Vivien still with a dish-cloth in her hand.

'I 've got the best possible news,' said Mrs Farthing the moment she saw them. 'Daddy 's coming home.'

'Coming *home*?' They could not believe it. 'When?'

'On Monday.' Mrs Farthing sounded as if she could hardly believe it either. 'I 've got to arrange for an ambulance to fetch him. A nurse is to come every day and give him injections, and of course he can't go to work or walk about for a long time yet. But he is coming home—he really is.'

'Oh, Mummy, how absolutely frightfully nice,' said Dinah, taking Mrs Farthing's arm and hugging it tightly. 'Come in here and tell us every single thing about it.'

They were still talking about it when John arrived home, scarlet from fresh air and exercise, very dirty, and very cheerful. When they told him the news he stood stock-still in the doorway, gazing incredulously from one to the other.

'On Monday?' he said at last. 'On Monday? Mummy —can he eat whatever he likes, do you think?'

'Yes. Anything he wants to. The doctor said so. Why?'

'Well, what could he have for dinner?' said John, his face solemn and preoccupied. 'Do you think he would like to have stew?'

With great efficiency by the ambulance men, and much co-operation from Mr Jones at the lift, and extreme interest from a small crowd of messenger-boys on the pavement Mr Farthing was brought up to the flat with out the slightest discomfort and installed on the sofa in the sitting-room which Vivien had prepared with sheets and blankets and pillows and two hot-water bottles.

When at last everybody had gone, the flat returned to its accustomed silence, and Vivien, watching a little anxiously saw her father gaze slowly from the door to the table, and from the table to the dome of St Paul's outside the window, and at last give an enormous sigh.

'Oh, this is grand,' he said. 'I can't believe it, you know.'

'Aren't you tired? Are you sure?'

'No, not the slightest bit in the world. I think this is a perfectly lovely little flat,' said Mr Farthing, going on looking and looking at everything as if he must make up for lost time. 'It 's even nicer than I had imagined it.'

There was so much to see and to talk about that the day passed quicker than any day had passed for months. A nice quiet nurse, called Nurse Rymer, arrived just before lunch to give Mr Farthing an injection, and looked with a professional eye at Vivien's arrangements for his comfort, but apparently found nothing to criticize. The great Sir William himself came a little later, tall and smiling, and after a short visit went away saying that he would come twice a week until further notice. Vivien made a light lunch, of omelette and fruit and coffee, which Mr Farthing said was nicer than anything he had eaten for months, and after it he was tired enough to lie resting and dozing until almost tea-time.

By the evening he had quite recovered again, and was well able to enjoy the stew which John had insisted Vivien should make for him. That night after dinner, as he lay enjoying the last half hour before he was to be helped to bed, Vivien felt so immensely and incredibly happy that more than once her eyes became suddenly full of tears. Mrs Farthing was sitting on the couch at her husband's feet. Both of them had books, but although they looked at them occasionally they looked at each other a good deal more, and she did not believe they had the slightest idea what they were reading about. John, his nose peeling violently from Saturday's sunshine, sat brooding over some homework at the table; and Vivien, sitting opposite him, began a long and conversational letter to a school friend whom she ought to have written to several months ago, and who would not have the slightest idea why Vivien was so cheerful all of a sudden, and such a good correspondent.

' "Oranges and lemons," say the bells of St Clement's; "You owe me five farthings," say the bells of St Martin's. . . .' The words and the tune kept running in her head as she wrote—and no wonder, she realized suddenly, for they *were* five Farthings again now, if one counted Dinah, which one very reasonably might. And it was the bells of St Martin's who were asking for them: of Wren's own St Martin's, one could be allowed to think, only a few yards away down Ludgate Hill. Smiling to herself, Vivien remembered an old and long ago worn out joke from their nursery days—a family signature. She took a slip of paper, scribbled on it '1¼d.,' and passed it across to John.

CHAPTER VII

MESSRS BROADSTREET ARE WORRIED

WITHIN a very few days it seemed as if Mr Farthing had been at home with them all for as long as they could remember. They would sometimes refer to 'when we used to come and see you at the hospital,' or 'when you weren't here,' but as if that had been almost years ago, when they were very young. Things were not right yet, for it seemed even stranger, now Mr Farthing was back, that Mrs Farthing should go out to Greencoat's every morning; but they were much, much better.

Mrs Jones and Mr Farthing liked each other as soon as they met, and had long conversations about how things had changed since some time which they amiably but vaguely referred to as the 'good old days.' Mrs Jones now came up to the flat every morning, and did so much work in the hour or so which she 'spared' to the Farthings that Vivien had scarcely any more to do than she had had before Mr Farthing came home.

If Mr Farthing was tired of his illness, or worried as to when it would end, he managed to give no signs of it. He was always peaceful and always cheerful. He read, he looked out of the window, he took a keen interest in everything Vivien was doing and inquired about the progress of each thing she cooked. He heard all John's gossip from school, and all Dinah's when she came home on Saturdays after her orchestra practice, and everything Mrs Farthing could tell him about the peculiarities of the women from Mayfair and Hampstead and the home counties who came to buy their clothes at Greencoat's.

He was a little tired each day after his injections, but he soon recovered, and he was always ready to hear about the peculiarities of the Wilkinses or the strange people Vivien saw when she went out shopping.

As for Vivien, while she cooked and washed up and shopped and fetched new library books for her father, her mind was half the time not on what she was doing at all, but somewhere round the corner in the firm of Messrs Laurence Broadstreet. She thought over and over again about all she had seen and heard on her visit there, and above all, of course, of young Mr Broadstreet's suggestion and the way he had smiled when he made it. It was all so thrilling that she could hardly believe it—or rather, it would all be so thrilling, if only she heard something more.

But now a week had gone by, and she had heard nothing from anybody. Even Mr Blueley had not appeared. To be sure, he knew that her father was coming home, and most likely had kept out of the way on purpose, but still . . . Busy scraping a particularly dirty saucepan, Vivien came suddenly to the conclusion that it was high time Mr Blueley and her father came to know each other.

Mr Farthing, when she asked him, said he would like it very much if Mr Blueley could come in one day for half an hour for a quick City lunch, and a note to Mr Blueley at Broadstreet's produced a prompt acceptance. Mr Blueley had never been up to the flat before, and he looked round him with great interest when they had been introduced and Vivien was bringing in her father's lunch tray.

'It 's a grand little place you've got up here,' he said, crossing to look out of the window. 'Do all your rooms face out this way?'

'Oh, no—some look out to the back. How 's Broadstreet's getting on?' said Vivien, unable to wait a moment longer.

'Oh, rubbing along, thanks.' There was such a lack of conviction in his voice that Vivien was surprised. He sat down at the table, took a good helping of salad with the ham and tongue she had put out, and stifled a very large sigh. 'Fact is, things are a bit at sixes and sevens, for the moment,' he added.

'Why? What 's the matter? Has something gone wrong?'

'Nothing 's gone *wrong*, exactly, no, but——' Mr Blueley looked up doubtfully. 'Look here,' he said, 'you don't want to be bothered with our difficulties.'

He sounded as if a little encouragement would produce the whole story, and sure enough, when Vivien assured him how much she would love to be bothered with Messrs Broadstreet's difficulties, he began without more ado. He managed to eat a very good lunch meanwhile, but there was no denying that he was not the ordinary, cheerful, Wren-loving Mr Blueley to whom she had grown accustomed.

Broadstreet's it appeared, had one firm of publishers above all others who were their deadly rivals. Several times in the past they had fought over the same authors or the same ideas; and now, all of a sudden, their rivals had plunged them into a first-class crisis.

'I 'll name no names,' said Mr Blueley darkly, 'but they 're people who ought to know better. An old firm, with a good reputation. Well, now, what do they go and do? No less than steal the best series we 've had in mind for years, name and all, and snaffle the very authors we had in mind for it by paying them a ridiculously high advance. That 's what they do!'

With an angry snort Mr Blueley looked down at his plate, found that he still had some salad, and began thoughtfully to eat it. Vivien looked at her father, but he did not seem to understand any better than she did.

'Please,' she said, 'could you explain a bit more? I mean, it sounds awful, but——'

'Oh, of course, yes. I ought to have thought. Well, you see, it 's something like this. Broadstreet's think up some series or other which they think would sell— let 's call it the Yesterday Series, just to give it a name. They 're going to make a big thing of it—plenty of advertising, special sales campaigns, and so on. They think they 'll have one book called *Yesterday in the Theatre* by a well-known actor, and one called *Yesterday in the Country* by somebody else, and *Yesterday in Dress* by a dress-designer, and so on, and they 'll pay them all so much money if they 'll sign a contract to write the book for them by a certain date. See? Well, we 'd planned out all our books and the authors for them, and even approached one famous person, who had agreed to write for us—and then these other chaps walk right in, announce a series called (so to speak) the Yesterday Series, go to the very authors we 'd thought of, and offer them so much money that it 's impossible they should refuse. Can you beat it?'

'Haven't you any legal redress?' inquired Mr Farthing.

'Not the slightest. No contracts were broken, or any thing like that. If it were an accident we shouldn't be so upset about it—it often does happen that publishers get very similar ideas. But this other firm obviously knew all our plans—that 's what 's so worrying. There 's only one thing it can possibly mean—someone in the firm is giving them information.'

'Good heavens,' said Vivien, 'they can't be.'

'It does seem improbable, I agree. Every one in

155

Broadstreet's likes being there, and one can't imagine them deliberately going and telling tales to our worst rival. But there it is. And now, of course, every body 's looking at everybody else, and wondering, and suspecting, and talking in whispers which stop when somebody else comes in—it makes me sick,' said Mr Blueley with emphasis.

'How frightful it must be,' said Vivien. 'What does— what does young Mr Broadstreet think about it?'

'Mr Irvine? Oh, he 's ramping around in a fine old rage. He 's quieted down a bit to-day, but my goodness, he was angry. And by the way, come to think of it,' Mr Blueley added, 'he sent his compliments, and said he 'd be glad if you could step in for a moment this afternoon or to-morrow.'

'Me? He said that?' In an instant the misfortunes of the firm paled into the merest nothing. 'Does he really want me to come? Do you think it 's some work?'

'He wants to have a talk with you, anyway. He 's a nice young fellow,' said Mr Blueley as if young Mr Broadstreet was the most ordinary man in the world, 'and he 's said to me twice what intelligent eyes you had.'

Mr Blueley looked across at Mr Farthing on the couch. They exchanged a profound glance and an extremely middle-aged smile; then suddenly realized that Vivien was looking at them, and got hurriedly on with their coffee.

CHAPTER VIII

THE FARTHINGS JOIN IN

GOING to Broadstreet's alone was a very different matter from being taken round it by Mr Blueley. The whole place looked bigger and more formidable, and Vivien was much relieved when Miss Ramsay greeted her with a friendly smile as she walked across the echoing floor of the show-room.

'I would like to see Mr Irvine Broadstreet' she said. 'At least, he said would I come in and see him.'

'Oh, yes. Well, if you will ask the girl over there, she 'll telephone up for you.'

Miss Ramsay nodded towards the corner, and Vivien saw that there was a lift there, and a girl sitting at a telephone switch-board in a little glass cubby-hole beside it. The girl, when she asked for Mr Broadstreet put in a plug and telephoned up 'Miss Farthing to see you, sir'; then waved towards the lift, said 'First floor,' and turned back to her switch-board to deal with an impatient-sounding buzz.

The lift put Vivien down just beside the big room full of typists, and in the moment while she stood waiting for someone to come forward she felt that they all of them took in every single detail of her appearance, from her hat and hair down to the very tips of her shoes. It did not last more than a second, though; then one of them got up from her machine, inquired whom Vivien wanted, and took her at once to the door of young Mr Broadstreet's burrow.

'Ah, Miss Farthing—this is very nice of you. Mr

Blueley said you were coming.'

Polite, but a little preoccupied, a large pair of spectacles in his hand, Mr Irvine pulled up a chair for her, and they both sat down. Vivien felt quite calm now that she had actually arrived: quite calm, but a little out of breath, as though she had been running.

'I 'll tell you what it 's all about,' he began, swinging his spectacles thoughtfully in his hands. 'You see—well, you know we get our manuscripts read by outside people to see if they 're worth our while to publish?'

'Oh, yes.'

'Well, we have one here on which I 've got three reports, all rather different, and we can't make up our minds. It 's a woman's story—the sort of thing my uncle and I are really not competent to decide about, as we neither of us have a wife to try it on. Could you be so kind as to take it home and read it and just tell me in a few words whether you like it or not? We 'd like it back in a day or two, if you could manage it. Of course we should offer you our ordinary fee.'

Somehow or other Vivien managed to indicate that she could be so kind, and that he should have the manuscript back as quickly as possible. Mr Irvine smiled at her.

'That 's grand,' he said. 'Tell me—you do belong to a lending library, don't you?'

'Yes—to Boot's. And sometimes we go to Smith's for an occasional book or two, and I have been to a twopenny library. And we buy a lot of Penguins, of course, and other books when we can afford them.'

Mr Irvine nodded approvingly, and had just begun to speak when somebody knocked at his door.

'Come in,' he said. 'Oh, it 's you, is it, Day? No, do come—you 're not disturbing us. Is it the Sunday stuff?'

'Yes, Mr Irvine. I 've brought you a rough lay-out.'

Vivien, sitting in her corner, watched the new-comer with a little frown of perplexity. Where had she seen that man before? Large, red-faced, rather anxious looking....

The two men bent over the desk and began to consult together, sketching things and crossing things out on the paper in front of them.

'It looks so extremely uninspired,' Mr Day was saying in a worried voice. 'Just exactly what it is, and nothing more—another half-double for the *Observer* and *Sunday Times.*'

Vivien gasped. Just in time she managed to stop herself from exclaiming aloud. She had certainly seen Mr Day before—and heard him speak, too. She had heard him say those very words. He was the man in the office opposite the kitchen window; the man who telephoned strange words, and got rather angry, and had his window open when the weather was warm.

She said nothing about it to Mr Irvine when Mr Day, a little cheered up by his help, had at last gone away. It could hardly interest any one that her kitchen overlooked some of Messrs Broadstreet's premises. But she had an idea, nevertheless, and far-fetched though it certainly was, she meant to investigate a little further.

'Yes, but who would have heard him?' said John. The Farthings were in conclave over Vivien's new suggestion. Dinner over, they had cleared away, and were sitting, John and Vivien at the table, Mrs Farthing in the arm-chair, and Mr Farthing as usual on his couch, to discuss in full detail the strange idea which Vivien had just put forward.

'You say you 've heard Mr Day talking when the window was open, and that somebody might have overheard and pinched Broadstreet's new series that way. But then, it would have to be someone who knew about publishing, or they wouldn't have understood what he was talking about. You didn't understand a word when you heard him first.'

John plonked his elbows on the table as if to say that he would like to see how she could explain all that. Vivien sighed.

'Yes, I know,' she said. 'But I can't help feeling that it is a possibility—and it would be so lovely if we could go to Broadstreet's and tell them we 'd found out the solution.'

'And then young Mr Broadstreet would give you a good hug and reward you with the half of his kingdom!' Mr Farthing laughed. 'Sorry, Vivien! I do really see that you want to find out, but I don't think we 're in a very strong position. There must be dozens of other possible channels for the information to have got through— people at Broadstreet's talking to their friends in other firms, or the authors themselves giving things away, and so on. Do we know what the name of the rival publishers is?'

'No—Mr Blueley was being so careful, don't you remember, that he didn't tell us any names at all.'

'Well, are there any publishers in this house, anyway? This is the only place where Mr Day can be heard from— and then, mind you,' said Mr Farthing gravely, 'the heads of the firm would have to be lurking under the window-sill and listening attentively at the very moment when Mr Day made his shattering disclosures. And there would have to be a heat-wave, or his window wouldn't be open.'

'Lurking under the window-sill...?' To Mr Farthing's surprise, Vivien took no offence at his latest suggestion. 'Daddy, what about the Nilpils? The Wilkinses, I mean—

those red-headed boys upstairs?'

'What—are they publishers?'

'Er—no, I don't think they are. But nobody knows what they are. They might just as well be that, and they do look rather unscrupulous, and they 've only got one hat between them, and nobody ever goes up to their flat to see them. And I often see them looking out of their window and laughing.'

'Very like publishers,' commented Mr Farthing.

'Daddy, you 're not helping a bit. You 're horrid. John thinks it 's possible, don't you, John?'

John, not at all sorry that the possibilities of drama had survived his criticisms, indicated that, on consideration, he did. Mrs Farthing looked up from the pillow-case she was mending.

'Ask Mrs Jones about them,' she said. 'Mrs Jones is sure to know everything, or Mr Jones.'

Vivien agreed that this would be much the best thing to do next, and after a little more discussion the topic was dropped for a time. John got down to his homework, Mrs Farthing went on mending, Mr Farthing took up his novel, and Vivien, turning from one exciting thing to another, opened the manuscript Mr Irvine had given her, and went on from the point she had reached just after tea. It was a silly book, in her opinion: a love story, full of misunderstandings and noble renunciations which need never have happened at all if the heroine had had the elementary sense, at the beginning of the book, to tell the man she loved that she had once been engaged before. Vivien began to feel like giving her a good smack; but it was an interesting book, all the same, written with an ease and fluency which she heartily envied, and she read on, oblivious to everything else, until Mr Farthing began to hint loudly and strongly that it was time he had a little drink of tea.

'The Mr Wilkinses?' Mrs Jones gave a final rub to the floor she was polishing, and looked up, her face as benign, her thin white hair as tidy, as if she were entertaining visitors. 'Well, that 's a funny thing, Miss Vivien, I was just saying to Phineas yesterday, we 've neither of us seen inside their room since they first came here. And that must be nearly a year.'

'Don't you know at all what they do?'

'No, I can't say as how we do. One of them told me once that it 's to do with selling boilers, but whether he meant it or not I couldn't make out. They don't get many letters—only circulars, and an occasional letter from the country, and they all have to be put in the box in the hall.'

'Do you like them? Do you think they 're nice?'

That was a difficult question. Mrs Jones inspected her floor-cloth with great care before she answered.

'Like is not hardly an easy way to put it,' she said. 'I think they have been well-brought-up young gentlemen. And I think they have very little money.'

And with that Vivien had to be content, for Mrs Jones would say no more. She had another piece of news, however, and when Vivien, after tidying up Mr Farthing's bedroom, came into the sitting-room where he was now installed for the day, she found Mrs Jones and her father deep in a neighbourly conversation about the King and Queen.

'Ever so good, I think they are,' Mrs Jones was saying. 'So friendly, and natural-like. Yes, in three weeks' time they 're both coming to St Paul's, and the little Princesses too. And there 's going to be uniforms and soldiers and men from all the Dominions—these windows around St Paul's will be worth a lot of money, for those that likes to let them out.'

'That 's very exciting,' said Mr Farthing. 'Vivien—did you hear that? The King and Queen are coming. I really think we ought to have a party.'

'Oh, Daddy. But who could we have?'

'Well. . . . Aunt Rosamund and Uncle Charles, and Aunt Harrison, and Mr Blueley, and any one else we could think of.'

'But wouldn't you be too tired?'

'No, not the slightest bit. I 'd enjoy it.'

Mr Farthing was determined that there should be a party, and when Mrs Farthing came home that evening the whole thing was arranged. As the service at St Paul's was to be at three in the afternoon neither Mrs Farthing nor John could be there to watch, but Dinah, they thought, might get special leave for the afternoon and come over with her great-aunt. Within a very short time the guests had been asked, and had accepted, Colonel and Mrs Edmonthorpe saying that they would make it the excuse for a short holiday in London after the hard work of moving in. And then Vivien got the brilliant idea that she and John should go up and invite the Nilpils.

'They very likely won't come,' she said. 'In fact I hope they won't, rather. But we may get a chance of seeing into their room,' she added shamelessly.

So before dinner the next evening, feeling a little apprehensive, she and John went up the narrow stone and iron staircase to the fifth floor back. There were two doors there, and after some hesitation they knocked on the nearer one.

There was a scuffling sound inside, and after a moment or two the untidier Wilkins opened the door. He was so much surprised when he saw them that for the fraction of a second he held the door wide open. They

163

caught a glimpse of the room inside: an unmade bed, and a plain wood table with no cloth upon which there stood a typewriter, three novels in bright-coloured jackets, and a plate.

'Excuse me,' said Vivien, 'we 're—we 're the Farthings, you know, from downstairs. We wondered—that is, we 're having a small party when the King and Queen come to St Paul's, and we wondered if you 'd like to come and have a look.'

Mr Wilkins pulled the door to behind him so that it shut with a bang. His mouth opened twice before he could decide what he was going to say.

'Er—er, thank you,' he said at last. 'Thank you. But, as a matter of fact, my brother and I work so hard that we—we never go out at all.'

He opened the door as little as possible, edged in through it, and shut himself firmly inside. Vivien and John, after gazing at the closed door for a moment, turned round and went downstairs.

'One up to him,' said Vivien when they had reached their own flat again.

'Yes, but one up to us as well. Vivien, didn't you see the three books on the table? And the typewriter?'

'Yes, I saw them. And the plate. And the sheets all over the floor. Publishers don't look like that,' said Vivien out of the depths of her experience.

'Well, but what about those novels? How do you suppose they got those?'

'Stole them, perhaps,' said Vivien without enthusiasm. 'Or even just simply got them out of the library. No, John, it couldn't possibly be them.'

And with a sigh of disillusion Vivien turned from the detection of crime to deciding why the blue-eyed heroine of Messrs Broadstreet's typescript novel seemed to her to be such an annoying little fool.

CHAPTER IX

ROYAL VISIT

MR IRVINE BROADSTREET said that he was extremely pleased with her comments on the manuscript he had given her. They had not much chance for conversation, as his uncle was interviewing somebody in the big room upstairs and they had to talk in the showroom with Miss Ramsay and the telephone girl for audience; but Vivien went away feeling exceedingly happy, and scarcely able to believe that a cheque for the work she had done was going to be posted to her the following morning.

'That 's quite decided me,' he said as he saw her to the door. 'If you say that girl in the book was a silly little fool, then that settles it. I thought just the same, but I couldn't be sure. Good-bye—good-bye. We 'll meet again soon.'

If life had seemed full before, it seemed twenty times fuller now. Mr Farthing was at home, and getting better. The King and Queen were coming. And—incredible thing—Vivien was working for a publisher. True, it was not much work, but it was a beginning. Writing began to seem unimportant in comparison with it, and she could not help hoping that one day, when Mr Farthing was well and Mrs Farthing could stop going to Greencoat's, there might be a chance for her really to join the firm and have a proper, full-time job.

Mr Blueley's advice, and the sight of all those manuscripts at Broadstreet's had made Vivien think a lot. Thousands of other people, it seemed, were just as sure as she was that they could write books or stories—and with just as good reason, and much about the same chance of success. And that, it seemed to her, was not much. She could not forget those packages which the fair-haired girl was parcelling up. For the moment, at any rate, she would much rather that Broadstreet's thought of her as an ordinary reader than as an ordinary writer. The notes for her novel still lay in her drawer, but the great scene between Richard and the girl was not yet finished, and she felt in no hurry to get on with it. Vivien's thoughts for the time being were entirely centred on Broadstreet's. She longed to hear more from them; and she was so anxious to talk to Mr Blueley that she was just about to write to him when, to her relief, he rang up and asked if he might come up to the flat and see them.

'You 've caused a wonderful lot of gossip in the office' he said cheerfully when he had shaken hands with her and Mr Farthing. 'Our Mr Irvine isn't given to being so impulsive! I 've told them you were a. young writer I knew.'

'You 've told them I was a writer? But—but it was a secret. I mean, I 'm not.'

'Oh, you needn't worry. They won't ask any more about it. It 's just that it sounded more probable.' Mr Blueley took the cigarette he was offered, and sat down where he could have a good view of St Paul's and the pigeons who were taking their after-lunch tour around the dome. 'And anyway, what about that book on architecture that you 're going to help me with one day? On Wren, and so forth? You haven't forgotten, I hope?'

'No—oh, no. As long as you didn't tell Mr Irvine....'

'Oh, him? No, not a word. He 's quite satisfied with you as you are! But talking of Wren,' said Mr Blueley, as if that were far more interesting than young Mr Broadstreet,

'I was told by a chap in the City that almost exactly where this house is standing now Wren used to have his club.'

'What—here? Just where we are?'

'Yes, so he said. Interesting, isn't it? But mind you, I don't quite know what he meant by club. Perhaps it was simply the coffee-house or pub where he used to come when St Paul's was being built.'

> 'He said, "If anybody calls,
> Say I 'm designing St Paul's," '

quoted Mr Farthing. 'Sensible fellow, Wren.'

There was a pause, and Mr Blueley became rather thoughtful. Vivien waited for a moment to see if he was going to say something, but as he did not begin she started off hurriedly herself to tell him the whole story of Mr Day and the open window.

Mr Blueley was undeniably startled.

'Good heavens,' he said. 'What 's that? You 've been hearing Day on the phone? People upstairs may have heard? Well, that 's something quite new, certainly. How did you say it happened?'

Vivien carefully repeated all that she had said so far, and continued the story with a description of the Wilkinses and of her visit to them with John.

'It wasn't them, we 're pretty sure, but it might have been someone,' she finished. 'Come into the kitchen, and I 'll show you.

Mr Blueley followed her, looking large and bear-like in the tiny corridor and kitchen. He nodded as she pointed out Mr Day's window—which was now closed at the bottom, and almost closed at the top, as nothing less than a heat-wave could incline Mr Day to fling it open.

'Yes,' he said, 'I see. It would be perfectly possible.

You heard him quite clearly talk about the Sunday advertising?'

'Yes, absolutely—about half-doubles in the *Sunday Times* and *Observer*, and a lot more too.'

'H'm,' said Mr Blueley. 'Let 's go back and sit down. I want your father's advice on this as well.'

'Mr Day did know about the series,' he began the moment they got back into the sitting-room, speaking to Mr Farthing and Vivien both at once. 'We all did, though we were under strict orders not to talk about it. And he might have mentioned it over the telephone. But even if he was talking to someone in the building (it 's a house phone as well, you know), I can't imagine why he should have given a complete list of all the proposed books and their authors, and it 's nothing less than that that the other chaps know.'

'Then you 're inclined to think that the information didn't leak out this way?' Mr Farthing nodded, his own opinion confirmed.

'I 'm not saying anything,' Mr Blueley replied cautiously. 'I really don't know.' He scratched his chin slowly, first on one side and then on the other. 'Look here—I might as well tell you. You both know so much already. I need hardly say that this is entirely between ourselves, and that no one else at all must know about it for the moment. The fact of the matter is, I think I gave the show away myself.'

He gave an enormous sigh, as if it had been a relief to be able to speak of it. Vivien and Mr Farthing stared at him.

'I know it sounds mad,' he went on. 'I didn't say much, and then it was only to one bookseller—a chap whom I 've known and got on well with for years. But he wanted a little encouraging, and I was fool enough to tell

him that we 'd got a fine new series up our sleeves. I told
him a few of the authors, too—but I 'm sure, as sure as I
sit here, that I didn't give him the whole lot of them, or
the name of the series either.'

'Then it mightn't have been you, or rather him,' said
Vivien. 'Because wouldn't he then have had to tell
someone else, who would have had to find out all the rest
of the details and then go and tell them to the other
publishers?'

'Yes, something like that.' Mr Blueley sounded
depressed. 'It doesn't hang together very well—your Mr
Day theory is just as good. But if he *did* happen to let on
to somebody from Perryforth's—'

'Is that the other publishers?'

'Oh, yes—I forgot you didn't know. Well, if he did,'
said Mr Blueley, reaching the very depths of his gloom,
'then there 's no telling what might happen, for where
Broadstreet's are concerned Perryforth's have neither
manners, morals, nor conscience. Oh, well . . . we don't
know. But I 'll tell Day to be a little quieter about his half-
doubles, and thanks very much for the tip.'

'Do tell me—what is a half-double?' said Mr Farthing,
perceiving that Mr Blueley's meditations had come to
their gloomy end. 'We 're all of us longing to know. We
looked at the Broadstreet advertisement in the Sunday
papers.'

'A half - double?' Mr Blueley looked up. 'Oh, that 's
half the full length of a double newspaper column.
Publishers buy so much space from week to week, you
see—a half double, or a full triple, or perhaps a small
space like three inches double. It 's expensive space, and
there 's great competition for the best positions in the
paper. Half the publishers in London probably spend
their Sunday breakfast-time hating the other half for

having got the positions they would like to have had themselves.'

'What a dramatic trade it is, when one gets to know about it,' observed Mr Farthing, much pleased by this. 'Are the best positions the ones on the outside of the page?'

'Yes. And at the top of a page rather than the bottom. And of course everybody wants to be next to the leading articles. Day spends half his week doing striking layouts and breath-taking chat for the Sunday advertisements, and yet we all seem to think more or less like play producers are said to tell their actors: "Reckon that one half of your audience is deaf and the other half blind, and you 'll be all right."'

And, cheered up already by this dip into the technicalities of another department than his own, Mr Blueley settled down to tell them as much as they liked about the way in which the hundred or so London publishers set to work to outdo one another and bring their books to the notice of a public ninety per cent of which was probably unaware that their firms existed at all.

The day of the King and Queen's visit to St Paul's was fine and sunny, and warm. Ludgate Hill and St Paul's Churchyard were hardly recognizable. The roads were empty, the pavements already almost full, though it was well over an hour until the procession was due to arrive. There was an iron railing all round the big pavement of the Churchyard, keeping the crowds away from the place where the royal party was to draw up, and leaving a big open space which at the moment was occupied only by the statue of Queen Anne, indignantly pointing her sceptre down Ludgate Hill, and by a few surprised-looking pigeons. There were crowds at many of the windows, and the growl of the traffic had been replaced by the strange, quiet, scrunching noise of thousands of footsteps.

The people who were to be present inside St Paul's had already taken their places. For the past hour and a half they had been arriving in crowds, with small blue tickets which were carefully inspected by the police at the barriers before they were allowed to go through. There had been uniforms of every kind, from the modest khaki of the Boy Scouts to brilliant scarlet and gold affairs with nodding white feathers whose wearers were so grand that, unlike the mere ordinary congregation who had to arrive on foot, they came driving in huge, shining cars up the deserted sweep of Ludgate Hill. There were men and women, soldiers, nurses, old ladies, brown-skinned foreigners, and solemn-looking men in morning coats and top-hats. It was fascinating to watch them all, and everybody was kept very busy pointing out the ones who looked famous and deciding who they might be.

'See—that 's Lloyd George—I 'm sure it is.'

'How do you know it is?'

'By his hat. Down there—just going in.'

'*That* 's not Lloyd George's hat. It 's much more likely Mr Eden.'

In the sitting-room of the flat the party was almost complete. Mr Blueley was there, still a little depressed, but sufficiently trained by his profession to keep up a good flow of talk and produce one or two jokes every now and again. Colonel and Mrs Edmonthorpe were there, as nice as ever, having arrived in time for a picnic lunch which they had insisted on being allowed to help wash up afterwards. John was there, as the King and Queen had obligingly chosen a day when by a little wangling he could manage to be free, and with him he had brought a friend called Grigson and Mr Moore the history master, a tall, handsome young man with straw-coloured hair whom Vivien privately thought rather dull.

Only two people were missing—Aunt Harrison and Dinah. They had been expected at least an hour ago, but as no telephone message had come from them Mr Farthing supposed that their car had got delayed somewhere in all the crowds.

'But it 's so late now that I don't think they 'd be allowed to drive up here,' said Colonel Edmonthorpe. 'No cars have come by for twenty minutes or more.'

'No, but they might come round by Newgate Street and down Ivy Lane at the back here. Ropes is a very clever driver.'

By this time there were fresh excitements outside in the street. Little squads of soldiers, each led by an officer, came marching up the middle of the road, and fell into a single line along the edge of the pavement. In a very short time there was an unbroken line of soldiers as far as the eye could see, from Ludgate Hill right round to the back of St Paul's, standing motionless on each side of the street in front of the peering, murmuring crowd. The officers stood a little in front of them, one every few yards, waiting calm and alert for the signal for the royal salute. It really began to look as though things were going to happen.

Soon afterwards a military band came swinging up Ludgate Hill, playing *Land of Hope and Glory* and greeted with scattered cheers from the onlookers. It took up its place at one side of the Steps of St Paul's, and stood there, looking almost too fine to be true, waiting to burst into music again when the royal procession should appear. Then there was a pause. Little parties of policemen in white gloves strolled around talking to one another, discussing, pointing, arranging final details; but it seemed now that everything was ready, and that in ten minutes more, as the time-table in the papers had stated, the King and Queen should arrive.

And still Aunt Harrison and Dinah had not come. Vivien was beginning to get really anxious, and so was Mrs Edmonthorpe.

'Can you see anything, Aunt Rosamund?' Vivien joined her aunt at the window, where John and his friend Grigson were keeping watch.

'No, not at the moment. I 'm just trying to see if they 're standing in the crowd anywhere. It would be very hard to push through all those people, you know.'

'Something 's coming!' John turned round eagerly, motioning to everybody to be quiet and listen.

'I can't hear anything,' said Mr Moore. It was the fourth or fifth time that John had been certain the King was coming, and they were beginning to get a little suspicious. However, they all crowded to the window, and once again looked out.

Vivien declared afterwards that she had seen the conductor of the band hold up his arms, and that in another moment the National Anthem would have burst out. That, however, would never be known, for very soon everybody, the band included, was gazing down Ludgate Hill to where, at the bottom, something decidedly curious was taking place.

For a moment the watchers at the window could not see what it was. There was a little laughter, and a cheer or two, and one of the soldiers so far forgot himself as to turn his head to see what was happening. Then, up the empty curve of Ludgate Hill, came, not the escort of Life Guards or the royal procession, but two people, on foot.

One was an elderly lady, very dignified, dressed in

black and walking with a silver-handled ebony cane. The other was a small girl with red hair, who looked from side to side, and down at the road, and up again, as if she was half proud of her latest achievement, and half embarrassed. A little way away from them, shepherding them up the hill and seeing that they kept to their bargain, walked a large, fat policeman.

'But Dinah, how *did* you do it?'

Dinah and Aunt Harrison arrived up in the flat four minutes before the procession was due to appear. They were both rather scarlet in the face, and Aunt Harrison, after the briefest possible explanation, had refused to think that there was anything at all strange in the way they had arrived, and settled down at a chair in the window as if to say that nobody properly brought up would consider it in the least out of the ordinary.

Dinah, however, had a good deal more to say, and now that everything was safely over her high spirits had returned again in full force.

'I told them I lived up here, and that Daddy was ill,' she said, with a beaming smile which included Mr Moore, Mr Blueley, and her uncle and aunt as well as the family. 'It was true, you see. I had a letter in my pocket, and I showed them the address. They were frightfully nice. A superintendent on a horse came up, and all sorts of people.'

'What was it like, coming up Ludgate Hill like that?' Grigson was gazing at her curiously, as if she were not at all the sort of younger sister he was used to.

'Oo—grand.' Cheerfully forgetting all her recent embarrassment, Dinah began a glowing description, which would no doubt have gone on for a long time if they had not suddenly heard outside, in the distance as yet but clearly audible, the first outburst of cheers. Dinah stopped abruptly, and, everything else forgotten, they all thronged to the window.

The excitement down in the street was increasing every moment. The crowds packed close together on the pavement rippled like a field of corn as people turned their heads to see what was coming. The soldiers stood, if possible, more still than ever.

There was a roar of engines, and a patrol of police on motor bicycles came up the hill and round the corner, making perfectly sure, to the very last minute, that the royal route was in order. Then everything began to happen at once. To a burst of cheering a troop of Life Guards came sweeping into sight, their white plumes nodding, the sun blinking on their harness and lighting up the brilliant red of their uniforms. They came almost underneath the window: even four stories up one could hear the chink of the harness and the hollow little clatter of the horses' hooves.

Behind them, superb with its coachman and footmen and outriders, came the royal coach. The King and Queen were in it, bowing and smiling to the crowds on either side, and opposite them sat Princess Elizabeth and Princess Margaret Rose, smiling a little also and taking a good look at everything that was going on. There were other coaches also in the procession, but who was in them nobody knew, for they were all busy watching the royal family.

The coach swept round and drew up. The King and Queen and Princesses got out, and while the military band played the National Anthem until it seemed as though it would burst its lungs, they were received by the waiting dignitaries, and went up the steps and in at the big, dark door of the cathedral.

'Well, that was fine.'

'A splendid sight.'

'Yes, when it comes to processions, there 's nobody quite like the British.'

'Funny how tired one gets, simply standing and looking.'

'Yes, and we 're in luxury compared with all the crowds down there in the street. They 're having an easy now—see all the paper bags coming out, and the oranges, and some of the sensible ones have brought a bottle with them!'

At the mention of a bottle every one began to look rather thirsty, and Mr Farthing produced a perceptible stir of pleasure when he said that they were now going to have some tea. Vivien had already disappeared to see about it in the kitchen. The kettle was almost boiling, the cakes which she had made the day before were all ready on their plates, and by the time Aunt Rosamund, Uncle Charles, Dinah, John, Grigson, and Mr Moore arrived to see if they could help her, there was very little left to do.

This was perhaps lucky, as the helpers had no room to do any more than stand around and talk and abstract an occasional crumb or small biscuit from any plate they could reach. Soon they and the food and drink were all transferred to the sitting-room, and every one settled down to the serious business of restoring their strength until the King and Queen should come out again. They had no wireless, so they could not hear the service relayed from inside the cathedral, but they were perhaps not sorry to have time to talk and entertain themselves.

Vivien's cakes proved extremely popular, and the party was undoubtedly a success. Everybody was looking very cheerful, and talking very hard. Even Aunt Harrison was listening with a smile to the conversation of Mr

Moore, and Mr Farthing and Colonel Edmonthorpe were talking about horses and cricket and books with all the vigour of kindred spirits who have not met each other for a long time. Dinah was busy astonishing Grigson, which she did not find very hard, and John was looking on a little uncertainly, not at all sure whether he approved or not.

'Vivien, my dear, when 's your birthday?'

Vivien looked up to find that Aunt Rosamund had settled down beside her.

'Next week,' she said. 'It 's astonishing how quickly it 's come.'

'Next week? Is it really so soon—I 'd forgotten. Well, that fits in beautifully. Bridget and Hugh are both having exeats next week-end, and we 're staying up in town—would you care to come out with us and have a little birthday celebration? I thought we might go to dinner somewhere, and then all go to the Russian Ballet.'

'Would I care to come? Oh—I 'd simply love to.' Vivien could scarcely believe it. 'How terribly exciting,' she said, her eyes shining with pleasure.

They had no time to talk of it more, for Aunt Harrison required more tea, Colonel Edmonthorpe wanted to remember the name of a certain hunter, and Mr Moore wanted, apparently, to come over and talk to Vivien about the weather; but she remembered it with a delicious feeling of excitement all the time, and felt that the days would never pass quickly enough until next week end should come.

CHAPTER X

COVENT GARDEN

PUBLISHING and Mr Farthing and parties seemed all of a sudden to fill up the days so thoroughly that Vivien had practically no leisure left at all. She regretted very much that for the time being there could be no more expeditions with Mr Blueley, and no long lunch-hours on her own, exploring for Wren churches and the other delights of the City. She did however manage, while Mrs Jones was in the flat or Mr Farthing was resting to go on many days back to one of her old favourites, and find some thing new about it or remind herself of its design and look for a moment or two at some organ or window or roof that she specially enjoyed.

St Sebastian's was still her favourite of all, and she had got to know the one-legged Mr Persepolis quite well. He no longer switched on the lights for her, but he had done her the special favour of taking her into the vestry, a beautiful little room which Wren had also designed.

'He used to use it himself, so the story goes, when he was working up in this direction,' Mt Persepolis said as they admired together its light-coloured panelling and its fine plaster-work ceiling.

'What, after the Great Fire, do you mean?'

'Round about 1670 to 1675 it would be, I suppose, when he was busy on all the churches. It 's a certain fact that he was very particular the vestry here should be finished before any of the rest of the church. They say he used to sit in here and drink coffee—he was a great one for coffee,' said Mr Persepolis as if he were describing a personal friend.

Vivien was beginning to know quite a lot about Sir Christopher Wren's tastes and habits. Her interest in him had led her to read every book she could get hold of which bore on the history of those strange times after the Great Fire, and also on the Roman, Italian, and French architecture from which he had got many of his ideas—a course of reading which led her into many enthralling second-hand bookshops, and caused a good deal of surprise to the library assistants. She used often to think of those days which seemed so long ago and yet so extremely close: of the fire itself, as Pepys described it, and Charles II helping to put it out: of Wren afterwards drawing up a whole new plan for the rebuilding of the City, which was never used: of how the people must have grumbled at the tax on all coal that came into the City, out of which Wren's masterpieces had been paid for. She felt sometimes that she could almost see him, picking his way among the scaffolding and the workmen and the stacks of brick and rubbish, and watching St Paul's grow up before his eyes as he had planned it.

She and Mr Farthing often talked of it all, and in many ways her father got almost as much pleasure from her hobby as she did herself. But it was tantalizing, to both of them, that he could not come out and see all the places which they talked about: places which he had not been to for some fifteen or twenty years, and which lay almost in sight just outside the window. He was getting better, Sir William said, but there was no denying that it was slow work. There was talk now of his being allowed to go out to work again in September. He was able to walk about a little—a very little—in the flat, which was a great step on; but it was not enough, and they all longed for better times.

However, as they often said, they seemed to enjoy life pretty well all the same. 'We haven't much money, but we do see life,' as Mr Farthing would observe. They were all in good spirits at the moment except Dinah, whose violin exam was just about to take place and who was much more nervous about it than she had ever been before.

As for Vivien, it took her approximately four days to get ready for her evening out with the Edmonthorpes. They had said it was to be a real proper party evening, in evening dress, and she spent one and a half days considering the only evening dress she had—left from last Christmas down at Berrings—and trying to work up a little enthusiasm for it. She could not succeed, and at last Mr and Mrs Farthing insisted that she should buy herself a new one.

'There's the money you've earned—it's a shame you shouldn't have something nice for it,' said Mrs Farthing. 'We'll add whatever more you need, and I think I can manage for you to get discount if you come to Greencoat's.'

So the next morning, as soon as Mr Farthing was settled for the day, Vivien set off for Regent Street, full of delicious excitement. The bus-ride was fun, the shop windows were so alluring that she felt convinced she could find the very dress she wanted in any of them, and it was so intoxicating to have money to spend that she could not restrain herself from humming a little song as she walked along to Greencoat's.

Mrs Farthing was too busy when she arrived to have more than a smile to spare for her. She was serving an elderly lady up from the country, and Vivien could hardly recognize her mother in this solemn and elegant person, dressed in navy blue and white, who carried dresses about over her arm and said 'Madam' to the customer and 'Miss

181

Perkins' to the timid-looking young girl in green who was supposed to be helping her. They all three disappeared into a fitting-room after a little discussion, and soon afterwards Mrs Farthing came out again.

'Hullo, darling,' she said, suddenly for a brief moment looking like her ordinary self. 'I 'll get Miss Watson to help you—she 's nice and not a bit alarming.'

Miss Watson proved to be very nice, and very helpful, and by her special cleverness Vivien was provided with a little French dress—a sample, she was told—which was quite enchanting and suited her extremely well. She knew in an instant that that dress, and no other, she must have. As she stood gazing at its soft pattern of pale green and lemon and gold Mrs Farthing came hurrying in to see how they were getting on.

'Darling, how lovely.' She and Miss Watson exchanged a quick nod of pleasure. 'You really will be a credit to the family.'

Vivien's spirits, already high, went up even higher, and as soon as her buying was finished she went off and wandered in a blissful dream round every department in Greencoat's, admiring gloves and hats and shoes and scarves and artificial flowers without any desire to spend any more money on any of them. The rest of her four days went on washing her stockings, polishing her shoes, having her hair washed and set, deciding which handkerchief to use, and reading and re-reading two books of Dinah's, *Ballet Shoes* and *Felicity Dances*, and the Penguin book on ballet which she had given herself for a treat.

The evening came at last, and Vivien, having spent almost two hours on getting ready, was just putting the finishing touches to her face when the bell rang from downstairs. She pushed the switch which would open the main front door, and a minute or two later Hugh Edmonthorpe appeared at the bend of the stairs, with his sister Bridget a little way behind and their father and mother following at a less headlong pace.

'Hullo, Vivien. What fun to live in a place like this.'

'Yes, you really ought to have a name painted on your door. All the others have. Messrs Farthing, Farthing, Farthing, Farthing & Farthing, or else just Five Farthings, Limited. Advice Given. Private.'

All four Edmonthorpes had by this time arrived, and they came into the sitting-room to say how do you do to Mr Farthing and John—Mrs Farthing being not yet home. Hugh and Bridget were twins, just a little older than John: Hugh had just gone to Rugby, and Bridget to a boarding-school at Eastbourne. They were a lively couple, not specially good-looking but always full of animation. The Farthings got on well with them, though they did not often see much of one another.

'Well,' said Uncle Charles, 'are you ready for us, Vivien?'

They complimented her warmly on her dress and said how well it suited her, to Vivien's great pleasure; and a few minutes later, after a little talk with Mr Farthing, the five of them set off downstairs to the waiting car. It was a fine big car, specially hired for the evening as Uncle Charles said it was hopeless trying to drive oneself to and from a theatre.

'We 've no distance to go, really,' he said as they all settled in. 'We 're having dinner at the Savoy, as it 's nice and near for Covent Garden.'

Vivien, sitting back in her corner, sighed with excitement. She had never been to the Savoy—never even thought that it was possible she might go there, although she passed it often when she was walking along the Strand. But now, for one evening, she was really going to parade about in Cinderella-like luxury. She meant to make the most of every single moment of it; and though to-morrow she would be back in the world of mackintoshes and umbrellas and bus tickets—the ordinary, real-life world—there would be something to remember, and something to write about, too, perhaps, one day.

The car turned in at the Savoy courtyard, and drew up at the door. Out in the Strand it was till broad daylight, but in here twilight seemed somehow to have come already, and the golden light from inside the hotel was shining out strongly through the glass. The commissionaire came forward and opened the door. Another moment, and they were all inside.

It was all like a dream to Vivien. She could remember every detail clearly if she tried, but the memory that stayed most vividly in her mind was just a delicious confused scene of lights and soft colours, vast rooms, tables, hurrying waiters, parties of people in lovely clothes sitting talking and laughing and eating. She saw bottles of champagne in little tubs full of ice, and brandy in glasses ten times too big for it, and caviare and smoked salmon and liqueurs, and all sorts of other things which she knew mainly from the pages of novels. Hugh and Bridget were almost as excited as she was, and a good deal more voluble about it, so that their dinner-table was fully as lively as any of the others around them.

Uncle Charles was an excellent host. He reminded Vivien very much of her father, although they were not related to each other, and although Uncle Charles had a fine military moustache which disguised a good deal of his face. But they had the same easy and quiet yet entertaining way of talking, and one felt perfectly safe with them that things would go as they were meant to. As for Aunt Rosamund, she was a darling; younger than Mrs Farthing, and much fairer, always sweet and lively, and looking to-night, Vivien felt certain, quite as elegant and beautifully dressed as all the other elegant women in the room.

At last the time came when Hugh had regretfully to admit that he could not eat any more; and this, his father said, was a very good thing, as it was just about time for them to set off to Covent Garden. The bill was paid, Vivien and Aunt Rosamund and Bridget went and powdered their noses in a palatial ladies' room, and they all got into the car again for the long drive to Covent Garden.

'Ordinarily it would take us about two minutes, I suppose,' Uncle Charles said as the car shot across the Strand. 'To-night is a specially good night, though, so there will very likely be a queue.'

'What do you mean, a specially good night?' demanded Bridget.

'I mean there's a very good programme. *Sylphides* first, which every one loves, and *Coq d'Or* next, which every one enjoys, and *Beau Danube* last, which every one adores. Ever seen them, Vivien?'

'No,' said Vivien, feeling almost ready to sail up through the roof with excitement. 'I've never seen any ballet. I've read a lot about it, and seen pictures, but that's all.'

'Here we are,' said Aunt Rosamund a moment or two later. 'Yes, there certainly is a queue.'

The car had turned into a sloping street where two long lines of motors were slowly making their way towards a big, high portico—the Royal Opera House itself, said Uncle Charles. One queue put down its people outside the portico, the other inside, at the door of the theatre. The Edmonthorpes' driver firmly made for the inner queue, and after not too long a wait they were safely put down at the big doorway.

Car doors were banging, people talking, waving, gesticulating, hurrying about to find one another—there was such a crowd that Bridget clung hurriedly to her father's arm, afraid of getting lost. Inside the vestibule it was just as bad, or worse; half the people were determined to push through and find their seats, and the other half were just as determined to stay where they were and wait for friends who had not yet arrived.

They made their way through somehow, Uncle Charles produced tickets, and all of a sudden they had got out of all the racket and were in the theatre itself. It was an astonishing place. Four ordinary theatres, Vivien thought, would have fitted inside it easily. It was so huge that from where they stood it really looked like a long walk down the centre gangway to the orchestra and stage, and when she turned her head she saw balconies rising one above the other into the dim distances of the roof.

Their five stalls were about in the middle of the vast open space, and they settled into them full of anticipation, watching all the other people come in, listening to the tuning-up of the orchestra, and gazing around to take in their surroundings. The theatre seemed to be composed entirely of crimson and gilt. The seats were all crimson, and all round the balconies and boxes there was gilt, with cherubs or classical ladies, also gilt, hung on wherever a corner could be found for them. Hugh said it was very Victorian, but Vivien thought it was perfect: just what a theatre ought to be like, she said stoutly, and her aunt and uncle laughed and agreed with her.

It seemed a long time, and yet much too short a time,

before the lights in the auditorium went down. A hush of expectation fell suddenly on the audience. Something happened in the orchestra pit, there was applause, and then Vivien saw the black shape of the conductor outlined against the faint light, and heard the sharp little tap of his baton. The orchestra began to play.

She knew the music well—it was music of Chopin's —yet here, in this huge, waiting place, it sounded strange, unearthly, and exciting. She listened, and hardly knew when the curtain went up; but suddenly she found she was watching, as well as hearing—watching dim, graceful white shapes who seemed almost to be the music itself come to life.

They floated about the stage, they dreamed, they combined into rings and patterns and floated apart again, while the lovely music went on. They were girls—there must have been about twenty of them—in long, full white filmy skirts, with ridiculous little wings, but she could not think of them as human. They were what the name of the ballet said they were, sylphides. One occasionally detached herself from the others and did some specially lovely movements, and often a man, golden-haired, dressed in black and white with big sleeves, came on to the scene and danced with them. There were two sylphides who were even more graceful to look at than all the others, and the excitement in the audience was extreme every time either of them danced.

Vivien sat spellbound, gazing at it all and listening; so did everybody else, and when at last the dancers formed into their last pattern, the music came to an end, and the curtain slowly came down, there was a moment when nobody moved at all before the storm of applause broke out. Then there was such a noise that it sounded as though everybody in the theatre had gone mad with enthusiasm; the curtain rose and fell, the dancers came forward and curtsied, and all the people who knew what to say turned to each other and began to exchange expert exclamations about how good it had been.

'Did you like it?' said Aunt Rosamund.

'Oh, Mummy——'

'Oh, Aunt Rosamund——'

'Pretty good,' said Hugh. 'Can we get some ginger beer, do you think?'

They joined the queues of people who were making their way to the exits, all talking as if the fifteen minutes' silence had been a terrible strain on them. They walked along a crimson-walled corridor, and out into the vestibule, and up a wide, grand staircase which was so crowded that Vivien had great difficulty in preventing her dress from being trodden on.

'We 'll get a drink up here, if we 're lucky,' said Uncle Charles. 'There 's always a terrible crowd.'

There certainly was a crowd, and eventually Aunt Rosamund and Vivien, who did not want anything to drink, gave up the struggle and stood in a corner at the top of the staircase while the other three pushed on to the buffet. It was much more fun standing still; one could watch all the people, and study their clothes, and they had a very pleasant few minutes commenting to each other in a low voice upon everybody they could see.

'There 's a young man staring at you very hard,' said Aunt Rosamund suddenly. 'Do you know him?'

Vivien looked in the direction she was pointing out, half-way down the staircase. There, talking to a group of people among whom was his uncle, stood Irvine Broadstreet.

He saw her at once, and waved up at her with a charming smile which did much—though not by any means all—to offset the fact that he was standing with an extremely attractive girl on either side of him, and seemed to find their company very pleasant.

'He looks nice.' Aunt Rosamund studied him closely.

'He is nice. He 's a publisher in Magnificat Alley. I—I do work for him sometimes. Mr Blueley took me there.'

'Oh, I see,' said her aunt, in tones that were almost as admirably casual as her own. No more was said; the drink-hunters arrived back a moment later, triumphant but exhausted, and it was very soon time to start the journey back to their seats.

The next ballet was in its own way quite as lovely as *Les Sylphides*—it was a Russian story, with several things in it that made them laugh aloud, and a beautiful golden bird flashing through it like a streak of fire. If Vivien got it rather mixed up in her mind with thoughts of Irvine Broadstreet she enjoyed it immensely nevertheless, and she felt almost angry, as if she were being cheated, when the curtain came down and there was no more to see.

They went out in this interval also, but only as far as the vestibule, where they stood near the open doors to get a little breath of fresh air. People were strolling out into the street, and quite a number of other people in every-day clothes—girls and young men, mostly—had come in and were standing around in the vestibule, gazing at everybody and talking.

'They 're from the upper balconies,' said Uncle Charles. 'They think we 're all Philistines down here, who don't know how to appreciate ballet or anything else—but they come in and have a good look at us, all the same.'

Vivien, watching them, saw two faces which somehow seemed familiar to her; but at that moment a voice just behind her made her turn round with a start.

'Hullo, Vivien—I can't call you Miss Farthing, you know, I really can't.'

Irvine Broadstreet .held out his hand, shook hers warmly, and looked with interest at her aunt and uncle and the twins, who were all talking together, separated from them by a very fat woman in pale pink satin who had just pushed her way in.

'Is that your family?'

'Oh, no—it 's my aunt and uncle, at least.'

Young Mr Broadstreet said 'Oh' and submitted that he had thought they might be her parents. Vivien thereupon, after hurried and anxious thought, inquired if he would care to come up to the flat one day and meet her father and mother: which he accepted so promptly that she began to think that was what he had meant her to say.

'Blueley 's told me how delightful it is,' he said. 'I 'll make so bold as to come up now, next time we have a small job of work for you. Grand show to-night, isn't it?'

'Oh, heavenly.'

'Do you often come? I 've never seen you here before.'

'No—this is the first time in my life.'

Mr Broadstreet looked concerned, and apparently began to say that he hoped it need not be the last; but all of a sudden he broke off with an exclamation.

'Hullo,' he said. 'There are two of the girls from the office.'

He waved, and Vivien now realized why the two she had seen by the doorway had seemed familiar, for it was they who waved back. One of them at any rate she remembered as one of the secretaries who sat in the room outside Mr Broadstreet's private office.

She turned to say something more to Irvine Broadstreet, but he had gone. He was several yards away already, hopelessly lost in the crowd. He waved at her from behind the back of a tall man with flowing grey hair, and made a comic gesture as if to show that he could not help being pushed around like this. But she wondered, all the same. It had looked so very much as if he did not want to be seen talking to her by the girls from the office....

However, perhaps she was imagining the whole thing. Vivien shrugged her shoulders, and turned to gaze at the various celebrated people her aunt was pointing out to her—most of whom got lost again in the crowd before she could identify them. Never in her life had she seen such a solidly-packed crowd of wealthy and prosperous-looking people. If they had had to stand so closely packed together out of doors, or in a lift, they would have been furious; but in here they were clearly enjoying every moment of it, and the slimmest, most frail, most elegant women pushed and cried out and laughed and got around with quite as much success as the tough, stout elderly ones and the athletic young men This was quite a new aspect of living in London, and like all the others, it fascinated her.

In response to some signal which she had not heard, the crowd began to push back into the auditorium again for the third and last ballet. Vivien and Bridget, side by side, allowed themselves to be carried along by the stream at its own pace, and by this simple method were very soon delivered back at their seats in the stalls.

Le Beau Danube, as this last ballet was called, was in many ways the most delicious of the three—though Vivien had only to remember the sylphides of the first one, or the gold bird and absurd soldiers of the second, to feel that it was impossible to say anything but that they were all three perfect. It took place in a park, where a number of people in nineteenth-century dresses came frolicking in and out for apparently no better reasons than that the weather was fine and they felt cheerful and the music was so lovely that they could not help dancing to it There was a gardener, airily and ineffectually sweeping up dead leaves. There were girls skipping, and young men dancing, and an exquisite hussar, very romantic, in a pale grey uniform, who fell in love with a girl in white and danced a mazurka with her. There was a miraculously lovely street-dancer in dark rose-red velvet, who came in with two comic men and danced the unforgettable *Blue Danube* waltz with the pale grey hussar.

The dancers on the stage twirled and frolicked and quarrelled and loved each other again. The music became more and more exciting, the pale greys and browns and lavenders wove and rewove into newer and lovelier patterns. The whole huge audience of Covent Garden sat silent, holding its breath, forgetting everything except the music it heard and the dancers it was watching: until at last, with a final flourish, the frolic was over, the curtain came down, and as the music stopped the audience woke up, and the thunder of clapping broke out.

CHAPTER XI

CITY BIRTHDAY

VIVIEN always looked back on her eighteenth birthday as the end of one stage of their life in the City and the beginning of quite a new one. Most of the things that had happened up till now had been inside the family, so to speak—Mr Farthing's illness, settling in the flat, Mrs Farthing going to Greencoat's, Dinah to Kensington, and John to Whitefriars School, and the cooking experiments, exploring, and other affairs which had filled up their time. Life had been exciting, but not dramatic. But now the outside world suddenly began to take a hand in things. The beginning could be traced, in Vivien's opinion, to one exact moment—a moment which seemed very little at the time. It all began on the very day after her birthday, when Irvine Broadstreet went to the kitchen window.

Her birthday, the Sunday, was a fine day, but much too hot. The City was stifling on these sultry summer days when not even the faintest breeze moved the dust in St Paul's Churchyard or the big old tree in the corner of Stationers' Hall Court. They were all tired, and thought of the cool sea winds and the green trees of Berrings much oftener than any of them admitted. But they were pretty cheerful, all the same. They were always cheerful at week-ends, when they were all together and did not have to hurry around; and to-day there were two extra good reasons why they should be so. Dinah was safely through her Intermediate, having got Distinction and passed higher than any of Mr Hepplewhite's pupils ever had before: and Vivien was in such extremely good spirits

193

that, as Mr Farthing said, she would have made them all feel lively even if they had been suffering from colds in the head, sleeplessness, and acute indigestion.

There was a lot of work, as there always was on Sundays when Mrs Jones did not come to help them. But on the other hand, Dinah and John took a hand in it, and Mrs Farthing always made the lunch. Vivien careered about the flat with a mop and a duster, now meditating, now talking to any one who was handy, now singing snatches of the music of *Beau Danube* or Chopin's *Sylphides.*

'I 've never heard you so vocal,' said Mr Farthing as she dusted round his chair. 'Gay life seems to suit you!'

'Oh, yes, it does,' said Vivien fervently, having spent most of her time since Friday night thinking over every single thing that had happened then, from the street-dancer's waltz with the exquisite hussar to Irvine Broadstreet's sudden departure in the foyer. 'And I like having my birthday on a day when everybody 's at home.'

She collected some ash-trays that needed emptying, and went off again, pausing on the way to admire the book on London, the book on Sir Christopher Wren, the new cookery book, and the fine silk stockings which the family had given her for her birthday. Mr Farthing, settling down again to his Sunday newspaper, heard her telling Mrs Farthing something new about the dresses on Friday night in the kitchen, and then, a moment later, singing vigorously in her bedroom and breaking off to help Dinah chase a wasp round the room and out of the window.

The only member of the family who was not altogether cheerful was the one who might have been expected to be even more pleased with life than Vivien. Dinah had taken her success in Inter with a quietness which seemed, to Vivien at any rate, to be totally unlike her. Yes, it was nice to be through, she said, and yes, Heppie was pleased, and Miss Carruthers had congratulated her in prayers before the whole school; but she sounded so unenthusiastic, so little pleased with herself and what she had done, that Vivien could hardly believe that the rest of the family did not notice it too.

When the wasp had at last sailed off in the direction of the Nilpils' window, Vivien suddenly decided to venture a question.

'Has there been a row or anything?' she asked. 'I don't want to butt in, you know.'

Dinah sat down on the foot of her bed.

'No,' she said. 'At least, I mean there has been a row. I 've told Heppie what I thought of him.'

She looked up at Vivien. There was real unhappiness in her small, vivid face.

'I disobeyed him in the exam. I didn't play as he 'd told me at all. I played all my pieces as I 'd always *wanted* to play them. I 'm sure I 'd never played them so well before, and that 's why I came out so high. But then yesterday, when I went for my lesson, he was being so annoying that I got angry and told him!'

Dinah sighed heavily.

'He said he 'd tell Miss Carruthers, but of course he won't—it 's not much credit to him,' she said shrewdly. 'But I can't learn with him any more. Can't and won't.'

'Oh, Dinah.' It was something, at any rate, to know what the trouble was, but Vivien hated to see her so miserable. 'But what can you do?'

'Oh, I 'll find something. If only I had some money. Look here, Vivien, you mustn't say a word about this to anybody. Do you promise?'

'Yes.'

195

'Strike you pink?'

'Strike me pink.'

'You can go away now, if you like,' said Dinah kindly. 'I want to think.'

Dinah seemed to cheer up now that she had confessed to somebody. By lunch-time she was argumentative, and by tea-time she had apparently forgotten her troubles, and was as lively as the rest of them. She and John, bare-legged and wearing canvas shoes, held a long secret consultation in the kitchen after the tea was made, and emerged chanting and carrying a large, heavy plate.

'Here you are, Vivien—here's your cake. Come and look at it.'

They set it on the table with a flourish, and stood back for every one to admire.

'Oh, how beautiful,' said Vivien. 'I never saw any thing so elegant. What are they—mice?'

'They 're instead of candles,' John explained. Eighteen, you see. They 're pink sugar.'

'It 's much better, because we can eat them,' added Dinah. 'Candles do make such a dribble. Now read what it says.'

Vivien went round the table to get the message the right way up. The cake itself she and John had made together, but the icing of it had been done entirely by him and Dinah.

"Many Happy——" no, it 's "Hoppy." "Many Hoppy Returns to Vivien.'"

'It 's not "Hoppy," it's "Happy," of course.'

'It says "Hoppy,"' said Vivien meekly 'You told me to read what it said.'

'Does it really say "Hoppy"? Oh, how frightfully funny. That was you, John. Hoppy Returns—oh, dear, oh, dear.'

Dinah clung to John in a paroxysm of laughter. John, after one sad glance at his masterpiece, began to laugh too, and for several minutes they both giggled helplessly. At last they stopped enough to sit down to tea, though Dinah's giggles burst weakly out again every few moments. They began a prolonged discussion as to what a hoppy return would be, but before they had decided, it was time to cut the cake, and the rest of the meal was more peacefully spent in eating their handiwork and observing how nice it was.

'You make me feel hotter than ever,' said Mrs Farthing, when calm had more or less descended again. 'Who 'll come for a walk with me after tea?'

All three of them would, it appeared. Mr Farthing said he did not mind at all being left alone, and so as soon as tea was over they went off, down an empty Ludgate Hill, through a deserted Ludgate Circus, to Blackfriars Bridge and the Embankment.

'I like the City on Sundays,' Mrs Farthing observed as they walked along. 'One gets a better idea what it 's like without so many people in.'

'Sir,' said John suddenly, 'when a man is tired of London, he is tired of life; for there is in London all that life can afford.'

There was a startled silence.

'Where did you get that from?' said Mrs Farthing at last. 'It sounds like Dr Johnson.'

'It is Dr Johnson. I got it from Mr Moore—you know, the history master.'

In conscious pride John walked on, his soft-soled shoes plodding softly on the asphalt pavement. It was lovely down by the Embankment. There were more people there, for one could, if one considered it carefully enough, feel a distinct breeze blowing off the water. The

197

Thames was grey and quiet, the sky a little misty, and the buildings on the southern bank looked far away. They strolled along towards Waterloo Bridge, past the cool-looking Temple Gardens, and after a time turned back, as they always did about here, to see the dome of St Paul's looming softly over the City with the spires of Wren's churches all around it. It was very peaceful. If one could not have country, at any rate one could get here something that no country scene could offer; and the remark which John had quoted from Dr Johnson was in all their minds as they gazed, and turned again, and strolled on, past the eighteenth-century splendour of Somerset House, past Cleopatra's Needle, to inspect the flowers in the little Embankment Gardens.

On Monday Irvine Broadstreet turned up. He came just after tea, when Mr Farthing was reading, John doing some homework, and Vivien beginning to think it was time she went out to start the dinner. He sent a message up first by Charlie, who was on duty at the lift, and arrived as soon as Vivien's reply had been taken down, carrying a book under his arm.

Vivien went to the sitting-room door to meet him, well aware of the two interested people in the room behind her.

'Hallo,' he said. 'This is nice of you.' He smiled as if he was really pleased to see her. 'How are you? Did you enjoy Friday night?'

'Oh, it was wonderful.'

'Yes, wasn't it? Couldn't have been better. We had some friends from New York with us, and they loved it. I was sorry I left you so abruptly, but the crowd was really terrific—they do know how to shove!'

Not knowing whether to say that she had been sorry

also or that it did not matter at all, Vivien pushed open the sitting-room door and took him in to be introduced, reflecting as she caught sight of John's face that there were times when brothers would be much better out of the way.

Mr Farthing greeted him with great interest.

'So you 're the famous firm of Broadstreet he said as they shook hands. 'I 've been hearing a lot about you lately.'

'Oh, I 'm not the firm—I 'm only "young Mr Irvine," or "that there Irvine" if they get too much annoyed with me. Most of the older ones knew me when I was in my cradle!'

He sat down and talked for a minute or two with Mr Farthing, who, Vivien could very well see, liked him at sight. He then produced the book he had brought up with him, and held it out to Vivien.

'It 's from the United States,' he said. 'We like it, but we 're not sure if it isn 't a little too American. Will you have a look at it and tell us what you think?'

Vivien said she would be delighted to do so, and young Mr Broadstreet then produced some samples of patterned book cloth which he said they were thinking of using for the binding of novels.

'You may be interested to see them,' he said, holding them out to Mr Farthing. 'They 're something quite new. I thought I 'd try them on Vivien, as she 's kindly said we can use her as a sort of thermometer to find out what the public likes!'

Mr Farthing looked up with a distinct twinkle in his eye at the sound of Vivien's Christian name. John coughed. Whether Irvine Broadstreet heard him or not, he went on amiably:

'By the way, Irvine 's a hopeless name—it ought to

belong to a public trust company, or at the very least a peer. All my friends call me Tim.'

This confused Vivien so much that she was hardly able to give any attention to the patterned book-cloths. However, she managed an opinion of some sort, and after a few minutes more Tim, or Irvine, or young Mr Broadstreet got up to go.

'It is charming up here,' he said, looking around him. 'One wouldn't expect to find a real home like this on the top of all those offices. And I 'd no idea we were such near neighbours. The buildings must almost back on to each other.'

'Yes, they do, almost,' said Vivien, not thinking what she was saying. When Tim, having said 'Au revoir' to her father and John, was out on the landing again, he noticed the open door of the kitchen, and looked at it with interest.

'I should so like to see how we look from here,' he said. 'Would you awfully mind if I went in?'

Before she could say anything he was at the kitchen window, gazing eagerly out.

'Oh, you can't see much,' he said. 'In fact you can't see any of it, can you? Oh—yes, you can, though. Isn't that Day's room down there?'

He leaned out as far as he could, absent-mindedly pushing aside some stewed fruit which Vivien had put on the window-sill to cool.

'Yes, my goodness, it is—and old Day in it too, walking about as large as life and twice as natural. You must almost be able to hear what he says, can't you?'

Vivien had not the least suspicion that he was asking for any special reason—he was fascinated to see what could be seen, and she was perfectly sure his mind was on that and not on anything else. But hardly had she begun to say yes than she stopped abruptly. What might it lead to if she let him know that Mr Day had been so indiscreet?

'Yes, we—— at least, no, not really, you know. I mean, he never has his window open except when it's very hot, and we can hear a lot of other people too. So that we don't really hear anything, at least not anything specially——'

Mr Day, Mr Blueley, trouble inside the firm, trouble with Messrs Perryforth—the whole collection of facts began to buzz around in her head, and the more she remembered of them the harder it became to know what she ought and what she ought not to know. Tim Broadstreet recalled his gaze from the lead roof and the rows of windows, and turned round and looked at her curiously.

'You knew Mr Day belonged to our firm?' he inquired.

'Er—oh, yes. I saw him in your room, you know, when I came to see you. And I'd heard Mr Blueley talk about him.'

'Do you mean you recognized him when you saw him in our office because you'd seen him from here?'

'Yes, of course I do,' replied Vivien with spirit. 'One can't help getting to know what one's opposite neighbours look like, or what they talk about either, if they have their windows open.'

'You didn't tell me.'

'No, but really, why should I? It didn't matter to you.'

Tim Broadstreet was frowning thoughtfully. Vivien, a little resentful and more than a little uneasy about Mr Blueley, stood clearly waiting for him to go. He looked up again, and smiled, but he was still abstracted.

'No, of course not,' he said. 'Silly of me. Well, thanks

very much, Vivien. I must dash off now. Will you drop that book in with Miss Ramsay as soon as you can?'

And he was gone, almost as quickly as he had left her at Covent Garden. Vivien listened for a moment to his footsteps on the staircase, then with a minute shrug of her shoulders went back to the sitting-room.

John and Mr Farthing were both longing to talk to her. 'Nice young fellow, that,' said Mr Farthing. 'I thought publishers never washed or shaved.'

'Oh, Daddy!' Vivien nearly embarked on a spirited defence of publishers' standards of cleanliness, but caught sight just in time of the grin on her father's face.

'Tim, indeed,' commented John, planting his elbows comfortably on the table. 'Well, it 's better than Irvine, I must say. But Vivien, I 'm disappointed in you. Do you know that 's the very first person we 've met that I can't collect?'

'What do you mean?'

'He isn't queer. He 's simply ordinary!'

With a smile of the purest triumph, John watched his sister's indignation.

He isn't ordinary,' she protested instantly.

'Well, then, is he queer?'

'No, of course he 's not queer.'

'Well, then, he must be ordinary. Q.E.D.,' observed John blandly. Vivien spluttered a little, but could find no possible answer. At last with a look which should have reduced John to shame and sorrow, she went angrily out to begin the dinner, and his loud, contented laughter pursued her down the landing.

BOOK THREE

CHAPTER I

DISASTER

TWO days later Vivien took the American novel back to Broadstreet's with a short note about how she had liked it. She went into the showroom, and took them both across to Miss Ramsay, who was sitting in her usual corner keeping a watchful eye on a man who was strolling round looking at the bookshelves.

'Sometimes they want advice about what to choose, and that 's what I 'm here for,' she said in a low voice to Vivien. 'But sometimes they rather want to pocket the books without any further formalities. Oh, by the way,' she added, noticing the book Vivien had brought, 'Mr Irvine said when you came in with this would you please go up to him.'

'Go up to him? Oh—oh, yes, of course I will.'

Vivien went over to the telephone girl, asked for Mr Irvine Broadstreet, and was sent up at once. She felt distinctly uneasy, though as she reminded herself on the way up in the lift, there was really nothing for her to be uneasy about. But she wished she had seen Mr Blueley in the last day or two, all the same.

She got out of the lift, and the slim, haughty-looking secretary came towards her—the one whom she had seen at Covent Garden. Her name was Haddon, Vivien suddenly remembered.

'Oh, Miss Farthing,' she said at once. 'Mr Irvine is free to see you, of course, but he 's just on the telephone. Would you mind waiting a moment?'

There was nothing in the words themselves, but there

was undeniably something in the way she said them: a slight, slight emphasis on the 'of course,' and a sidelong glance which caused Vivien to redden angrily. As she stood waiting, the girl went back to her desk and sat down again at her typewriter; but instead of beginning to type she leaned over and asked her neighbour for a pencil. They fell into a low conversation, which Vivien could not hear and did not suppose she was meant to hear. Then Miss Haddon slightly raised her voice.

'...really magnificent dancing,' she said, still leaning across to her neighbour's desk. 'You and Bill ought to go. Of course, not everybody has money enough to do the thing in style, or perhaps I ought to say rich friends to take them there in style. . . .'

Her voice sank again, and without a glance in Vivien's direction she went on with her conversation. Vivien's flush deepened. There was nothing in these words also, but she had not the slightest doubt why Miss Haddon had said them, or what she meant them to imply. Hating Miss Haddon, wishing with all her heart that something would happen to stop her, Vivien stood and longed for Tim to finish on the telephone.

At last there came a faint tinkle on Miss Haddon's phone. The call in the inner room had come to an end. Miss Haddon got up, and with impersonal dignity conducted Vivien to the door of Mr Broadstreet's office.

'Ah, here you are. Come in.'

Tim was in his uncle's big room, Mr Broadstreet, no doubt, being out at a business lunch. He came forward, but waited until Miss Haddon had shut the door before he said any more.

'Is that the book? Oh, thanks. Sit down, won't you— over here.'

There was not the slightest doubt that something was

wrong. His manner was very stiff—he was clearly feeling awkward about something. They sat down, he at the desk and she in the big visitors' chair.

'Look here, Vivien—we 're in a bit of a difficulty here, and we think it just possible that you can help us to clear it up.'

He smoothed down his thick dark hair, which sprang up again immediately. He seemed to find things easier now he had actually begun.

'I don't know if you know about it, but information which is rather valuable to us has been going astray from here lately.'

'Yes,' said Vivien.

'What—you did know?' Tim looked at her keenly. 'How was that?'

'Well, Mr Blueley told me something about it—but only in the most general way.' Vivien had thought a lot about what she should say if such a question were asked, and this seemed to her the safest possible answer.

'Oh, I see. Well, now—the thing I want to ask you is this. Do you think it possible that, either from Mr Blueley or—h'm—from Mr Day's office, or from what you 've heard talked about while you were in this building, you could ever have heard anything which didn't seem important to you, but which you might without thinking have told to somebody to whom it would be very important, and very interesting and useful?'

Tim looked at her, his eyes grave, his fingers playing a little tattoo on the arm of his chair. Vivien slowly reddened.

'So that 's what you think!' she said at last. 'You think I 've been giving your stuff away?'

She gazed at him, unable to say another word. Tim shook his head.

'No, it 's not what I think. I must say I was shaken for

a moment when I saw how much you could pick up of old Day's concerns. But I know you well, don't I—and for me it 's unthinkable. Only—oh, look here, Vivien, this is horrible for both of us, but it must be said. There 's a lot of talk going on in the office, and a lot of suspicion running around, and because you 're a new-comer here, and because they see that I like you and have given you work, they say that it must be you who 's been giving away our information.'

He sighed, glanced quickly and almost apologetically at her, and looked away again, his gaze going slowly round the outside of the big window-frame. Vivien took a deep breath.

'So that 's why you ran away at Covent Garden— because they saw us together. I thought so. And Miss Haddon, just before I came in here . . . Oh, well———'

Making an enormous effort, she calmed herself down, locking her fingers together on her handbag.

'I can see they *might* think it,' she went on more slowly. 'They know I 'm from outside, and I might have friends in all the other publishing firms, and tell them things. But I haven't. And I wouldn't tell them anything at all, even if I had.' In spite of herself, her voice began to rise. 'And if I 'd been you I should have told them it was all lies, since you were so sure yourself. But you *weren't* sure—that 's what it is. That 's just what it is! You thought it might be me all the time. Well, all right.'

Vivien got up, breathing very fast, her cheeks scarlet and her eyes blazing with anger.

'I didn't ask to come and work here, did I? You asked me to. Well, now I don't want to come any more. You can call this notice, or whatever the proper word is. I 'm going. Good-bye.'

Before young Mr Broadstreet could fully take in what

was happening, the door to the staircase had banged shut, and he heard footsteps running down the stairs and across the hail to the showroom. Then they died away, and he could hear no more.

Vivien, out in the street, had not the slightest idea in what direction she was going. She was angry, and upset—angrier than she had ever been in her life before, and deeply upset that Tim, whom she liked so much, and Broadstreet's, where she loved to feel she belonged, had suddenly turned against her in this unbelievable way.

She plunged on down the street, seeing nobody, hearing nothing, unaware whether she crossed other streets or turned to the right or the left. She must have walked for twenty minutes before she slowly came back to a realization of her surroundings; and then, when she did so, she saw that she was in Watchman Lane. She must somehow have gone in a circle, and now was back again very near Magnificat Alley, and very near home.

She stopped short, wondering what to do. To go home was unthinkable. To walk about was not much better, now she had realized that she was doing it. She looked around, and saw she was standing only a few steps from St Sebastian's. That was the place—the very best place of all. She ran up the steps, and went in.

There was nobody inside, as far as she could see, and that suited her well. She did not want to talk to Mr Persepolis. She found a pew in a quiet corner, crept into it, and after kneeling for a moment sat there thinking, arguing with herself and with Broadstreet's, trying to see both sides of the matter, trying to calm herself down.

An occasional visitor came in, went quietly round the church, and went out again. Mr Persepolis did not appear. Slowly the peace and the ordered design of the church made its never-failing effect on her, and she began to feel happier again. She forgot about Broadstreet's, and began thinking about all the people who had worshipped in here in the two centuries and a half since Wren had built it— of how they must have come in here with every kind of trouble, and anger, and preoccupation. Old people, and young people, and children wanting to get out and play again in the sunshine....

She heard voices, and a man and a woman came in, talking rather more loudly than most of the visitors did. They came up the aisle, exclaiming and admiring, bringing with them a strong mixed smell of cigar-smoke and scent.

'See that, Ella?' said the man, waving his arm towards the dome. 'Pretty, isn't it?'

'Yes. Must be ever so old, don't you think?'

They walked briskly round the church, not seeing Vivien, saying how pretty everything was and how cold it was inside these queer old buildings. When their tour brought them back to the door again they went straight out of it, and she heard their exclamations fading away as they went down into the street. Silence and peace came back to the church again.

It must have been about ten or fifteen minutes later that she first noticed something was wrong. The smell of cigar-smoke had hung in the air so heavily that she had not realized how long it was taking to die away. Suddenly, with a start, she became aware that it was not dying away. It was getting stronger. . . . It was turning into something quite different.

She lifted her head and sniffed anxiously. It was very strong now. It was not tobacco-smoke at all any longer. It was——

'Fire!' said Vivien aloud, and ran down the church.

It was just inside the doorway, in the inner porch, which was shut off by swing-doors from the outer porch and the steps. Smoke was pouring out now, coming into the church in little purposeful clouds and streaks, and bringing with it a sharp, bitter smell of burning.

For a moment that seemed endless Vivien stood and stated at it. Her heart seemed to be right up in her throat. She could hardly breathe.

She took a step forward, thinking that she could dash through and get out into the street to call help. But she saw as soon as she thought of it that that was no good. The whole mat in the inner porch was alight. She could not get through.

Someone outside must surely see—the smoke must be getting through the door. Help would come: they would ring for the fire brigade.

As she stood there she saw a little tongue of flame creep forward and lick round the heavy curtains which hung in the archway. It played for a moment at the foot, then suddenly caught, and shot up the material as if it had been some living creature. The smoke grew denser every moment. The flames began to make a spitting, muttering sound that was terrifying to hear.

In a very few moments, if it went on like this, the fire would catch the panelling on the wall; and then, Vivien realized with a gasp of horror, it would burn through. And on the other side of that wall was the vestry—Wren's vestry, the room which he had worked in....

Gathering together all her self-control, thinking furiously, Vivien left the fire and ran off down the aisle to the right. Next to Wren's vestry was the choir vestry: and in there, she half remembered, was a washbasin, where she had once seen a big jug standing.

She found the basin, and the big jug standing beside

211

it. The one small tap ran terribly slowly, but the jug was half full already. While it was filling she looked frantically around, and saw on the table a big, heavy tablecloth. She pulled it off, upsetting an inkstand and several books as she did so.

In a moment she was back at the porch. The fire was strong, the smoke was tremendous, but it did not seem to have got much further since she went away. Choking and gasping, she shot the water into the hottest part of the fire, and flung the big tablecloth down on the burning mat.

The flames sizzled angrily, and a cloud of still blacker smoke shot out. But she had done some good. The fire on the further half of the mat was out, and the flames were less violent. She plunged in, blinded by the smoke, her eyes stinging till she thought that they too were on fire, and taking the heavy curtain by its still unburned edge she pulled and pulled until with a sudden rip it began to come away from its rings. Another pull, and it was down.

She staggered back, covering her eyes, and when next she was able to look up saw that just beside her on the wall hung a small fire extinguisher. It was too dark, too smoky, too hot, to read its directions; but with dim recollections of fire drill at school she got it somehow from its holder, hit its end on the stone floor, and with shaking hands directed the stream of liquid which shot out of it at the outer edges of the fire.

The flames were strong, but the extinguisher was stronger. With a violent fizzling sound they died down as the liquid met them, and Vivien, aware of nothing in the world but heat and smoke and the need to aim carefully, went on until the wall was quite free, the curtain was out, and nothing was left but a small ring of flame on the mat.

Her hands began to shake so violently that she could hardly aim at all. Everything began to go black.

Through the crackle of the flames and the noise in her own head she heard shouting, and footsteps, and the clang of a fire-engine bell. Dark shapes appeared through the glass of the swing-doors. They were flung open, bringing in a blast of cold air which made the flames leap out at her. She saw firemen's helmets, and the horrified face of Mr Persepolis, very dark through the smoke. Then her legs gave way, the blackness came down on her, and with a little choking sound she collapsed.

CHAPTER II

BEAUTIFUL MYSTERY GIRL

'IT 'S quite all right, dearie—nobody can come up. Phineas won't let them.'

Mrs Jones pulled the pillows straight and tucked in the bedclothes, which were once again falling off. It was the morning after the fire. Vivien, lying in bed with her arms bandaged and a cracking headache just above her eyes, took a final gulp of orange juice and lay back again.

It was not the fire itself which had been so shattering. If only she had been allowed to come quietly home somehow, and rest, she thought that by now she would be perfectly all right again—except of course for her burned arms and hands, and they did not hurt for the moment now the doctor had dressed them. But the commotion all those people made had been simply incredible. She could hear some of it even now: men shouting, women screaming out, a policeman saying 'Stand back, there— stand back. Let her get some air.' Someone had asked her where she lived, and she told them, and someone else said 'Oh, you mean you work there?' and she said 'No—live,' and then fainted again. When next she knew what was happening there was a large white ambulance in front of her eyes, and a woman was saying 'It 's a shame, that 's what it is—a poor little thing like that,' and a young man was insisting 'Excuse me, but I must have her name.' Then she was lifted up, and after that she remembered nothing distinctly until she was in her own bed at home, with Mrs Jones and a doctor standing beside her.

'Now you take this pill doctor left for you, and then you 'll go right off to sleep.' Mrs Jones held out the little white tablet, and Vivien swallowed it meekly enough with a drink of water.

'What about Daddy?' she asked when she had taken it. 'Are you sure he 's all right?'

'He 's as comfortable as could be. Don't you worry about him for a moment. Nurse Rymer 's coming back later on to see to you both, and he 's coming in here to see you himself when you wake up.'

'That 's nice. But are you sure those reporters can't get in?'

'Not a single reporter sets foot on this landing, not if it was ever so. Now shut your eyes, dearie, and don't think about anything any more.'

Feeling more or less relieved, Vivien shut her eyes, and heard Mrs Jones quietly drawing the curtains. She took a deep breath, and then another. She was asleep.

It seemed only a moment later that she opened her eyes again. Mrs Jones had gone, and in place of her someone quite different was standing beside the bed.

'Daddy! How did you get here?'

'Walked. Nurse Rymer 's in the other room, tidying up. How are you, darling?'

'Oo, I feel fine,' said Vivien, stretching herself luxuriously down the bed. 'That was a lovely sleep. What 's the time?'

'Five o'clock. You certainly did sleep. John 's back, bursting with inquiries about you, and what would you say about some tea?'

Vivien's opinion about tea was that there was nothing in the world that she would like so much; and so, five minutes later, Nurse Rymer brought in a tray for three, and John appeared after her from the other room.

The tea was so reviving, and it was so nice to have her father and John sitting with her, and her headache was so immensely much better, that a little while later Vivien inquired almost without nervousness whether the reporters had really put anything in the papers.

'They *were* disgraceful, pushing their way in like that,' said her father, knowing how much they had upset her. Two of them had come up to the flat actually with the stretcher-bearers, and their questions had distressed her so much, half unconscious as she was, that for hours afterwards her one fear had been that they would get in again. 'The doctor told them exactly what he thought of them when he sent them away.'

'Good,' said Vivien. 'Did they put anything in the papers really?'

'Did they!' John had been bursting to speak, and now could not keep silence any longer. 'Every single paper had it in—all this morning's as well as the evening ones last night. I 've got them all. Every one at school knew that you were my sister. Even the provost asked me about it, and how you were getting on.'

'What did they say—the papers, I mean?'

'You don't want to see them?'

'Oh, no, I 'd hate to. Just tell me.'

'Oh, they made a wonderful story of it,' said Mr Farthing. 'How a woman passing by smelled smoke, and then they saw the fire, and the fire-engines came at once, and they found you inside putting the fire out all by yourself.'

'Yes—"Beautiful Mystery Girl," one paper called you, said John, who found his father's account much too unexciting.

'And they had photographs of the porch, and an interview with Mr Persepolis—he 'd gone out for his

216

usual late lunch, and his substitute hadn't turned up. Of course it was wrong of him to leave the church without waiting to see if he came. And there was an interview with the rector, who lives out in Kensington, and several pictures of the fire-engines——'

'One paper has a picture of you, too—quite a decent one. In fact,' said John, 'it 's the one I had myself. Mr Blueley asked me if I 'd lend it to them.'

'Mr Blueley?'

'Yes, he was round here almost immediately. I don't know how he heard of it. He dealt with most of the chaps who tried to get in.'

'Oh, dear,' said Vivien, feeling suddenly exhausted. 'How queer it all is.'

She put down her cup, and lay back. Mr Farthing, with a meaning glance at John, stopped talking about the fire and began to give her news of Dinah and Mrs Farthing and the Edmonthorpes. Vivien lay and half listened, with a little frown on her face. The mention of Mr Blueley had reminded her of something... something. .... She could not remember what it was, but she could remember very clearly that it was unpleasant.

By the next afternoon she was so much better that she was allowed up, and the doctor told Mr Farthing that she was making very good progress.

'She seems a little out of spirits,' he said, 'but no doubt that 's the shock. She ought to get away to the country somewhere for a rest and change.'

Shock it might very well have been, to a large extent, but Vivien herself knew better than any one why she was feeling so miserable. She had remembered now all that had happened before the fire; and the more she thought of Messrs Broadstreet's and of what Tim Broadstreet had said, the worse it seemed and the more dismally unhappy she became. A huge bunch of carnations had come for her from Tim and his uncle: but when she read the card and saw whom they were from she said that the smell made her sick, and the moment she was left to herself again she burst into tears. She felt so unhappy that she thought she wanted to die. She wandered about from the sitting-room to the kitchen, and from the kitchen to her bedroom, and sat down a little, and stood looking out of the window a little, and could settle to nothing; and Mr Farthing, who knew nothing about the interview at Broadstreet's watched her anxiously, and would much rather the whole of St Sebastian's should have burned down than that she should have been so much harmed by saving it.

All sorts of strange visitors came to the flat in the days after the fire. They were severely weeded out by Mr Jones downstairs, but those who did come up Mr Farthing dealt with, and now that he was so much better there was no doubt that he enjoyed seeing all these unaccustomed people. A queer old man with white hair came to tell him that Vivien belonged to the Ten Lost Tribes of Israel, and drew little diagrams of the Pyramids which he said undoubtedly proved it. The rector of St Sebastian's came, much distressed and full of gratitude to Vivien, and he and Mr Farthing had a very good talk together. The agent of a film company came, to inquire whether Vivien had ever considered acting for the cinema, and to leave his card in case she wanted a trial: a visit which filled Dinah with terrible envy, but which only made Vivien smile weakly and say 'How ridiculous.' Several earnest young men called to invite Mr Farthing to insure against fire, to his great entertainment, and a middle-aged lady of impressive dignity found her way up and proved to be an agent for corsets.

These visits amused Vivien a little, in a mild sort of way, but none of them really interested her until Mr Jones's boy, on her second day up, brought a message that Mr Blueley was waiting downstairs and would be very pleased if he might see her.

'Oh, yes,' she said. 'Send him up, please.' When Charlie had gone she turned quickly to her father, who was unwillingly taking his afternoon rest with his feet up. 'Daddy, if you hear anything you don't know about, I 'll tell you after. There was—there was a little trouble at Broadstreet's.'

A very short time afterwards she heard the lift arrive, and in a moment more Mr Blueley knocked and came in. But he was not alone, and at the sight of his companion Vivien turned suddenly white. It was Tim Broadstreet.

'Oh,' she said. 'I didn't—I didn't——'

'Please excuse our both coming,' said Mr Blueley, looking as if he did not quite know what to say or do. 'But Mr Irvine said he had something so very urgent to say to you. . .'

'And that was that I 'm simply most terribly sorry,' said Tim. 'You will forgive me, Vivien, won't you? We 've come to explain.'

He looked into her eyes with an expression in his own that she found it quite impossible to resist, and Mr Farthing, watching with the greatest interest, saw her nod faintly and even smile. Both the new-comers gave what looked like a sigh of relief, and began to inquire how Vivien was feeling, looking with obvious concern at her bandaged arms and wrists and her unnaturally white face.

'It really was a grand bit of work,' said Mr Blueley with the idea of cheering her up. 'You 're a heroine all over the City, you know—people point out to each other as they go by that this is the place where you live.'

'Do they? Well, I hope they 'll very soon forget that I exist at all. I hope there 'll be an earthquake, or a murder, or quintuplets, or something else jolly for them to talk about.'

Vivien was clearly not cheered up at all, and Mr Blueley looked rather nonplussed. But Tim meanwhile had been asking Mr Farthing if it was all right to talk shop to Vivien, and Mr Farthing, with a sudden suspicion of the kind of things that had been happening, answered that it might be the very beet thing they could do.

Tim gave a preliminary cough and plunged right in.

'I say, Vivien—Blueley 's told us the whole story now. About how you think that Day may have been giving our business away, and how he thinks—how Blueley thinks, I mean—he may have done it himself. We 've all had a terrific talk together, and nobody suspects anybody any more.'

Vivien's pale face turned a delicate shade of rose-pink, and Mr Farthing said afterwards that the temperature of the room went up at least ten degrees as her hostility died away. She sighed deeply, and all of a sudden began to look, if not like her old self, at least like the recognizable ghost of her old self.

'Oh, good,' she said. 'That 's *much* better.' She thought it over for a moment. 'But—but that doesn't clear it up, all the same. Have you any more idea of what might be happening?'

'Yes, we have, in a way. We know now that it isn't only Broadstreet's who are suffering from this strange plague. I 've heard things from friends of mine in their firms.... And, Blueley, tell her about your stationery friend.'

'Yes, that 's a queer thing,' said Mr Blueley, leaning forward with one large elbow on his large navy-blue knee.

'I 've got a stationer pal up near where I live in North London—stationer, tobacconist, a few books, mostly crime stuff. You know the sort of place. Used to buy my tobacco there, before we moved further out. Well, he takes an occasional Broadstreet book, but never more than a single copy—I 've almost given up calling there now. Yesterday I was driving past, and what did I see but a. whole window full of books. I stopped the car and had a look, and when I saw that no less than four were copies of *Night-time*—you know that novel Broadstreet's did so well with a couple of months back—well, then I thought the matter could do with a bit of looking into.

'I dropped in for some tobacco,' he went on, clearly enjoying his story, 'and got the chap into conversation. He didn't want to talk at all, and when I said something about *Night-time* he did all he could to change the subject. I said he might have given me the order, and he said he wrote straight in to the trade department. I said that was very funny, as I was sure I 'd have noticed his order or been told of it. He said well perhaps he 'd forgotten—yes, of course, he ordered the copies with a lot of other stuff from Simpkins. And as I know very well,' said Mr Blueley with conviction, 'that a man like that would never order books like that if he lived to be a hundred, what was I to conclude?'

'What?' Vivien and Mr Farthing were both listening with breathless interest

'Why, that he 'd got them somehow that wasn't quite. above-board. I couldn't say anything, of course. I just asked after his wife—she 's terribly ill, poor fellow—and came away. But putting a case like that with the other things Mr Irvine 's heard and I 've heard, well——'

He looked at Tim, as if to say Now it 's your turn. Tim nodded.

'Well, in point of fact we 've come to the conclusion that there 's a pretty big organization at work, making money out of little odd corners of the book trade. I know it sounds like a detective story,' he added, with an apologetic glance at Mr Farthing. 'But it 's not only books that have been going astray, though there seems to have been quite a lot of that too. It 's ideas. That series of ours which Perryforth's got, for instance—and then I 've heard of at least two other cases when ideas which an author was definitely working on were pinched and used by somebody quite different.'

'But can you really be sure it was done on purpose?' Mr Farthing inquired.

'Oh, yes. I know ideas are difficult things to trace, but here there was no more doubt than there was over our series. Publishing and the book world generally are run very much on what my uncle would call gentlemanly understandings. If one firm announces a book by a certain title—say we announce one called *Clock Tower* to come out in the autumn—then it 's pretty well understood that no other firm would bring out a book called *Clock Tower* in the months in between. And if we use a certain kind of type in our advertisements, we can be fairly sure that nobody else will copy us. And it 's like that all the way through. But if once somebody gets the idea of *not* being bound by these gentlemanly agreements—well, you can see what would happen.'

'He 'd rake in a nice little lot of cash, if he knew how to use his information properly,' said Mr Farthing thoughtfully. 'But he 'd also have to know how to get hold of the information. You mean that you think it 's some men, or association of people of some kind, who are right in the centre of things.'

'Just exactly that,' said Tim cheerfully. 'Probably some

thoroughly decent chaps whom we all like and whom we tell more than we ought to when we meet them at cocktail parties and lunches. We 're going to have a gay time in the next few months or so, suspecting all the publishers and literary editors and reviewers and booksellers one after the other. So you see, Vivien,' he concluded with a grin, 'you 're right out of the running now. You 're not nearly famous enough! And that reminds me, by the way, you 'll have to do that book on Wren and so forth one day.'

'The book on Wren? But—how did you know about it?'

'Oh, Blueley got it into the papers, or some of them at any rate. "Beautiful Mystery Girl a Lover of Art— Studying Architecture in the Sacred Building she saved." Wasn't that right, Blueley?'

'That 's it,' said Mr Blueley, entertained by the expression on Vivien's face. 'Advance publicity, you know. It was a wonderful opportunity—we couldn't have missed it.'

Well,' said Tim, reluctantly making a move to go, 'be sure to let us have a look at the manuscript, when there 's anything to see. Broadstreet's have the first claim on it, I really do think. When are you going to begin?'

'Give the poor girl a chance,' said Mr Farthing. 'The next thing that 's going to happen is that she 'll be packed off to the country for a holiday.'

Tim looked delightfully sorry to hear that she was going away, but agreed that it was only the proper thing. He and Mr Blueley went off, having done Vivien as much good as several days in the country, and she and Mr Farthing, much intrigued by all they had heard, settled down to discuss it.

'But you really are going away,' said her father before

223

they began. 'Mummy 's telephoning to Aunt Rosamund before she comes home, and I know they 'll say you're to go down the moment you can travel.'

Vivien thought of the country: of sunshine, and shady trees with comfortable chairs underneath them, and roses and apple trees and big green lawns. She thought of the hot City streets, and the stuffy City air: and then of Messrs Broadstreet's, particularly including young Mr Broadstreet, and of the promising-looking plot that they had unearthed. She wished vehemently that it were possible to be in two places at once, and hoped very much that the unknown villains would take a long summer holiday, and do nothing more until she got back.

CHAPTER III

SUMMER HOLIDAY

IT was really the greatest fun, staying with Aunt Rosamund and Uncle Charles. They had a very nice house, called the White House, in a village called High Melvin which was less a village than the outer edge of a little country town. The garden was lovely, the roses in full bloom, the apples ripening, and hundreds of pinks giving off their delicious sweet smell all along the edges of the flower-beds. Vivien spent half the morning in bed, and the rest of the day sitting or wandering slowly about out of doors in the shade and the sunshine.

For company she had her aunt and uncle, whom she was never tired of being with; and for entertainment she had the rector's family, the Bascombes, who lived just round the corner. They were a comic and very charming family, already the best of friends with her aunt and uncle, and she got on well with them at once.

'They 're rather like all of you,' her aunt said one day. 'They say what they think and they do what they like and they manage their own affairs.'

'Are they like us?' Vivien thought them over. There was a dark-haired girl of about her own age, Jean: a young, fair child, a cousin from Canada, whose name was Anne, and an elder sister of hers who had recently married but seemed to be always about at the rectory all the same: a boy rather younger than Dinah, called David, who had been sent home early from school owing to an outbreak of mumps, and was extremely pleased about it.

'Not to look at, or anything. But you know they took

on the running of that big house all by themselves, rather like you took on the flat. They didn't know anything about housekeeping or anything, but they decided they wouldn't have any maids, but run the whole place themselves. They still do it all.'

Vivien looked with particular interest at the rectory when she was well enough to go there to tea, and was much fascinated by the various arrangements the Bascombe family had thought out for making their work easier. They had a lot of rooms to look after—but, on the other hand, they had a lot of space to work in, and she began to feel she would gladly exchange the tiny City flat for this big, friendly, three-hundred-year-old house with cupboards and queer little rooms cropping up everywhere. They had a big garden, and grew their own vegetables and fruit. They had a car, even if it was, as they said, the oldest Morris known to be running.

She compared notes with them about everything, and they seemed as much interested to hear about living in the City as she was to see how they managed every thing. The rector and Aunt Rosamund, when they all met at tea-time, were highly entertained to find Vivien in animated discussion with David and Jean as to the best kind of enamel saucepans to be bought at Woolworth's.

But when she got back that evening there was a letter from her mother saying how much they missed her, and a note at the end of it from John to say he had made a *soufflé*, and a letter from Tim Broadstreet to say that when she got back she must come to a literary party or two with him and do a little spying. All at once the country seemed to lose its charm. It was very nice, no doubt, for a short change: she really did feel all the better for the fresh air and quiet days: but London was better. The City might be stuffy, and the flat cramped, but it was there that she belonged, and things were happening, and likely to happen, that she simply could not bear to miss.

She went back to London, when the last day of her holiday came, like a horse with its head turned for home, as her uncle put it. It was grand to arrive in the dark, smoky depths of St Pancras, thrilling to tell the taxi-driver to drive to St Paul's and stop just by the pavement on the left. They drove along shabby slum streets, and past Gray's Inn into Holborn, and down to Ludgate Circus, and when Vivien got her first glimpse of the dome of St Paul's as the taxi swung round into Ludgate Hill she felt that she was really coming home.

Mr Jones welcomed her with delight, and took her suit-case from the taxi-driver as if he could not possibly allow any one else to carry it.

'You're looking bonny, miss—real bonny,' he said as he pulled the lift cord and they began to go up. 'Quite your old self again. And your father's walking about like a nathlete, and everybody's been as well as could be. Here we are, then. I'll put your suit-case along in your room for you.'

His description of Mr Farthing as an athlete was perhaps a little too optimistic but Vivien did at an rate find her father standing up when she went into the sitting-room, and when he heard her he walked over from the window almost as if it was no effort for him to do so.

'Daddy!'

'Vivien—I wondered if that was your taxi.'

'Oh, it's lovely to be home,' said Vivien, hugging him. 'It's almost the best part of going away! How's everybody? Is there any news?'

'John and Dinah both break up in a couple of days. Mummy's very well. Sir William says we can certainly go away in September, and then, after that, he thinks I can try and begin to work.'

'Oh, Daddy—that really is lovely.'

'Yes, it will be—if I can still get the work to do,' said her father soberly. 'However, don't let 's worry about that for the present. There 's a big box of chocolates waiting for you over there on the table. Of course I can't imagine who it 's from!'

It seemed very much as if villains did take summer holidays just like the rest of the world. At any rate, nothing at all dramatic happened in the book trade for the next few weeks: in fact, if one could believe Tim and Mr Blueley, nothing happened of any kind, not a single person anywhere wanted to buy any books, and it was only by some miracle that Broadstreet's and all the other publishing firms escaped bankruptcy.

'Of course, we say this every year,' said Tim in a moment of honesty. 'But trade is slack, all the same, and I don't wonder the Enemy is taking a bit of a breather. He 's probably cruising in the tropics on his ill-gotten gains!'

He was going away to the Hebrides himself in a very short time, and talked of a business trip to America later in the year; but for the moment he was here, and not too busy, and he and Vivien seemed somehow, almost without noticing it, to have progressed from acquaintances to being very good friends. They were no more than that, and if Vivien sometimes wondered what they really felt about each other she came back always to precisely the same conclusion: that she liked things very much as they were. They went for drives together in his car. Often they had lunch together, twice he took her out to dinner, and once to the ballet at Covent Garden again and once to a play. He was often away at week ends, and played a lot of tennis if he was at home; but now and again, if he was free on Sunday, he would take not only Vivien but any of the rest of the family who cared to come, for a drive in the country.

There was one notable day when they all came—not only Mrs Farthing, Vivien, Dinah, and John, but also Mr Farthing. They went to Hampton Court. Mr Farthing was strictly forbidden by Sir William to do any walking about, but he and Mrs Farthing sat in the car with the roof open while the others explored, and he enjoyed the fresh air as keenly as one only can after months of being indoors. Vivien paid tribute to Wren, admiring the magnificent red brick building and recognizing his hand in it in many different ways. John and Dinah tore about, finding strange stone animals to marvel at, and birds and flowers, and the enormous old vine beyond the Knot Garden. It was very much an out-of-doors day, with a tiny cool breeze to offset the late summer dryness, and they strolled up and down the long green walks, and looked at the Thames, and talked, and idled, and would not have changed places with any family in England. Vivien and Tim fetched some tea from a little tea-shop which the four senior members of the party ate in the car while John and Dinah, large slices of cake in their hands, plunged into the Maze and with squeals from Dinah and shouts of instruction from John found their way to the centre and out again.

Another day Tim, as he had promised, took Vivien to the Ivy Restaurant to see celebrities eating their lunch. She was much astonished to find so grand a place at the corner of two dingy-looking streets behind Charing Cross Road, but when they got inside she found that it fully came up to her expectations, and she gazed with reverence while he pointed out Dame Marie Tempest at one table, and Gladys Cooper at another, and famous writers and publishers by the handful all over the room. She came regretfully to the conclusion that famous writers looked and behaved just exactly like ordinary people. One day he took her to a literary cocktail party, and she met and talked to some of them; and when once she had stopped expecting them to look great she found they were very easy to get on with, and full of information as to how the books of all their famous friends were selling.

'Oh, Tim, they are funny,' said Vivien, after a middle-aged gentleman had been explaining to her for five minutes why poor Something-or-other's books did not sell as they used to.

'Funny, indeed. It 's easy to see you 're not a writer yet, or you 'd be much more respectful! But you see how easy it would be to pick up information.'

'Yes, indeed. It simply rushes at one.' Vivien gazed round at the crowded room, at the groups of people talking vigorously together, and the solitary ones, glass or cigarette in hand, who were prowling around looking whom they might pounce on next for a little neighbourly talk.

'Do you suspect any one here?' inquired Tim, watching her.

'Oh, all of them. They all look either so lean and discreet that one feels sure they must have something to hide, or so fat and cheerful that one can't help suspecting them of some secret plot.'

'Would you suspect me, if you didn't know who I was?'

'Oh, yes, instantly. Lean and discreet. But really, Tim, I don't see how you 're ever going to find any thing out—not at this sort of place, at any rate.'

'No—we 're only amusing ourselves,' answered Tim frankly. 'Though I must say one never knows where a clue may pop up. But we and several other firms are sitting like spiders in a web, just longing for someone to come and offer us a nice new idea, or a series that sounds a little too good to be true. That 's really the only thing we can do—wait and look out. But we might as well entertain ourselves in the meantime!'

Whether they entertained themselves or not, Tim Broadstreet and Broadstreet's in general certainly entertained Vivien. She was, though she did not know it, looking a very different creature from the rather frightened young person who had arrived with her family at that dingy hotel in South Kensington. It was not so much that she had settled down, though having the flat and being settled in it certainly made an immense difference. It was more that there was always some thing to look forward to, expected or unexpected; one woke up in the mornings, not nervous of London, but waiting with real interest for whatever the day might bring.

John put her thoughts into words much better than she could.

'It is much more fun being in London than I ever thought it would be,' he said one day when they were all three dangling their legs in a row on the sitting-room table, trying to get a draught from the open window. 'It 's not as *nice* as Berrings, but it 's more interesting, because there are always a lot of queer people, and nobody bothers us, and yet there 's always plenty going on for us to watch. I never thought we could have such a good time now we haven't much money any more.'

'Well, I could do with more money, if you couldn't,' said Dinah. 'But I think you 're quite right. London 's like a free play, going on all the time. Even Aunt Harrison 's

231

like something out of a play. Do you know, I know now almost exactly what she 's going to say to every single remark I or any one else makes to her. I bet myself on them, and I 'm always right.'

'I can't think how it is you haven't come to blows with Aunt Harrison long ago,' said Vivien candidly. 'You 're not her kind at all—even less than we are.'

'Oh, aren't I? You ought to see. I just get into the play too,' said Dinah with obvious relish. 'If she wants a sweet little girl for her visitors, clever but shy, then I 'm that. If she wants a rather overworked one, working too hard at her music, then I 'm that, and she brings me up hot milk herself when I 'm in bed. And just now and again I burst out, and say something a bit rude, and I 'm not sure she doesn't like that best of all, though of course she pretends not to.

'Dinah, you are the limit. You 'll come to a horrible end.'

'Oh, no, I shan't. I 'll simply get what I want,' answered Dinah, so calmly that both John and Vivien turned and stared at her. 'People do, if they want things hard enough. I want to be famous.'

It said a lot for Dinah that John did not instantly utter some impolite retort. He sat swinging his legs, and thinking, and at last said nothing more devastating than 'Well, I want to get cool.'

'Let 's go out, then. It ought to be cooler up at Hampstead.'

Dinah and John had both broken up, and they were making full use of their freedom and of all that London had to offer in the way of entertainment. Dinah was to practise three times a week, but otherwise she was having a well-earned rest. Mr Farthing was so much better that he did not at all mind being left for lunch or tea, or both, and Vivien and Dinah and John made a number of most satisfactory expeditions to such places as Richmond, Kew, Hampstead, and nearer home to Billingsgate, Southwark, and the Tower of London. Holidays were in the air. Mr Blueley had gone with his wife and three children to Margate. Aunt Harrison had gone to Buxton. Tim Broadstreet had gone away now, leaving a terrible blank in Vivien's everyday life. There was nothing to do but get out as often as possible.

But after a time Dinah and John began to grow restive. The flat was small, London was cramped and stuffy. They began to quarrel a little. They needed fresh air and room to spread themselves. London ceased to amuse them, and the entire Farthing family was much relieved when the time came for them in their turn to go down and stay at High Melvin with Aunt Rosamund and Uncle Charles.

Their holiday was an immense success. Hugh and Bridget were of course at home, and the two Farthings so ardently enjoyed running wild with them and with the family from High Melvin rectory that Mrs Farthing was persuaded to let their fortnight lengthen into three weeks, and then into a month. When they at last came back, brown and muscular and so full of vigour that the flat would hardly hold them, it was September, and school was not far away. Mr Farthing had twice been out for a walk, Sir William said he could go for his holiday, and when he came back again he would almost certainly be well enough to work.

CHAPTER IV

THE VILLAINS RETURN

THE fine weather held for many weeks, but autumn came early; the dry brown leaves began to fall from the planes and the chestnuts, and there was a cold tang in the air in the early morning and evening. Mr and Mrs Farthing went down to the ever-hospitable White House, and enjoyed High Melvin as much as the rest of the family had. Hardly had they gone than it was time to get Dinah ready to go back to Aunt Harrison's and school— a performance to which she submitted so mildly that Vivien felt perfectly certain some mischief or other was brewing. Soon after she had gone John went also, and Vivien found herself with an empty flat and the whole day to herself. All she had to do was to get breakfast for John, and a good meal for him to come back to in the evenings. Otherwise, for the first time since they had come to London, she could really do what she liked.

Delighted with this sudden freedom, she wandered about, revisiting the places she liked best in the City, shop-gazing up in the West End, sitting sometimes for hours on end in Hyde Park or St James's Park with a book which she did or did not read. She watched the crowds of tourists, now slightly fewer, being taken round the biggest city in the world and making remarks about it. She watched the office workers coming to and from their work, the less important ones arriving early and leaving late, the grander ones arriving comfortably late and leaving early. She watched small children playing around their prams and staggering with squeals among the trees.

She watched gulls and ducks, and grubby-looking sheep grazing among the deck-chairs, and dogs being taken for walks, and people riding. She got to know London in more and more of its aspects, and the more she knew of it the more there was still to find out.

Now and again, while she was sitting at home waiting for something to boil, or bake, or stew itself, she tried her hand at writing some of it down. Her interest in fair men with piercing blue eyes had somehow dwindled steadily, and the novel lay where it had been for weeks past, under a pile of handkerchiefs in her drawer. She was making her first attempts to write about life as she really saw it, and difficult, even exasperating, though it often was, it was fascinating work. But after a few days of this agreeable existence she began to feel that some thing was lacking. She missed her parents, all the time—the sitting-room without her father in it seemed positively unnatural. But it was not only that, and after a little while more she had to admit that it was Tim, and the fun of being with Tim and the fun of going to Broadstreet's, that she was missing so badly.

It was better at the week-end, when John was at home and comparatively free from homework. On their first Saturday evening alone they went up to Piccadilly Circus to the cinema, and after a very satisfactory laugh at a Walt Disney film and the new Gary Cooper went into a big Lyons and had orange squash and sandwiches. And on the Sunday, having got up late and done no more than the bare minimum of housework, they decided to make some sweets.

They had never made sweets before, all their energies having gone to more serious matters; but it seemed just the thing to do at this particular moment, and they were so well provided with cookery books and equipment that they felt pretty sure they could produce something eatable.

'Let 's make some fudge,' said John, after serious study of the books.

'All right—if you do the beating. And we might do some peppermint creams as well.'

They set to work, and very soon the kitchen was in the familiar state of tidy muddle which meant that some thing important was being made. There were newspapers on the floor, and basins and plates standing everywhere with weighed-out quantities of the sugar and butter and other things that they were going to use. John rolled his sleeves up more tightly, Vivien lit the gas, and the fun began.

Everything went well, though beating fudge was such hard work that John said it was a very good thing he was in training. They had almost finished, and were still feeling so energetic that they talked of making a cake, when they heard footsteps coming up the stone staircase.

'There 's someone coming up,' said Vivien. 'I wonder who it could be.'

'It 's not Mr Jones—it 's too heavy. Perhaps it 's the Nilpils.'

'No, it isn't. They 're up in their room—I 've heard them. It might be a visitor for them.'

'Well, if it is,' said John, 'it 's the first visitor they 've had since we came to live here. Much more likely it 's somebody for us, bother them.'

'For us? Yes, but oh, I wonder if it might be!' Struck by a sudden hope, Vivien dusted her wet and sugary hands on her apron, and rushed to the door.

'Oh, it is—it is! Hullo! Hullo, Tim!'

'Hurray, Vivien—I 'm so glad to find you. How are you? How 's everything?'

They were so pleased to see each other that it seemed the most natural thing in the world to kiss each other. Not lingering on the landing, Vivien pulled Tim past her into the daylight of the kitchen, where they stood nodding cheerfully and seeming extremely well pleased with life. John, looking up from his beating to give Tim a friendly nod, noted distinct signs of sugar on his coat-collar, but being a nice boy at heart said nothing about it.

'What are you making?' inquired Tim, looking rather more at Vivien than at the work in progress. 'Vivien, you 're looking grand.'

'So are you, Tim. You——'

'We 're making fudge,' said John firmly. 'And you 're the very person we need. Would you like to beat this a bit?'

'All right—certainly.'

Tim took over the basin and began to beat, finding it much harder work than he had expected. It was not too hard for him to talk, however, and while he worked he asked for news of all the family, and of all that had happened since he went away.

'That 's grand about your father,' he said. 'I am so glad.'

'What about you, though? Have you had a good time?'

'Oh, wonderful. In a little boat, sailing round among the islands, seeing the most lovely places in the world. It rained every day except two, but that didn't matter. I went up a couple of pretty good mountains, too. I 'll tell you all about it some time. But, Vivien—things have been happening round the corner since I went away.'

'What? At Broadstreet's do you mean?'

'Yes, and elsewhere too, I dare say. The trade department reports that for months they 've been giving out books to a messenger who said he came from one of the big literary agents. He'd got their card all right, with a note scribbled on it, and his stories were always quite natural ones. He wanted a copy of so-and-so to show a film man, or three copies of something else for the author to take home with him to the country, or something of the sort. The books were charged to the authors' accounts, of course, and nobody worried any more.'

Tim had quite forgotten the beating, but neither Vivien nor John noticed.

'Go on,' said John eagerly, when he paused for a moment.

'His last haul was six copies of Headley Paris's new novel—you know the thing, Vivien. He said something to the effect that Mr Paris was just off on a cruise and wanted to autograph them before he left. Well, that was true enough—Paris did go on a cruise. But he left two days before the boat was officially scheduled to start, as he was going overland and only picking it up at Marseilles. Miss Ramsay happened to hear about the books, and of course she never misses anything. She rang up the agents at once. They'd never asked for six copies of his book for Mr Paris. They'd never asked us for any books since the end of last year.'

'Oh, how thrilling!'

Vivien and John were delighted. They could not pretend to be anything else, though they tried to look a little sorry for Messrs Broadstreet.

'And isn't there any trace of the messenger?'

'Not the slightest. The people at the trade counter can't even agree what he looked like, he was so ordinary. There's a hope—a faint hope—that he may come back again, as he very likely doesn't know we've found him out. But he's the Enemy all right, or one of the Enemy's underlings.'

'Oh, we must find out who they are. We really must—though I don't see how on earth we 're going to begin!'

'Nor do I,' said Tim soberly. 'Chaps who keep vanishing like this, and who know the trade so intimately that they 're up to every possible dodge—they 're not easy to lay hands on. But I will lay hands on them, all the same. I swear I will. I won't—I won't have any Christmas dinner next Christmas unless I 've found out who they are, the nasty little bounders.'

'Grand,' said John approvingly. 'We 'll help you. And we 'll say the same, won't we, Vivien. I don't much like plum pudding, anyway. That reminds me, Tim, you might get on with that beating. The stuff will get hard if you don't.'

'All right,' answered Tim, obediently taking up his spoon again. 'Death to all villains, and hurray for the Farthing family's cooking.'

'I wish we could really help you,' said Vivien, knowing enough about things to realize how unlikely it was.

'You help me by being yourself,' said Tim in a low voice. 'And if there 's any sleuthing to do, or anything like that, you 're the very first people we should ask. Come on, now—give me something to turn this out on to. I can't beat it any more. It 's finished.'

CHAPTER V

BOOK WEEK AHEAD

'Do I look like a City gent?' inquired Mr Farthing, turning slowly round for Vivien to admire.

'Yes, absolutely. I never saw anything so dignified in all my life. And that 's exactly the right kind of tie.'

'That was Dinah—she wouldn't let me have the one I wanted. Said it was too spotty.' Mr Farthing picked up a brand new bowler hat and a neatly rolled umbrella. 'Well, darling, I must go. Good-bye till this evening.'

Another moment, and he was gone, walking once more with the upright, soldierly carriage that Vivien had almost forgotten. The Farthing family was in the middle of yet another change—a change which, if things went well, would bring them yet further back towards normal conditions again. Mr Farthing was going out to work. And if he found that work was not too much for him, and was able to go on with it, then Mrs Farthing could leave Greencoat's and come back and look after them all again, and perhaps, perhaps—though this was looking very far ahead—they would leave the flat and go somewhere further out, where they could have a garden.

That Mr Farthing had a job to go to at all they owed, Vivien knew, to his cousin from Berrings. Cousin Raymond had an interest of some sort in a big firm for property management with offices in Chancery Lane, and he had said from the beginning that if Mr Farthing would go there for a time on trial he would help him to buy a partnership. The trial period had now to be six months, as there was always the danger that his health would break down again; but to have work to go to, in these difficult days when so many could not find work anywhere, was such good fortune that the Farthings hardly dated to believe it.

Pottering around at her housework that morning, Vivien paused a good many times to wonder how her father was getting on, and whether this really was the beginning of more settled times, and what she herself would do if times did become more settled; but she did not pause too long, all the same, for she was going out to lunch with Tim. It was late in September now. His visit to New York was beginning at the end of the week, and that meant that she would not see him again for at least a month He had to be back, however, for the big Autumn Book Fair Week—and it was to talk about that, he said, that he specially wanted to see Vivien to-day.

'At least I specially want to see you anyway, and any time,' he had corrected himself. 'But that 's to-day's good reason, you see.'

She was ready punctually, dressed in a fine new navy blue coat and slightly daring hat which Messrs Greencoat's had provided and Messrs Broadstreet's cheques had paid for. She went down in the lift with Mr Jones, and out into St Paul's Churchyard, and round to Magnificat Alley. The City was beginning to look like its normal self, its winter self, again now. The brief relaxation of hot weather and sunshine and holiday tan was over. Overcoats were beginning to appear, and sensible mackintoshes, and new winter clothes, and the light, on five days out of six, was the cool, grey, slightly foggy light which made the City look as if it and all who worked in it had really begun to settle down for the winter.

Arriving at Broadstreet's, Vivien went up the steps,

expecting to find Miss Ramsay alone in the showroom as usual; but Tim was with her, and they were both brooding over a large blue plan on her desk.

'Come and look at this,' said Tim. 'It 's a plan of the Fair. It 's a huge affair this year. We 're looking where Broadstreet's stand is.'

'We 've got a very good place, I think,' said Miss Ramsay in her pleasant, competent-sounding voice. 'Plenty of people passing by, and a cash desk just beside us.'

'Miss Ramsay 's running our share of things this year. She 's coming to lunch with us to-day so that we can get as much as possible settled.'

Vivien was not perfectly sure if she was pleased to hear that Miss Ramsay was coming too. However, when they were all three settled in the quiet little Soho restaurant Tim had selected as being good but out of the way, she had to admit that Miss Ramsay was a very good addition to the party.

'I thought this was a safe place to come to,' said Tim, looking up and down the long menu card with a practised eye. 'If we went to the Ivy or one of those places, we should certainly have a publisher at the next table, and I don't want any one else to hear all the bright ideas we have for our stand.'

'What do you do at your stand?' inquired Vivien. Ordinary publishing talk she was now beginning to understand, but all this was something quite new. 'Show Broadstreet's books?'

'Show them and sell them! We reckon to make our expenses at the very least. Book Fair Week is mostly a vast co-operative affair—publishers, booksellers, newspapers, libraries, and so on all getting together to make the public think of nothing but books for at any rate one week in the year. They are really managing it, too. Last year's was a huge affair, almost like the Motor Show, and there 's no doubt that people have got the habit now, and even more of them will come this year. My uncle 's on the Joint Committee, and Blueley 's on another, and Day on another—we 're doing our bit. But all the publishers have their own private stands too, to make a little splash on their own, and of course every one wants to make theirs better than anybody else's. And that 's where you come in.'

'Me?' Vivien was startled.

'Yes. We 've decoyed you with a literary lunch, you see, in quite the proper manner! Could you possibly manage to come and help at our stand?'

'Oh! … Er. . . Thank you very much, Tim. I...' She hesitated. Tim and Miss Ramsay both failed to understand why.

'Of course we 'd offer you a salary, you know.'

'Yes—I mean thank you. But I rather—well, you know, after all the things they said about me, I don't awfully want to be with them very much. The people in Broadstreet's, I mean. Miss Haddon, and the others.'

'Oh.' Miss Ramsay saw her point the instant she had spoken. 'Yes, that is rather difficult. But one thing about coming would be that they 'd get to know you better, and you them, and I really think you 'd find you got on with them quite well. They 're all a decent lot. A bit gossipy and a bit jealous, if they get half a chance to be, but aren't we all?'

'Vivien, darling,' said Tim in the kind of voice that was quite irresistible 'do do it! We 'd be lost without you, honestly. Last year we took girls from the office the whole time, and they loved it, of course, but it meant our everyday work went completely to pieces. They 'll hardly be there at all this year—if you come, that is. Only very

243

occasionally. Miss Ramsay would take the lion's share, and you 'd help her say for half the time...Think what fun it would be, finding out how to sell books to people!'

He did not need to say any more. Vivien agreed at once to come, and the rest of the lunch was spent very pleasantly by them all in discussing the various books they hoped to sell well, the way they should be arranged, and the innumerable technical details which had to be considered by even so small a part of Book Fair Week as a single publisher's stand. A hundred or more of these stands, side-shows too many to count, displays and advertisements all over London, lectures, plays, competitions—Vivien heard of more new aspects of Book Fair Week every minute, and very soon she was so much excited by it all that she quite forgot she had ever imagined that she did not want to take part.

Mr Farthing arrived home just before six that evening, tired but content with life. His first day had gone well, and exhausting though he had found it, he felt certain that he had got work he would enjoy.

'I can't tell you how good it is to be getting a grip on something again, after all these months,' he said when, his elegant City jacket thrown off, he lay stretched out in a dressing-gown on the sofa, resting his back. 'When I 'd dealt with a big rent problem, and really found out how it went, I felt better than if I 'd just had a big glass of champagne!'

They bad a particularly good evening that evening, talking about Mr Farthing's new office and about Vivien's job at the Book Fair. John wanted to know a number of precise details about it which she had of course either forgotten or never known.

'How many people went to it last year?'

'I don't know—thousands and thousands,' said Vivien hopefully.

'Of course they did, if it was at that huge place in Earl's Court. Do you know how much space in it they 're having?'

'I haven't the slightest idea. It 's the place Dinah can see from her window at Aunt Harrison's, isn't it? The one she calls Mount Earl's Court. That reminds me, I rather thought she was going to ring up this evening and ask how Daddy got on.'

'Why not go down and ring her up yourself? I 'm sure she 'd be glad to know.'

'All right—I might.' Vivien was feeling so pleased with life that she did not even mind disturbing her comfortable after-dinner laze. 'Give me twopence for Mrs Jones.'

'She 'll only let you pay a penny. She says she won't cheat her friends.'

'Mrs Jones wouldn't cheat a fly,' said Mr Farthing, getting badly tied up with his dressing-gown as he fished in his pockets for the money. 'Give her my love.'

Out on the landing, Vivien heard a quite unusual amount of activity going on upstairs in the Nilpils' direction—a tap running, the clatter of tin utensils, and somebody pulling furniture about. She did not think much about it, though, but ran down to the Joneses' rooms, knocked, gave her father's message and the news of the day, and dialled her Aunt Harrison's number.

Wheeler answered, as always, and when she heard his deep, solemn tones she asked if she might speak to her sister.

'Miss Dinah, miss? Has she left you, then?'

'Left us, did you say?' Vivien thought she must have misheard.

'Yes, miss. Like she always does on Mondays, and the other days too, when you want her. We never expect her home before nine at the earliest.'

'Wait a minute, Wheeler.' Vivien clung on to the receiver, thinking desperately. 'She always does, do you say?'

'So I have been informed, miss.'

'But—but—she doesn't. We never see her except at the week-ends.'

There was a pause. Vivien did not know what to say, and Wheeler appeared to be meditating.

'Look 'ere, Miss Vivien.' His voice was suddenly quite human. 'Don't you worry. She 's turned up safe every time so far, and she will to-night. Miss Dinah knows how to look after herself.'

'Yes, that 's true enough,' said Vivien, a little comforted.

'The important thing,' Wheeler went on, 'will be, if I may give an opinion, miss, not to say anything to Mrs Harrison.'

'Oh, *yes*. Can you see to that? Don't say I rang up, of course'

'No, I won't.'

'What shall I say this end, do you think? I don't want to worry my parents?'

'Misinform them, Miss Vivien,' said Wheeler without a moment's hesitation. 'There are times when misinforming people saves them a great deal of unnecessary disturbance. And if you hear no more from here in the morning, you may be perfectly at ease that all is in order again.'

His voice sounding guarded, as if one of the maids had come in as he spoke, Wheeler bade her a solemn good-bye, and they rang off.

Vivien was very thoughtful as she hung up, and more

than a little worried. She had to tell the Joneses what was happening, as they had already heard the greater part of it from her answers to Wheeler, and they reassured her by at once saying, as Wheeler had said, that Dinah was well able to look after herself.

'And I really wouldn't say anything to your parents to-night, dear,' said Mrs Jones, sitting very upright with the *Evening News* in her hand. 'Not with your father newly gone to business, and all.'

'Yes, but if anything *has* gone wrong——'

'If she isn't home by her usual time, then your great-aunt will be told at once, won't she? There can't be any risk, especially now that Mr Wheeler knows.'

Taking their advice, Vivien said nothing when she got upstairs except that she had given the news and that Dinah had been fine. Nobody seemed to notice any thing wrong in the way she spoke, and the subject was dropped at once, as the family was in animated discussion as to what plans they would think of making for the future if events so turned out that they *could* make plans.

'We 're not being rash, you see,' said Mrs Farthing, looking happier and younger than Vivien had seen her for a long time. 'We 're only saying that if Daddy gets on so well that we can begin to think of it we should like to have a place where the soil would be good for roses, and enough ground to grow our own vegetables.'

'And all the principal rooms facing south,' put in Mr Farthing. 'In fact I 'm in rather a fix, because the house I 'm planning has to have every room facing south except the bathroom.'

'And the larder,' said John, who was taking it all very seriously.

'Well, yes, the larder too. But even so it isn't very practicable. I must think again.'

CHAPTER VI

MIDNIGHT EXCURSION

VIVIEN could not sleep. She kept on assuring herself that she was not really worried about Dinah, but all the same it would have been a great relief to know, or even to be able to imagine, what she was up to. That it was something to do with her music one could be fairly certain. But without money, without any musical friends who could be helping her, what could she do that would keep her busy night after night like this?

Vivien turned over restlessly, and punched her pillow into a different shape. Pillows were the most maddening things—always flat when one wanted them humpy, or developing a crease that tickled one's cheek just when one thought one had properly settled down. In the adjoining room John snored the placid snores of one who had scored a goal in the last second eleven match and had not a care in the world. Envying him heartily, Vivien turned over again and went on worrying about Dinah. If what Dinah was doing were anything which she could in the slightest degree be proud of, the family would have heard every detail of it long ago. Dinah was not in the habit of keeping her triumphs and excitements to herself....

What was that?

Vivien sat up suddenly in bed, her blood tingling. She had heard something—something moving. Surely she had not been mistaken. She listened, not daring to breathe. Yes—there it was again. Someone was moving about.

After a moment that seemed to go on for ever, Vivien

slid down to the foot of her bed. Her door was ajar, and by leaning forward she could see through John's room to the door which led into the passage. The darkness seemed as thick as cloth; but even as she watched she saw the farther door suddenly leap into its place, outlined by a thin, bright streak of yellow light. Someone had switched on the light in the corridor.

Half curious, half apprehensive, Vivien put one foot out of bed and felt about for her slippers. It might be something to do with Dinah. It might be that Mr Farthing was not well. Whatever it was, it was hardly likely to be burglars, if they switched on the light like that. She must go quickly and see.

John did not stir as she crept past him, and in a moment she was opening the door. The light outside blinded her for the first few seconds: then she saw a thin figure in a dressing-gown standing just at the turn by the lift. It was one of the Wilkinses.

Vivien gave a little sniff, that might have been anger or might have been relief, and was just about to go back again. But he had seen her.

'Oh—please,' he said. 'Just a moment. I am so glad somebody's come.'

'Is there anything wrong?' Vivien paused with her hand on the door-knob.

'Yes, there is. My brother's ill. He's got a fever or something. I wondered——'

He looked somehow rather pathetic, standing there in a dressing-gown which was much too short for him, his gingery hair on end. He was Pete, Vivien decided: the tidy one.

'Do you want any help?' she inquired, still a little unwillingly.

'Would you really come? That would be kind. I can't

get him settled at all, and I think his temperature 's pretty high.'

'Yes, I 'll come, certainly. Just wait while I get a thermometer.'

She crept into the sitting-room, and took the family thermometer from the sideboard drawer, adding also, after thought, a bottle of aspirin, which she put in her dressing-gown pocket. She went out again to Pete Wilkins, and together they went up the stairs.

Roger Wilkins certainly had a high fever. Vivien could see that the moment she caught sight of his flushed cheeks and bright eyes, and the restless way he kicked and muttered in the bed. He said 'Go away,' feebly when she arrived, but clearly had not the least idea who she was, and allowed her without more protest to put the thermometer under his arm and hold it there—she did not dare to put it in his mouth.

'Count a minute, please,' she said to Pete. 'Have you a watch?'

Pete had no watch, it appeared, and there was not a clock of any kind in the place. However, they guessed the time, and when she read the thermometer Vivian felt they had left it in fully long enough, for it had gone up to 104°.

'Yes, he has got a high temperature,' she said. 'Wouldn't you like to get a doctor?'

'Oh, no, no. There 's not the slightest need,' said Pete instantly sounding almost alarmed. 'He 's sure to be better in the morning. He 's done this sort of thing before, once or twice.'

Vivien wondered briefly how it was that, if he was worried enough to come down for help, he was not worried enough to have a doctor. However, she said no more, but set to work to make the invalid comparatively comfortable. Pete, under her direction, helped to pull the sheets straight and get the blankets more or less in order. It was by no means warm in the room, and Roger's feet were as cold as his head was hot.

'Can you boil a kettle up here?'

'Oh, yes. There 's a ring. There 's a kettle too, somewhere.'

'Good. Then we 'd better give him a hot-water bottle. I 'll fetch mine. Will you put some water on? Then if he has two aspirin, or perhaps even three, I think that 'll be about the best we can do for him.'

The water was not yet hot when she came back with her hot-water bottle, and as she stood over the ring beside the broken-toothed gas-fire Vivien gazed round her with great curiosity, taking in as many details as she could without letting Pete notice her interest. The room was not much more inspiring than it had looked that time when she and John got a glimpse of it. It was small and narrow, with a sloping roof, and the two divans, the centre table, two chairs, and a big cupboard were almost all the furniture. There was a tiny cubby-hole at the farther end, in which she could see suit-cases and an old tennis racket without a press, but otherwise this appeared to be all the room they had. The gramophone stood just under the window, and there were no books to be seen except a novel spread-eagled on the floor beside Roger's bed, and a row on the mantelpiece just in front of her.

Waiting for the water to warm up, Vivien bent down and gazed at their titles. To her astonishment, she saw that they were a collection of uniform works, their binding as much out of date as their titles, which had been best-sellers in 1910 or thereabouts.

'Good gracious!' she said. 'Maria Higgins Wiltshire—I thought I recognized them, somehow.'

'Do you know them?' inquired Pete, who was standing by the table.

'Oh, yes. My mother had them all once. She used to read and read them when she was young. So did I,' said Vivian maturely. '*My Lady Nine o'Clock*, and all the rest of them. You must have almost the whole lot.'

'Yes, we have. As a matter of fact,' said Pete, as if he imparted the information unwillingly, 'Maria Wiltshire is my mother.'

If he had said Shakespeare was his father Vivien could hardly have been more surprised.

'Your mother?' Vivien bent down to turn off the gas, and took up the kettle and her bottle from the table. 'I—I thought she was dead. That is——'

'Oh, no, she's not dead. She's an invalid, and doesn't go about at all. She lives down in the country.'

Vivien studied the Wilkinses with quite a new interest as she gave Roger the hot-water bottle, dissolved his aspirin in water, and generally did all she could to finish putting him straight. It seemed incredible that these two thin, unagreeable, hard-looking youths could be the sons of Maria Wiltshire. Maria Wiltshire's tales were about young love, and moonlight, and sad little misunderstandings at picnic parties. She could not imagine the Wilkinses being romantic in moonlight, or on any other occasion for that matter.

'There,' she said. 'Now when the aspirin begins to work, don't on any account let him come out of the covers. He ll get terribly hot and damp, but it's the best way to bring his temperature down. He could have a sponge-down when he's really finished sweating, if you thought so. You don't want me any more now, do you?'

'Er—no. No, thank you.'

'Come down again if you want me,' said Vivien, going

to the door. 'I 'll come up to-morrow before breakfast, if you like, just to see how you 're getting on.'

Vivien slept like a log after her unexpected excursion, and woke full of charitable thoughts about the Nilpils. They really were rather nice, after all—nice and pathetic and unpractical. As soon as she was dressed she went out past the still sleeping John to go up and heat how Roger was getting on.

Their door was shut, and when she knocked she heard one of them mutter something to the other before it was opened. Then Pete came out. He did not smile, and he shut the door at once.

'Good morning,' he said. 'Thank you for your help last night. My brother is better this morning.'

'Oh, I 'm so glad. Is his temperature down? Did he sleep?'

'He is quite well, thank you.'

'Is there anything I can do for you?' Vivien's voice was a little doubtful. There was no mistaking the hostility in Pete Wilkins's replies. He spoke as if she were a tiresome stranger.

'No, nothing at all. Absolutely nothing.'

Nothing except go away, he was plainly implying. With a sudden rush of anger Vivien turned on her heel, and went straight downstairs again. To demand one's help at midnight, and be rude at eight the next morning...If the Nilpils were jobless and starving, then in her opinion they deserved all they got, and she almost hoped they would soon be obliged to go home to their mother, whom she felt convinced they did not like at all.

CHAPTER VII

MUSIC IN BADGER'S MEWS

POLICE-CONSTABLE NICHOL was a little bored. Kensington was, in his opinion, a dull district, and this was one of the dullest beats in it. It was almost impossible to make an arrest. Nothing more dramatic happened than an occasional car left without lights: and how was an ambitious young police officer to get on if he could not find any one to arrest?

He strolled on a little further, brooding on the injustice of fate, and turning a corner came to the narrow entrance of Badger's Mews. He knew Badger's Mews well. Nothing ever happened there either. It was inhabited by chauffeurs and their wives and families, quiet, law-abiding people who never even left a car without lights and whose lives were regulated by the wealthy people for whom they drove the big green and maroon and black cars housed in the garages underneath their tiny flats.

Someone in the mews seemed to have a wireless on, and Police-Constable Nichol, who was interested in music, paused at the corner to listen. It was a change from walking, anyway. It was a tune he knew—a funny little bit of Mozart—and he had just reflected how strange it was he should hear such a thing instead of the usual dance tunes, when he realized that it was not the wireless he was hearing at all. Someone was playing the fiddle.

He strolled a step or two down the mews, till he came to a curve in the entry. From there he could see the whole mews spread out before him; and the sight he now saw was so unexpected that Police-Constable Nichol stopped dead in his tracks.

The mews was busy. Two men had their big cars out, one of them exploring inside the bonnet, and the other one polishing with the careful energy of someone to whom the least speck of mud is an everlasting disgrace. Women were moving about on the wooden balcony that ran past all their front doors, resting after washing up their family's high tea. In one of the empty garages children were dancing, swinging and scampering about in time to the music. Even in the semi-darkness the whole scene was as clear as if it were daylight, for the car-polisher had turned on his lights, and they picked out the moving figures with the unreal vividness of a dream. And there was one figure especially, the centre of everything, whom they lit up so sharply that Police-Constable Nichol could see the expression on her face and the vivid grace with which she was playing.

She was quite a small girl, with red hair. Absorbed though she was in her playing, she was none the less well aware of everything that was going on around her, and he heard her, when her tune came to its end, call out 'Bill, twist those lights round—they 're too bright,' before beginning another tune for the scampering children. And she played extremely well. Police-Constable Nichol's own instrument was the clarinet, but he had heard enough good violin playing in his home to recognize it again when he met it, and this child had great talent, if not even something more.

He stood and watched and listened, quite forgetting his boredom, until the new tune also came to an end. There was a murmur of applause from the listeners in the mews, and the children clapped. No one seemed in the least surprised at her playing, though, and Police-

Constable Nichol concluded that she must belong to one of the families who lived there.

'Dinah, are you coming up again?'

One of the women leaned over the balcony railing. The girl looked up.

'No, thank you, Mrs Patterson. I said I 'd be back early.'

She ran up the wooden staircase, however, fiddle in hand, and a few moments later reappeared with a coat on, a hat—a black school hat with a striped band round round it—in one hand, and her fiddle in its case in the other. She went up to the big car, standing in shadow behind its own lights.

'Bill, dear, you owe me my money.'

There was a grunt, and a chuckle, and the clink of coins passing from hand to hand. Then the girl Dinah came round the car, and amid shouts of good-bye from every side began to walk up to the entrance of the mews.

Police-Constable Nichol was by now more interested than ever, and in his professional capacity. This girl did not belong to the mews. She lived somewhere else, she came there to play or for some such reason, and she was taking money. This was decidedly a matter he would have to look into. He faded neatly into the deep shadows while Dinah came out.

Dinah, walking contentedly back to her great-aunt's house with two new half-crowns in her pocket, became suddenly aware that someone was coming up behind her. She slowed down for a moment, hoping that the footsteps she heard would overtake her and go on. But they did not. They slowed down too. Dinah, turning quickly before she gave herself the chance to get frightened found herself looking straight at the bright brass buttons of a policeman's uniform.

'Oh!'

'Just a minute, please. I think you and I must have a bit of a talk.'

She thought of running, but it would not have worked. The policeman looked much too young and energetic, and then also, he might have blown his whistle. Dinah shook her hair from her forehead, tried to say something, found that she could not, and waited.

'Will you tell me your name and address?'

Dinah blinked.

'Mary Jones, 24 Kensington High Street,' she said rapidly.

The policeman snorted.

'That 's no good,' he said. 'I heard them calling you Dinah. Try again, please.'

'Dinah Farthing, Overton House, St Paul's Churchyard.' Whatever happened, thought Dinah with a sick feeling in her stomach, Aunt Harrison must be kept out of it somehow.

But the policeman was getting impatient.

'Now really,' he said, 'is this the way to St Paul's Churchyard? You must tell me the truth. It 'll be much better for you, you know.'

'But I do live at St Paul's Churchyard. I really do. We have a flat there, on the fourth floor.'

'Well, what are you doing over here?'

'I 've been seeing some friends,' said Dinah doggedly.

'Yes, so I heard. And playing for them. You played that Mozart beautifully, by the way.'

His tone was so dry and official that Dinah could hardly believe she had heard him aright. She looked up at him, a glint of hope in her eyes, but his expression did not change.

'That 's a St Monan's hatband, I see. Are you a boarder there?'

'No. I—I——' Oh, well, there was no way of getting out of it. 'I stay with my great-aunt in Queen's Gate.'

'Very well.' The policeman nodded, as if to say that now he did begin to believe her. 'I 'll take you back there, and we 'll discuss this little matter of your playing to those friends of yours and getting money for it.'

'I didn't get money for playing.'

'Well, what did you get it for, then?'

'For teaching two children to play. And they 're so terrible that I really have earned it,' said Dinah with feeling.

They were too far from a lamp-post for her to see whether this remark had moved him. He walked on in silence for several yards, then said:

'You must come while I telephone, please. Queen's Gate is still in my beat, but I must report before I take you there. By the way, what did you want to earn money for?'

'For violin lessons with a new master.'

'What 's the matter with the one you have now?'

'Oh, if you could only see him . . .!'

The dark shape at Dinah's side gave a quickly suppressed chuckle.

'But I still don't understand. People who live in Queen's Gate don't have to go and earn money in a mews. Couldn't you just have asked——'

'*I* have to—I have to earn money,' said Dinah darkly. 'It 's the only possible way.'

'But why down there, of all places?'

'Because they 're friendly people, and make a noise. You can't imagine what it 's like, living in Queen's Gate.'

'Oh, can't I?' retorted the policeman. 'Indeed I can. I

258

was born there.'

In startled silence Dinah took in this information. But interesting though this strange policeman might be, she was for the moment considerably more interested in herself.

She gave an enormous sigh.

'One gets so repressed . . .' she murmured, as one sufferer to another.

'Repressed?' It was his turn to be startled now. 'Repressed, indeed? You? That's a good one, I must say.'

Police-Constable Nichol glanced sideways at the small, red-headed figure plodding along the pavement beside him. He choked, tried to control himself, then gave it up. In the dignified silence of a South Kensington evening, he began to laugh.

'My dear, good man,' said Aunt Harrison slowly, 'will you kindly repeat what you said.'

Police-Constable Nichol drew himself up to his full height, which was six feet one inch, and looked as offended as he was. Dinah, whom Aunt Harrison had reduced to tears, gave a hurried snivel and a quick blow, and looked up sideways in the sudden hope that she might be going to enjoy herself.

'I said that your niece——'

'My great-niece.'

'Your great-niece, then, had a quite remarkable talent, and that it would be sad if no better outlet could be found for it than playing to children in a mews.'

'It would indeed, constable. No member of my family has ever before done anything so outrageous, and you do not need my assurance that it shall never happen again.'

'Thanks,' said Police-Constable Nichol shortly. 'But it wasn't that that I meant. I meant that it seemed a pity she could not get the kind of lessons she was longing for.'

Aunt Harrison gave him an extremely cold stare. She was sitting very upright in her usual straight chair, one hand on the arm of it, her white hair piled up in its accustomed wig-like folds. Dinah wondered whether, in some queer sort of way, both she and the policeman were not enjoying themselves.

'When I require the Police Force to give me advice in such matters,' Aunt Harrison observed with cold sarcasm, 'I shall be happy to ask them for it.'

'Oh, yes.' Police-Constable Nichol smiled amiably at her. 'I 'm sure you will. But you see, at the moment I really believe that I *can* help you. I shouldn't have spoken about it otherwise.'

'Indeed? May we perhaps hear how?'

'Of course yes, certainly.' Police-Constable Nichol turned to Dinah, whose tears had stopped running in all this excitement, and had dried all down her cheeks. 'You 've heard of Sir Barthelmy Nichol?'

'Oh, goodness, yes—why, he 's the composer. The violin composer. I play some of his studies.'

'That 's the one. Well, you see,' said Police-Constable Nichol simply, 'he 's my father, and I don't see why, if I told him about you, he shouldn't take you on as one of his pupils.'

CHAPTER VIII

THE FUN BEGINS

'ISN'T that just what I told you, Vivien—people get what they want, if they only want it hard enough.'

'Oh,' said Vivien disbelievingly. 'I suppose you wanted to be nearly had up by a policeman? I suppose you wanted to get in a row with Aunt Harrison? I suppose you arranged it purposely that the policeman was the son of Sir Barthelmy Nichol? It sounds to me more like the most outrageous good luck.'

Dinah was at the very peak, the very maximum, of her triumph. Sir Barthelmy Nichol had agreed to take her as a pupil. He had been not only nice but also understanding about her playing, so that she felt at once that she could learn from him. His son Jack, looking completely unlike a policeman in his everyday clothes, had taken Dinah up to his big house in Regent's Park for the momentous interview; and Aunt Harrison was so startled by all these events that she had invited both Sir Barthelmy and his son to dinner, had allowed Dinah to sit up for it, and had actually made two jokes in the course of the evening.

'But of course it was luck.' Dinah swung her legs up on to the sitting-room table, and sat there hugging her knees. 'That's just what I meant. And if it hadn't happened that way, it would have happened some other way. I'm perfectly certain that people almost always get the kind of luck they want to get.'

'What about people who get bombed?' John looked up sceptically from the newspaper he was reading.

'Oh, I don't mean that. That 's wars and things,' said Dinah, who in spite of Air Raid Precautions and the gas masks and equipment which Mr Farthing appeared with now and again could only regard wars as a very far-away terror. 'I mean ordinary people not in wars, like us. If you want anything terribly, terribly badly, and do all you can towards getting it, then it turns up. That 's what I mean. I wouldn't have got to Sir Barthelmy if I 'd sat at Aunt Harrison's like a good girl doing my homework.'

'H'm,' said John, turning over from the bombing to read the day's comic strip.

'Well, would I? John, don't be so stupid. Just because you don't happen to want anything, except to get into the second eleven—and anyway, when you wanted that you didn't mind going to bed early before the trials. No, but look at Vivien, too. She likes old buildings and books— she gets to know people who like the same sort of thing, and now she 's practically got into a publishing firm, just because of that.'

'It sounds a pretty risky theory to me,' said Vivien, thinking it over.

'Risky but true. We don't *do* things on purpose—it just happens like that.' Her philosophy of life worked out, Dinah swung her legs off the table. 'John, have you finished that paper yet? I want to see the new one about Night Starvation.'

The great Book Fair Week was coming near very fast. Behind the scenes in the bookselling and publishing trades preparations for it had been going on for months. It was to be something bigger and more exciting than anything of the kind had been before, though it would of course be based on the experience of past years and have the same experts to run it. It was to be not only the huge

Book Fair at Earl's Court, with its innumerable stalls, side-shows, lectures, plays, and special exhibits. All the London booksellers were joining in, as well as nearly all the publishers, and in each of their shops there would be a display of books for the whole of Book Fair Week, with competitions so thrilling that they almost obliged everybody to take the next bus or tube train out to Earl's Court. There were Book Galas at many of the restaurants. Special Book Buses would be running from Piccadilly and Oxford Circus, with a book lent to each passenger to read during the drive: there was no end to the ideas which had been thought of to make Book Fair Week the most exciting show of the year.

Broadstreet's were as busy as everybody else, and Vivien very soon became so much caught up in the excitement that she had practically not a moment to spare for thinking of anything else. She just managed to remember to cook the family meals and keep the flat in order; but otherwise she spent every spare moment either round at Broadstreet's or brooding at home over some new document or catalogue or plan of campaign which had to be considered from every possible angle.

Many hours of her time were spent in Broadstreet's show-room, prowling around all the shelves, learning what every single book that Broadstreet's published looked like, and cost, and what it was about and what kind of readers it would be likely to appeal to. Miss Ramsay of course could tell her all that she wanted, and when Vivien got stuck she had only to go over to the desk where Miss Ramsay sat making neat lists on odd pieces of paper, and say to her, 'Here, what on earth is this one supposed to be about!'

'Don't worry—you'll do splendidly,' said Miss Ramsay one morning when Vivien began to sound a little desperate. 'If you don't know say so, and if you feel sure the person who asks you won't like it, say so too. It 's much the best way.'

'Is it really?' Vivien was not quite convinced. 'Mummy was giving me a few tips the other evening— she sells dresses, you know—and she said the two unbreakable rules were "Never say no" and "The customer is always right." '

'Ah, but that 's different. With dresses and such things I can quite see that 's the way to do it. But with books the only thing is to try and really help people. You ask any successful bookseller.'

'All right—that 's much easier, then,' said Vivien, relieved, and went back to her prowling at the shelves.

She liked being down here in the show-room with Miss Ramsay, but she now felt much less frightened about penetrating upstairs to the other departments. Tim was away in New York, and, sad though that was, it did in a way make it easier for her to face Miss Haddon and the others who—whether she had imagined it or not—had seemed at times to resent her presence. She met Mr Day, and was soon on waving terms with him out of their respective windows. She saw a good deal of the taciturn Mr Tyson, who was responsible for the various decorative notices and posters on the stall, and for planning its colour scheme, and she got to know young Mr Sackville, the blurb-writer, a frail-looking, fair young man who never stopped talking if once he got started, but who at the moment was in a perpetual state of groaning over a series of snappy Broadstreet slogans which were to help the sale of their books.

As for Mr Blueley, he was almost busier than any one, for he was on the committee which linked up the booksellers' activities with the Fair, and whenever Vivien saw him he was either just dashing out of his car to run up and consult old Mr Broadstreet about some new point, or dashing into it again to hurry off to a meeting.

The plans grew and took final shape, and at last the excitement about Book Fair Week began to spread from the inner, professional world to the world at large. Posters appeared in the tubes, on hoardings, on buses and trams. There were advertisements every day in the newspapers, leaflets in the shops, intriguing letters arriving by post every morning in thousands of households. People were talking about it everywhere, and there seemed no doubt that it would be an overwhelming success.

Sooner than it seemed possible the day came when Messrs Broadstreet were instructed to go and prepare their stall. Vivien, Miss Ramsay, and Mr Tyson set off together, the packing-cases full of books having been sent by the firm's van the day before. The vast exhibition premises looked strangely empty and dead: there were a number of people hurrying around, officials like themselves, but in a place built for so many thousands of visitors they looked like the merest handful. Everything was queer and unfinished. Wooden framework stood where in twenty-four hours' time there would be brightly coloured stalls filled with books. Workmen were hammering, and in one part of the principal hall they were busy finishing off a pale lilac coat of paint on the walls. There were crates of books arriving every moment, carried up by sweating vanmen who dumped them thankfully down wherever they thought best. There were single, solitary-looking gold-painted chairs standing in the most unexpected places. People with large bundles of notes in their hands hurried from one hall to another, their foreheads wrinkled in anxiety. Vivien gathered from their scattered remarks that nothing was ready, nothing was ever likely to be ready, and when the Duke of Petersham arrived to declare Book Fair Week open all the entertainment he was likely to get was a cup of tea at the restaurant and a ride on the Book Token Roundabout.

It was incredibly difficult work to arrange the stand. Vivien had not expected it to be easy, but it was far harder than she had thought, and she began to understand why Miss Ramsay had darkly warned her not to promise to get home in time for dinner. They had drawn up a very careful plan of the whole stand in the office, marking just where every kind of book was to go; but when they found themselves confronted with their entire stock piled in untidy stacks on the floor, just as it had been taken out of the cases, it did not seem nearly so simple to begin arranging them.

'We 'd better turn them all right way up, so that we can read the titles, and then put them roughly in their places,' said Mr Tyson with a deep sigh. He worked very hard, as indeed they all did, but it was just as tedious as he had seemed to expect, and by the time they eased off for a quick lunch the stand looked in a far worse muddle than it had when they first arrived.

By five o'clock that evening the books were all in their places according to the plan they had made in the office. By a quarter past five they had unanimously decided that it would not do at all, as it gave them no possible method of keeping extra stock of every book near the section it belonged to. At half-past five old Mr Broadstreet arrived to see how they were getting on, regretfully agreed with them, and then and there took off his coat and set to work to help with the rearrangement of the entire stand. At a quarter to seven they were finished, and so tired they could hardly see or talk. The moment the last book was in place Mr Broadstreet gathered them all together in a fatherly way, put them into a taxi, took them to the Café Royal, gave them a good, quick dinner, and immediately after it sent them all off to their various homes, with no other ambitions in the world but to have a hot bath and a long night's sleep.

When Vivien got back to the exhibition at ten the next morning she could hardly recognize it. She had been much too tired the night before to take in the fact that other parts of the Book Fair besides Broadstreet's stand had been progressing, and now, as she showed her card of admission and got her first glimpse of it all, she was quite bewildered to think that this was the waste of scaffolding and dust-sheets and chairs she remembered from yesterday. The whole place was bright with colour, and full of life. There were posters, banners, pictures, signposts: the Fun Fair was being tried out by some very young assistants, who seemed to find it good: and everywhere, as far as the eye could see and beyond, there were books.

She walked slowly down through the publishers' stands, looking at them critically, delighted when she saw one that looked less well arranged than Broadstreet's, almost indignant when she saw one or two that were undeniably better. In front of Messrs Perryforth's she stood for at least a minute, studying their various prosperous-looking series and wondering which was the one that they, or the Enemy for them, had stolen from Broadstreet. She looked so forbidding that the young woman in charge there, who had come forward as if to talk to her, stopped abruptly and began in an uneasy way to arrange some catalogues. With a sniff of disapproval, Vivien walked on.

The Duke of Petersham would have something to open after all that afternoon, it seemed. One could see that everything was not yet ready. At every stand there were two or three people putting up last-minute displays or making some new arrangement, and assistants from the Magic Bookshop, the Houp-là, the Stop Me and Try One, and the various Book Rooms were continually running over to the stands to borrow some book that they had forgotten or inquire where some consignment had got to. But to the unprofessional eye the Fair looked finished enough, and Vivien realized that when it was crowded with visitors wandering down every aisle and into every room and display, the fact that a few books were out of line or that a shelf-ful did not correspond yet with the catalogue was hardly likely to be noticed by more than one person in a thousand.

She arrived at last at Broadstreet's to find Miss Ramsay in a brilliantly clean pink overall balancing a row of books up somewhere at the back while Mr Sackville stood about in a willing sort of way, meditating.

'How does it look?' inquired Miss Ramsay when she had greeted her.

'Lovely—really splendid. I am so glad we rearranged it.'

'Yes, so am I—though I 've redone a good deal of it again this morning, all the same. Look, Vivien, can you and Mr Sackville stand by here for the next half hour or so? I think I 'd better go and get tidy and have a cup of coffee, and then I can be here at twelve when the people begin to come. Mr Blueley said he 'd look in if he could, but there ought to be as many of us as possible all day to-day.'

'Of course,' said Vivien, taking off her things and stowing them under the stand. 'The official opening 's at three still, isn't it—the Duke and all that?'

'Yes, no change. Good-bye, then.'

There was nothing much left for Vivien and Mr Sackville to do. They stood gossiping and looking vaguely around for twenty minutes or so, and were very glad when Mr Blueley turned up, large and amiable, having been driving round on a last visit to the bookshops since nine o'clock that morning.

'Everything looks grand,' he said, joining them in front of the stand. 'This part of the Fair is in order, at any rate.'

'Why, isn't the rest of it?'

'The half-crown Book Room 's terrible, and some of the others too. Half their chaps are running about begging publishers for spares of everything they can give them. Haven't you had any here yet?'

'No, not yet. But isn't it because they changed the whole plan of it yesterday morning? They really haven't had time.'

'Oh, perhaps it is. By the way, Vivien, Mr Irvine 's back.'

'Oh, is he?' Vivien's face lit up. 'Is he coming here?'

'Yes, rather. He 's got at least six of our authors in tow, coming to hear the Duke, and he 's persuaded Headley Paris, and I think some of the others as well, to take part in the Author Hunt. We 're in for a lively afternoon, if you ask my opinion,' said Mr Blueley contentedly.

CHAPTER IX

FAST AND FURIOUS

THE loud-speakers hung in every corner of the Book Fair began to crackle and mutter. The crowds who were surging in at the turnstiles and down through the exhibition looked up at them apprehensively, as if afraid that at any moment they might hear the Duke give a preliminary cough. It was barely half-past two, and he was not due to arrive until a minute to three, but already the lecture theatre was full to the doors. Those who knew they could not get in to hear him in person were taking up their position in groups on the chairs beneath the loud-speakers, while those who considered that they ought to be able to get in pushed and exclaimed and argued with the two large janitors who refused to let them through the lecture theatre doors.

At every stand and exhibit which the Duke would pass on his way from the entrance the most exquisite order reigned. Not a book anywhere was out of place. Assistants and officials, elegant and prim, stood looking as if never in their lives had they done anything so undignified as stagger about in old clothes with large stacks of unsorted literature. Nobody talked, except to the occasional visitor who paused on his push towards the lecture theatre to pick up a book and look inquiringly into it.

But in those corners where the Duke would not penetrate until later on the order was decidedly less exquisite. Eleventh-hour arranging was still going on. Messengers were arriving, phone calls being hurriedly put through from the cash desk, lists being consulted and found not to tally with other lists. Someone had a ladder in her stocking, and was crying mournfully for some soap. Two young men were arguing hotly, their conversation for several minutes being limited to 'I tell you I did,' and 'I tell you you didn't,' repeated with furious monotony.

Vivien, standing at her post and looking almost too neat to be true, listened with great enjoyment to the quarrel, which was going on at a stand just round the corner from her own. What the young man had or had not done she had not as yet found out, but she hoped that in time they would come to it. Broadstreet's was in perfect order, Mr Blueley and Mr Sackville were standing by as well as Miss Ramsay and herself and though she had not yet seen anything of Tim she felt that the world, and the Book Fair in particular, was a rather good place.

'I tell you I did.'

'I tell you you didn't. Here—what's that?'

A new-comer had apparently come up; Vivien could not see unless she walked out into the centre of the aisle, and it was not worth while doing anything so untidy.

'Two more copies of *Wild Beasts I have photographed?*' said the first young man at the stand. 'But my good chap, we sent them one yesterday.'

'These beastly Book Rooms,' said the other young man. 'They never seem to know what they do want.'

'What's that you say? For display in a show-case? Oh, well, I suppose you must have them.'

'There was a pause, a curt 'Thank you' from the new-comer, and the first young man said, 'Now, what were we talking about? Oh, yes—now look here, Hugo, I tell you you *did*.'

But Vivien was not listening to them any more.

271

Struck by a sudden wild, inspired idea, she had darted out into the middle of the aisle. She looked to her left. There was nothing to be seen close at hand but the two young men; but far away now, down at the other end of the parallel aisle to Broadstreet's, a man was walking with two large books under his arm.

Vivien gave a frenzied exclamation.

'It is! It must be! "Running about begging books from publishers"——Mr Blueley, come here—quick.'

'What? What is it?'

'Look down there.' She caught his arm and made him look in the direction she wanted. 'You said something this morning, don't you remember?—it 's a man who takes books. I 'm sure of it. It must be the Enemy!'

She had caught his attention now, all right, and Miss Ramsay's and Mr Sackville's too.

'Where? Let me look. How do you know?'

Vivien pointed down the aisle, and Mr Blueley was just in time to see the figure rounding a corner to the right. In a few hurried words she explained, and the four of them held a brief, murmured consultation.

'We can see if he does go to the Book Rooms, at any rate,' said Miss Ramsay. 'You two had better go after him. We 'll hold the fort here. No, don't wait—go quickly.'

'Come on, then.' Vivien started forward. 'Oh, we 'd better ask these two, I suppose. . . . I say!'

The quarrelling couple looked at her in surprise, and were still more surprised at the question she seemed to be asking them.

'What was he like? Well, really, I didn't notice a thing like that. What was he like, Hugo?'

'Ugly,' said Hugo promptly. 'Thin and ugly.'

There was no more to be got out of them. With a quick thank you Vivien and Mr Blueley hurried across, hoping to reach their quarry by a short cut through the hall.

'We 've no idea where he 's gone.'

'No. But certainly not to the Book Rooms. They 're right in the other direction.'

They rounded a corner, and there, far away, just crossing an open space, was the same figure again: a thin figure, with two books under its arm.

'Run!' said Mr Blueley, and leaped forward like a stag.

They might have caught him then and there, had they not, by the greatest misfortune, run straight into the august procession which was proceeding to open the Fair. It was making its way with royal and dignified slowness down the carpeted aisle from the door. The Duke of Petersham himself, tall and benign, nodding his grey head as he listened to his escort's explanations of the Fair. The escort, high officials and noble personages connected with books and bookselling. And after them came a bevy of less important people, men and women all in their very best clothes, chattering in low voices to one another and happily aware of their own good fortune in being in this important procession and having important reserved seats waiting for them for the opening ceremony.

It was impossible to get across the hall while they were going by. Even had they dared to attempt it, they would not have succeeded, for a tightly packed crowd had somehow collected all down the sides of the aisle, and nobody could have got past. Almost five minutes must have been wasted while the procession went by. Vivien and Mr Blueley dashed forward again the moment the way was clear, but of course it was too late. The Enemy was nowhere to be seen.

Mr Blueley stood puffing and snorting, too angry to speak. But Vivien was by no means so despairing.

'I think he 'll be back again soon,' she said. 'He will if he 's got any sense, at any rate! That 's a good dodge about asking for books for the Book Rooms, and he 's almost certain to go on with it as long as he can.'

'Well, but how shall we find him?'

'Just wait about. There's nothing else we *can* do.'

Mr Blueley was not satisfied, but he had no better suggestion to offer. They strolled a little way, and then stood hesitantly by one of the rows of stands. The loud-speakers burst into a terrific roar of applause—the Duke had come into the theatre. The applause died down, and the chairman of Book Fair Week began his speech of introduction.

Vivien and Mr Blueley, standing a little apart from one of the groups of listeners, listened also, without hearing a single word. They were interested in one thing only: a thin, dark figure which should appear from some unknown direction and ask somebody, somewhere, for some books.

From where they stood they could see down three different aisles. Vivien had just inspected them all without result when, beginning again at the first, she saw something which made her clutch Mr Blueley by the arm.

'Look,' she said. 'Down there—right down at the end!'

Mr Blueley swung round. There he was again—not a doubt of it. The same thin, dark figure, his arms empty this time. But he had gone up to one of the stands: he was asking them something. A moment more, and he would walk off with another haul.

They began to run. Several people turned to gaze at them in shocked astonishment, but they saw nothing, thought of nothing, but the Enemy ahead of them. And as they came closer Vivien gave a startled little cry.

'But—but I know him,' she gasped. 'It is—it is! Then

it was them all the time! Mr Blueley—it 's one of the Wilkinses—the two who live over our flat!'

They were within ten yards of him now . . . within five. He looked up. For a moment his face was blank, without expression. He looked as he had looked when Vivien last saw him, on the night when he had had fever.

Then he saw her. He realized who she was. Instantly he sensed that something was wrong. An assistant had just come up to him with a small stack of books, and he took them automatically; but he did not stop to say thank you, or anything else. With a quick, ducking movement and a last look behind, he was off.

He ran at tremendous speed, but they managed to keep him in sight. Up one aisle, down the next, across the hall at right angles, and out into the Fun Fair—he was heading straight across it for the door that led behind the scenes.

'Stop him—Stop him!' cried Mr Blueley as they ran. But the sound of his voice was completely lost in a new outburst of applause from the loud-speakers. The chairman had finished: the Duke had risen to speak.

'Stop him—oh, stop him!'

They stared, they gaped, they pointed, but they did not stop him. He plunged between the Houp-là and the Book Token Roundabout, fled neatly round it, gained the big door, and was out in the concrete corridor. The door slammed in their faces, and they lost precious instants pushing it open again. When they were through he was still in sight, but he had doubled his lead.

'Where 's he going?' gasped Vivien, panting for breath.

'Down there—I don't know. Oh, in at that little door.'

Roger Wilkins had paused, and with the swiftest possible look over his shoulder pulled open a door on his right. His pursuers, expecting to see him disappear instantly, saw with amazement that he suddenly stopped.

From the half-open door came the sound of a voice—a grave, dignified voice, speaking in the slow phrases that carry to thousands of listeners.

'. . . this magnificent Fair, a living and vigorous tribute to the printed word which is one of the strongest forces in our present-day world. . .'

There was no loud-speaker this time. It was the Duke himself that they listened to, and inside that door was the platform from which he was speaking.

For a moment—a moment that was infinitely long—Roger Wilkins stood with his hand on the handle. He looked behind him again . . . he looked in front....

Then, with a sudden resolution, he raised his head high, pulled open the door, and went in.

'He 's caught—he 's caught!' Vivien hardly knew if she spoke the words or not. She and Mr Blueley looked at each other.

'How is he caught?' said Mr Blueley, still gasping for breath.

'Don't you see! I 'll go in after him. You go round to the other side—get someone with you. I 'll stay on this side of him, you come in and stay on the other side, and then, the second the Duke has finished, we grab him. Go on. We must be quick.'

Mr Blueley nodded in sudden comprehension.

'Good girl—good girl,' he gasped. Then he was off again, running back the way they had come and round to the left. Not stopping to consider, not daring to think, Vivien smoothed an automatic hand over her hair, opened the door, and stepped after Roger Wilkins into the gaze of hundreds of eyes.

CHAPTER X

MESSRS BROADSTREET ARE CONTENT

THE Duke of Petersham was making an extremely good speech. Even outside the theatre, in the groups round the many loud-speakers, the listeners were sitting as quiet as mice to hear him. Inside the theatre, the fortunate ones who could see as well as hear him sat watching every word that he said, gazing admiringly up at the tall, grey-headed figure who stood so erect and calm among the semicircle of important persons on the platform.

'...when one is told that as many as eighty books are sometimes published in London on a single day, one begins to realize . .

They nodded unconsciously, absorbed in what he was saying. Nobody's attention was distracted even for a moment when a door at the back of the platform quietly opened and a young man edged in. He sat down unobtrusively on the ledge that at that point ran right across the platform to the door on the other side, and put a small stack of books down at his side. He looked like some minor official.

The Duke had barely finished another sentence when the door was opened again. This time a girl came in: a pretty girl, very young, with dark hair and a flushed face. She sat down instantly between the young man and the door. Several people's eyes wandered for a moment, and the Duke, who could sense every reaction in the many audiences he spoke to, decided he had been giving too many statistics and skilfully worked up to a joke.

The audience laughed, and was completely recaptured.

The Duke went on. The various officials who had noticed the two come in perceived that one of them had books with him and that the girl wore a stand-assistant's badge. An important bookseller who sat at the farther end of the platform abandoned his idea of sending an urgent note to one of the janitors. Someone must have given the two permission to come in. It was unorthodox, but it did not really matter.

He had just settled down to listen again when the door immediately behind him was pushed open: not the farther door this time, but its twin on this side of the hall. He half turned round, scandalized at so many interruptions, and saw a large man in a navy-blue suit creeping along as quietly as a squeaking pair of shoes would allow him. The bookseller blinked angrily, looked again, and saw that it was no other than Walter Blueley, Broadstreet's London traveller, who sat on the same Book Fair committee as himself.

Behind Mr Blueley came another man whom the bookseller knew—Irvine Broadstreet, old Mr Broadstreet's nephew. And with Irvine Broadstreet was someone whom not only the bookseller but the entire audience recognized the moment they saw him: Headley Paris, the famous author, the great author, every one of whose books was a certain best-seller.

If it had not been for Headley Paris there would undoubtedly have been trouble. Every official in the hall was by now watching the intruders. It was shocking, it was unheard of, that they should come creeping in like this when the Duke was speaking. The Duke himself was aware of them: he had half turned his head at the sound of Mr Blueley's squeaking shoes. It was a disgrace to the whole Book Week.

But if Headley Paris was with them, then everything

was all right. Authors, if they were famous enough, could do slightly peculiar things, and nobody would mind in the least. All five intruders were by now sitting quietly on the ledge, very close together, making no disturbance of any kind. Headley Paris was gazing respectfully at the back of the Duke's grey head. The audience now had not only the Duke to look at, but the round, thoughtful face of Mr Headley Paris who was sitting behind him. With a sigh of relief which could almost be heard, the officials throughout the theatre allowed themselves to relax.

The Duke brought his speech to an eloquent end, and his listeners broke into a tumult of applause. He bowed, smiled, sat down, got up again, bowed, and smiled. The chairman escorted him down through the audience, and all the other important personages followed them. People began to grope about for hats and coats and umbrellas, eager to get out and explore the Fair. No one had any attention to spare for a strange little drama which was taking place at the back of the now deserted platform, where the young man who had come in first gave the girl a violent jab with his elbow, got past her to the door, and was there captured by the large man in squeaking shoes and Mr Headley Paris, who promptly sat on him.

'And how are you, Vivien—none the worse?'

'Good gracious, no—all the better,' said Vivien, as if being jabbed in the ribs was the exact sort of treatment she found best for her. Old Mr Broadstreet smiled.

'As your future uncle, I must say that I 've never seen you look better, or prettier either. Do you find it quite—er—tolerable to be engaged to my nephew?'

Vivien's answer was not very easy to follow, but the gist of it clearly was that never in the world had anything been so lovely before. Old Mr Broadstreet nodded approvingly, and seeing his nephew approaching went tactfully off to talk to somebody else.

Messrs Laurence Broadstreet, Limited, were giving a party. The Book Fair had been such an enormous success, and the excitement over the capture of the book thieves and the engagement of young Mr Broadstreet to Vivien Farthing had reached such a pitch, that as old Mr Broadstreet said it was the only thing they could possibly do.

It was held in a suite of rooms at a big West End hotel. It was meant first and foremost for the staff of the firm, all of whom had come, and who were apparently enjoying themselves very much already, though the evening had only just begun. But there were numbers of other people whom it had seemed essential to invite as well: people from Book Fair Week, Mr Headley Paris and several other authors, and, of course, the entire Farthing family.

'Enjoying it, darling?'

Tim took Vivien's hand, and tucked it under his arm. He looked as well, and cheerful, and pleased with life, as Vivien did herself, and that was saying not a little.

'Oh, I never thought anything could possibly be so exciting.'

Vivien gave a little sigh of contentment. Arm in arm they stood looking around, enjoying it all with the immensely heightened enjoyment which Vivien had discovered that being engaged gave to everything. In the room where they were, and the one next to it, people were standing about and talking—talking, if one could judge from the sound of it, not to make conversation but because they had such a terrible lot to say. In the room beyond they were dancing, and the sound of the piano, saxophone, and violin came pleasantly through the hubbub of laughter and talk.

Everybody was there. Mr Broadstreet and Tim and Tim's parents, of whom Vivien was still a little frightened, although they had been extremely nice and Tim kept on assuring her they were harmless. Mr and Mrs Farthing, looking so young and handsome that people would hardly believe they were Vivien's father and mother. Dinah, absolutely in her element, allowing first Mr Tyson and then Mr Paris and then Mr Sackville to take her over to the ices, and cracking jokes with them which were clearly a huge success. John had developed a warm attachment for Miss Ramsay, with whom he had danced twice already, to the chagrin of Mr Blueley, who wanted to dance with her himself. Miss Haddon had proved to have an ardent admirer in the firm's north country traveller, and every one prophesied that another engagement would be heard of before they were very much older.

'There's only one person missing,' said Vivien at last. 'Or two people, rather. The Nilpils.'

Tim laughed.

'Yes, poor chaps. Well, the next party we have they may be able to come to. Shall we ask them to our wedding? I wonder how they're getting on up in Yorkshire.'

'I do think it was nice of your uncle to fix up that job for them. No one else would have done such a thing.'

For Mr Broadstreet had absolutely refused to have the two Wilkinses prosecuted. Several other firms had wanted them arrested at once—particularly Perryforth's, who found they had suffered from their attentions quite as much as they had benefited from them. But Mr Broadstreet was firm.

'No,' he said. 'If they're once sent wrong they'll stay

wrong. We've got a chance with them now we shall never have again. They know such a lot about books that they might well turn out two of the most useful men in the trade, if once they begin on the proper side of the law.'

Further inquiry had proved that he was right. The Wilkinses did seem to want to go straight, if only they could begin.

'We tried it, when we first came to London,' said Pete frankly, 'but it didn't work. We had letters of introduction from my mother, and so forth. But nobody wanted us, so when we'd learned our way about we started the other thing. We had to have money somehow. Mother always thought we were reading for publishers and reviewing.'

Their business had been quite highly organized, in its own strange way. They had got hold of an astonishing number of books, from all kinds of sources, at no expense to themselves, and had without difficulty found other places where they might be disposed of at a profit. One of their neatest tricks had been their imitation of the literary editor of a well-known paper. Roger could copy his husky voice to perfection, and when he rang up publishers to say he urgently wanted a certain book of theirs to consider for a very special review, he invariably found the book waiting when he himself, as the paper's special messenger, called for it a little while later. 'They'd have given us a bunch of roses too, if they'd had any,' he remarked with the enjoyment of a true artist when he was telling his story.

Among their earliest and most successful ventures was the Broadstreet series which they had sold to Perryforth's. They had first heard of it—as Mr Blueley learned to his great confusion—in the dark City restaurant where Mr Day, Mr Blueley, Mr Tyson, and one or two others gathered almost every day for lunch, and where they found it impossible not to talk shop, and impossible not to get a little excited at times and speak louder than was quite discreet. Once on the track of Broadstreet's activities, the Nilpils were in clover, for any stray overheard half sentence might mean a lot to them now. They took the room at Overton House, were much obliged when Mr Day had his window open, and settled down to business. Pete generally did the calling upon publishers or editors. Roger, in his oldest clothes, was the messenger, and there were few trade counters in London which he did not know. They did not keep or redistribute any of their books from Overton House, but had an 'office' behind the shop of a small City newsagent, who shut his eyes to their doings and occasionally lent them his carrier tricycle.

The Book Fair of course was a godsend, though Pete felt that his features were a little too well known for him to be safe there, and had to turn messenger and sit on the tricycle in the goods yard while Roger collected the spoils. He had been found down there, after Roger was caught, sitting nonchalantly whistling, his carrier full of books from all over the Fair.

But now they were both up in Yorkshire, working in a big bookshop and printer's of which the manager, but nobody else, knew their story. Mr Broadstreet admitted it was taking a chance, but was convinced it was worth it; and the first letter he had had from them seemed to indicate that they were putting quite as much ingenuity into selling books to hard-headed Yorkshiremen as they ever had into defrauding the London publishers.

Vivien often thought about them, and bore Roger no malice at all for his jab in the ribs—quite the reverse, in fact, for it was after that that Tim had picked her up, and had somehow gone on holding her tightly long after she was on her feet again, and it was in the middle of all the hurly-burly that they had become engaged.

'But that just shows you,' she said happily, still thinking of the Nilpils, 'you must always believe what I say. I said they were up to no good in that attic of theirs. I even said they went there to listen to Mr Day out of the window, and you know they admitted that was true.'

'Yes, you were quite right. But you didn't know Roger had seen Blueley and me coming up to your flat—that must have been why they choked you off again, the morning after he 'd been ill.'

'Oh, I don't know everything,' admitted Vivien handsomely. Tim laughed.

'Do you know if you still love me to-day, just the same as yesterday?'

'Yes. I 'm absolutely perfectly certain of that, at any rate.'

'That 's lucky, because I simply don't know what in the world I should do if you stopped.'

They discussed this vital question a little longer, and came to the conclusion that neither of them would ever stop, as long as they lived, which they both found highly satisfactory. They had by now talked to everybody whom they ought to talk to, and been congratulated right and left ever since the party began. They felt they deserved ten minutes to themselves, and so, still discussing the wonderful, the incredible fact that they loved each other and were engaged to be married, they crossed to the dance floor and floated blissfully off to the mournful strains of a fox-trot.

Mr Blueley rapped on his glass with a fork from the buffet.

'Ladies and gentlemen!' he called.

The hubbub of chatter stopped suddenly, and every head in the supper-room turned to where he was standing, his face very red and happy above his gleaming white collar.

'Ladies and gentlemen,' he began again. 'It is with very great pleasure that I respond to Mr Broadstreet's kind suggestion that I should propose the health and happiness of the newly engaged couple, Miss Vivien Farthing and Mr Irvine Broadstreet.'

There was a murmur of approval, and several people shouted 'Hurrah!' Vivien, standing with Tim by the long gold curtains of one of the windows, began to blush, and Tim caught her unobtrusively by the hand.

'We old chaps have always liked Mr Irvine since he was so young he couldn't walk,' said Mr Blueley, looking happily round the room. 'We know he 'll be just such another as his uncle, and we couldn't have better than that. And as for Miss Farthing, or Vivien if I may be allowed to say so, I think she 's the most charming new inhabitant the old City has had for years, and there 's one other person, at the very least, who thinks the same as I do. And not only that, but it was she who saved one of the finest churches in the City from being burned to the ground. And as if that wasn't enough, she spotted those two young gentlemen at the Fair last week, and caught them too, and she nearly killed me in the process, chasing all through the place like that!'

Mr Blueley nodded several times, with a beaming smile.

'You know,' he went on almost confidentially, 'this is all my doing. Or perhaps with myself I may make so bold as to include Sir Christopher Wren. For it was Sir Christopher Wren who introduced me to her, and it was I who introduced her to Mr Irvine, and I think it was one of the best days' work I ever did in my life.'

There was tremendous applause, through which Mr Blueley stood beaming and Vivien stood blinking because her eyes had suddenly filled with tears.

'I won't say more,' said Mr Blueley, 'except that I know you'll all be more than delighted to join with me in wishing the two of them a long life and a very, very happy one together. Ladies and gentlemen—their health!'

Through a golden haze Vivien saw her mother and father, standing together, holding up their glasses and smiling at her. She saw John, solemn and happy, with a glass that looked nearly as big as his face, and Dinah, standing on a table where Mr Paris had gallantly hoisted her so that she could see. She saw a whole roomful of people, all of whom she knew, and liked, and felt at home with, but it was to those four that her eyes returned. So happy that she could not speak, and could hardly believe it was true, Vivien clung tightly on to Tim's hand, and every one began to cheer.